HEATHER BOYD

USAT BESTSELLING AUTHOR

THE WEDDING AFFAIR

REBEL HEARTS 1

Rebel Hearts Series

Book 1: The Wedding Affair
Book 2: An Affair of Honor
Book 3: The Christmas Affair
Book 4: An Affair so Right

THE WEDDING AFFAIR

Edited by Anne Victory

DEDICATION

For Anne, who never fails to straighten out my babbling. You have the patience of a saint (a naughty one) and my gratitude for your words of wisdom.

For Michelle, who makes the world brighter with every word she writes, no matter the medium. Thanks for being my dearest friend.

And for John, my beloved and long suffering husband. Thank you for making me lift my game every single day. Love you. Always and forever.

CHAPTER ONE

April, 1815
Newberry Park, Essex

I WILL BE BETROTHED TODAY.

The knowledge brought Lady Sally Ford intense satisfaction as she hurried toward Newberry Park's white drawing room where her future waited to be taken up.

The two footmen flanking the drawing room doors opened them silently, allowing Sally to make a grand entrance to meet with the earl whom she intended to give her hand in marriage. She noted the occupants arrayed in the afternoon's final suns rays—her mother and her future mother-in-law.

But no potential groom.

Regardless of the lack of future husband, Sally dropped into a perfect curtsy because she could not afford to make a bad impression. She had spent many additional minutes before her looking glass, making sure her dark hair was perfectly arranged and her lips slightly pinked thanks to a brush of tinted beeswax. She wanted to have utterly kissable lips when she agreed to become a bride.

Sally's mother, the Countess of Templeton, rested with her feet upon a padded stool and a scrap of fine cloth over her brow.

"Good afternoon, Mama. Lady Ellicott."

Mama started upright at the sound of Sally's voice. "Sally, what are you doing here? I thought you would be gone for hours yet."

Sally smiled, but did not want to be drawn into a conversation about the estate business before her future mama-in-law. "Where else would I want to be but with our important guests?"

Lady Ellicott, her beau's formidable mother, had also been drowsing in a comfortable high-backed chair and smiled somewhat warmly in return. A round woman with a pale puffy face, Lady Ellicott met her gaze and held it a touch longer than Sally found comfortable at first.

But Sally was becoming accustomed used to the intense scrutiny over the past weeks. After all, she was in the running to become a countess. Sally straightened her spine a touch more, determined to meet the Lady Ellicott's high standards of decorum. She felt she had almost won her over to approving the match, yet until the proposal had been uttered, and was accepted, she could not let down her guard.

"Is she not a vision of loveliness," Mama murmured, glancing across at Lady Ellicott.

"Indeed," Lady Ellicott agreed as her son stepped into the room from the terrace.

There he was.

Adam Belmont, Lord Ellicott.

The man she would give her hand and fortune to if he would but ask. "What do you think, Ellicott?"

"She is definitely a beauty," Ellicott agreed as he strode across the room, lean and handsome, smiling as he approached. He reached for her outstretched hand and raised it to kiss. "Good afternoon, Sally."

Sally had given him leave to use her given name a week ago, but the sound was still something of a surprise still. It was an intimacy she did not give lightly to anyone outside her immediate family.

Clearly his mother did not approve of such informality because she was frowning severely behind her son's back and shaking her head.

Sally blanched, hoping she had not set herself back in that woman's good opinion.

The sound of her first name tumbling from her future betrothed's lips should have excited Sally's happier emotions to life though. This was what she wanted after all. Lord Ellicott as her future husband and a marriage that would end her long spinsterhood. A state explained away by the war and fastidiousness on her part.

Sally looked up at Ellicott again and waited for anything resembling a heated awareness of the earl to sweep over her senses. After all the time they had spent together, shouldn't she feel something more, at least anticipation, for the pleasure of his future kiss and future together?

When Sally's heart and body failed yet again to become excited, she smiled and demurely lowered her eyes again. Making this marriage was more important than fleeting pleasures found in the marriage bed. Ellicott was her future, and he knew it, too given his smirk. "Thank you for the compliment, my lord. Have you had a pleasant morning shooting with Uncle George?"

"Yes, quite pleasant."

Her uncle George had lost a foot years ago, but that did not stop him from hunting on the estate several times a week. He was a dear man, and she felt confident he would only paint her character in the best light when pressed. "I am sure he enjoyed having the company of another man with him."

Ellicott laughed, and his eyes lit up with mirth. "I imagine so. The chatter of a dozen women must be overwhelming."

Sally smiled, but the jibe hit a little too close to the bone. Newberry Park consisted primarily of wives or spinsters plus one elderly duke and his brothers. "There are only ten Ford women on the estate to amuse three demanding men. It is an exhausting job indeed keeping that trio amused."

"I do not wonder why you are hardly ever come to London now. They must want to keep such beauty all to themselves." Ellicott kissed her hand again and looked deep into her eyes. He doted on her as much as almost-courting couples were allowed within the bounds of propriety in public, and in the brief private moments they had been granted she had found much to admire in him. He was very free with his compliments, and she felt them all sincere.

He needed a bride with a dowry like hers to bolster his estate's finances but was not so overwhelmed with debt to be considered an out-and-out scoundrel about it or desperate. Her family and connections were just as important to him. He was smart enough to keep up his end of a lively conversation in all settings, and he was active enough not to allow his figure to run to fat anytime soon.

Overall, a worthy catch for any husband-hunting woman from a good family.

Unfortunately for Sally, her head might say yes to marrying him, but her body and heart remained watching from the shadows. That lack of feeling was probably for the best. If there was any chance of love between them, Sally was convinced it would surface once they were husband and wife and without anyone, such as her nine female relations, watching everything they did and said together.

Finding quiet moments with Lord Ellicott had been a challenge during the week of Ellicotts' stay. Not one to let a little obstacle such as propriety overset her plans at this late stage of their courtship, she allowed him to take her hand in his and place it upon his arm. "You are too kind."

"Not at all, for it is the honest truth." He led her across the room and stopped, poised equally between their mothers. He cast his eye over them all and smiled. "Beauty runs in the family. In both families."

"True, but a woman's good looks must be cared for as if they were her greatest achievement," Lady Ellicott remarked, casting a stern look in Sally's direction. "I trust you rested in a dark room this morning. It works wonders for the complexion. Yours is looking a little too tanned of late."

"I did hope to, but unfortunately there was a matter that required my urgent attention, so I had no choice but to go out on the estate for a little while." Sally had also wanted to escape the house and find a useful outlet for her nervous energy. Pretending to be demure while waiting for a proposal was extremely difficult.

Lady Ellicott exchanged a long glance with her son that hinted at disapproval.

But in her brother's absence, Sally had no choice but to involve herself in the running of the estate more than most unmarried women her age usually did. There was a shortage of experienced men to manage an estate of this size, and not just theirs either. Sally had enjoyed the challenge but usually hid her activities from important guests who would likely disapprove.

Lady Ellicott clearly disapproved of women concerning themselves with matters beyond the household, or nursery. Even if it were necessary.

"What was amiss?"

"There were poachers in the northern field last night, but no sign of them this morning. I have had the flock moved closer to the others."

"If you think that best," her mother said approvingly.

"I hardly thing Rutherford allows," Lady Ellicott started but Mother raised her hand.

"It was his idea," she announced, and that ended Lady Ellicott's complaints immediately.

Sally exchanged a long glance with mother and sighed at her smug smile. Mother possessed a disposition as stubborn as Sally's and usually disliked airing disagreement in front of others. In her early fifties and mother of six children, five of whom still lived, there were ample signs of what had been considerable beauty in her mother's dear face. Determined that her mother and Lady Ellicott bicker today of all days, Sally crossed the room, perched at her mother's side, and took up her hand.

What Sally did for her family likely amounted to work by an outsider's standards, but she did it with love and pride. She hoped to involve herself in the running of her future husband's estate, but Lady Ellicott could not seem to abide the concept, and had already expressed her disapproval in so many subtle ways.

Today Sally was not so lucky.

"Surely Lord George could be making these decisions for the duke, or your father."

Sally met the woman's gaze steadily, resigned to yet another lengthy discussion on what women should do or not do. It was the worst possible time for it since Lord Ellicott was around. He never expressed an opinion on such matters, at least not around his mother. "Uncle George has his own concerns, father is barely ever away from the admiralty, my brothers are at sea. My grandfather cannot ride the estate anymore. What should we do, allow the flock to be fleeced and the estate fall to wrack and ruin while we play the harp in the drawing room?"

Ellicott coughed into his fist. "Never that."

His mother sniffed haughtily. "A lady should never be put in such a predicament. Practicing the harp is certainly more proper than traipsing around the estate at all hours. I always advise my acquaintances to spend as little time out of doors in the elements as possible to preserve their complexion."

Sally happened to love the outdoors, and she liked the way her skin looked—vivid and glowing with warmth during the summer months. She also loved to be useful, to be as involved as possible with what happened on the Newberry Park estate. Hiding her involvement in the running of the estate was not easy. Many of the servants came to her with their problems first and looked to her to make decisions. When she married Ellicott, she could never be an idle wife, but she had to tread carefully for now until the ring was on her finger. Then things would change.

"Sally thrives on challenges," her mother insisted loyally. To Sally she said, "You always make the right choices for the estate, and I could not be prouder of the woman you have become. Never doubt that, regardless of what anyone says to the contrary."

Sally struggled to hide her pleasure in the praise. Normally her mother would say nothing so openly approving about her or about the additional duties they undertook for the estate, certainly not around the Ellicotts. She had agreed that for Sally to make a good impression with the Ellicotts, she had to hide the more unorthodox aspects of their family life.

Hoping to turn the conversation into smoother waters, she smiled warmly at her mother. "Shall we take tea on the terrace today?"

Her mother's face lit up. "Yes, tea out of doors is just the thing to amuse us all."

"I think we should rather not. It is too warm outside and blustery," Lady Ellicott said in a firm voice. Outside, the wind was only gently stirring the bushes of the garden.

Lady Ellicott had a preference for eating all meals indoors. Not even picnics on the cliff tops overlooking the ocean pleased her. Sally had little choice but to agree with her assessment of the weather since she was trying so hard to win a place in the woman's good graces. "Well then, shall I twist Ellicott's arm and have him read to us from the new *London Gazette* while we enjoy the tea together here?"

Ellicott shifted toward her. "I was actually hoping you and I might stroll the grounds. Leave our mothers to drink tea while we stretch our legs a bit." He turned to Sally's mother. "All within proper sight of the mansion, of course."

Lady Ellicott stared hard at her son a moment and then nodded. "I am sure Lady Templeton will happily agree to your suggestion."

Sally's mother's expression grew flinty at being spoken for. "A leisurely stroll about the gardens is acceptable within sight of this room, but propriety must always be observed. You will take a maid with you."

Sally wanted the opportunity to be alone with Ellicott so he could propose, and her mother was not making it easy for her it seemed. A maid could gossip afterward, too. She would rather not receive a proposal with an audience present. "Mama, please. What harm could come from a short walk through the gardens without a chaperone? We are at home. The wisteria walk is lovely at this time of year."

"Indeed, that is true." Mama got to her feet and smiled. "I will have a shawl fetched and join you both outside."

Sally groaned. Why was Mama not helping her advance her claim on Lord Ellicott's affections? She had to know the right setting for a proposal was essential for many men to unburden themselves and reveal their desire for matrimony only in private.

Ellicott merely smiled at the news that her mother intended to join them. Lady Ellicott, of course, elected to remain indoors. "The more, the merrier. The breeze appears to have died down, too. We shall wait outside."

"Yes, that would be wonderful." Sally rushed to join him.

Arm in arm, they left their mothers behind in the drawing room. Undoubtedly Mama would catch up before too many yards had passed beneath their feet. Sally wouldn't normally dare try to escape her.

However, when Ellicott led her at a brisk pace directly toward the wisteria-covered walk, she laughed aloud at his haste.

When they stopped, he caught her hands in his and drew them to his chest. "My dearest Sally, Mother is right. You are the most beautiful woman. I must again convey my gratitude for inviting us both for the summer. It has been a pleasant interlude here with you."

"I agree," Sally agreed, staring up into his handsome face.

Waiting.

"I was thinking of you early this morning. Of how well you and I get along. And I do not know any other woman Mother has taken under her wing without hesitation." He laughed softly. "That is quite the coup, I must tell you. She normally never thinks anyone is good enough."

Sally's pulse raced, and she bit her lip as she waited for what she hoped might next spill from his mouth. But Ellicott suddenly appeared lost in thought. He was looking off into the garden, his lips pursed.

Sally put her hand on his forearm, reminding him she was still there and waiting. "Her good opinion means the world to me."

Not that she was sure she had his mother's approval yet, but...

He swallowed and smiled quickly. "I must say I never once thought we would reach this age and not be married to someone else." Ellicott sighed. "So, it seems plain that we must marry each other. What do you think of that idea?"

CHAPTER TWO

AS FAR AS proposals of marriage went, that was possibly the dullest Sally had ever heard of, but it was at least an offer, and she was already of the opinion she should accept Lord Ellicott. Therefore, she only had to reply and set her future in motion. "I would be very pleased to become your wife, Lord Ellicott."

Ellicott sighed. "Excellent. I must say, I appreciate all you have done to stay in Mother's good graces to this point. She can be difficult, and I know she can be a hard woman to warm to."

"Hardly that. Lady Ellicott has been very welcoming." Sally expected her heart to take flight now that her hopes for marriage had come true, but it sat dully in her chest, beating out the same rhythm of old. "We have been acquainted for such a long time that I often wondered if you would ever ask for my hand. I am so pleased you chose to speak up today."

He released her hands and stepped back. "Well, a man does not need to rush into matrimony like women do."

How right he was. Sometimes rushing was the biggest mistake a soul could make.

"No, he does not need to rush until he is sure," she agreed, speaking from experience that Ellicott did not know about nor need to ever learn. "I have often thought a hurried courtship a mistake for many women."

He smiled again. "Indeed, a man should wait his whole life for the right woman and might not even recognize her until his last days were upon him."

"But that is not the case with us." She threaded her arm through his and they started to walk along the path together, away from prying eyes and her mother's pursuit. "We have each other and will be happy together."

"We will indeed." He glanced at her sideways. "Mother can stop worrying for the succession at last."

Sally colored a little at the knowledge she would have to spend time in his bed to begin their family, but speaking about it today was not something Sally had anticipated. "And my family will be happy, too."

He sighed heavily. "I should like to speak to your father and arrange the marriage contract today."

"I have not seen Papa since dawn, and he said then he was not to be disturbed until midafternoon. Our butler, Morgan, will let him know you wish to speak with him. I feel confident he can have no objection to a match between us."

When they reached the protection of a stone archway at the end of the walk, Ellicott drew back and stared at her. "I should like everyone to know at once of course, and I am hoping the admiral will allow me to make the announcement to your family at dinner tonight before I have to go."

"You are leaving?"

"Nothing to worry yourself about." He patted her hand. "A pressing matter of business requires my return to London for a few days. Mother prefers not to travel with me so she will remain behind if that is agreeable. I should be back as soon as my business is finished, and with luck I will have time enough to speak with the archbishop about a special license while I am there. We can then be married and return to London before the May entertainments have truly begun."

Sally was a little surprised by his haste to wed. The end of April was barely two weeks away. He had never given the impression that he was so anxious for them to become man and wife. It gave Sally little time to prepare for her new life, but she could do it if she must. She wanted to be a wife, to have a home of her own, and someone specific to care for. "Yes, everything would be perfect for a dinner announcement. I am sure my father would be pleased to have you do so after your talk with him."

She took a step toward him, prepared for a kiss to seal their bargain. Ellicott saw her purpose and smiled gently before lowering his face to hers. His lips claimed hers softly, delivering a dry, close-mouthed kiss that lacked any spark of passion whatsoever. When he drew back after a moment, confusion filled Sally. It was an important day. Why did he not kiss her properly?

He squeezed her fingers and stepped back again. "We should return inside before your mother, or sister, or aunt, or any of your cousins come looking for us. I should not like to have them think us scandalous."

Her mother's voice hailed them urgently from the other side of the wisteria. "Lord Ellicott! Sally, darling!"

Ellicott glanced her way with a sly smile and then laughed out loud. "You see, barely enough time for a private proposal before we are sought after. The sooner you are mine, and away from here, the better."

Sally smiled until her face ached. "My mother is very protective and a stickler for observing propriety."

"I understand, but of course I cannot like it now." His eyes danced with mirth. "You, of course, would never allow liberties before marriage. Your brothers would be very quick to demand satisfaction of any who tried."

Sally's heart sank, but she kept her smile pasted on her face. Her brothers would not wait on any duel before obtaining satisfaction. They would take matters into their own hands immediately and teach the scoundrel a lesson with their fists. There might not even be a body to be found afterward. Sally's brothers were hard men and not to be crossed. Navy men, used to having their own way in all things. She was glad the war against France allowed for their absence from Newberry Park at such a time. Ellicott wasn't at all like them and needed to remain ignorant of their true natures for a little while longer or he might change his mind about his choice of bride.

"Not long now," Felix Hastings, captain of His Majesty's frigate the *Selfridge,* said to his companion as the end of their journey came in sight. Newberry Park, nestled on the windswept Essex coastline, had undoubtedly been designed to intimidate lesser mortals. Home of the Duke of Rutherford and his large family, the estate possessed a tree-lined drive that meandered through lush grounds and led to a large redbrick-and-stone mansion perched high on a distant hill.

He had never expected to see this place, let alone receive a summons of such urgency.

Manicured gardens bordered the grand home, but his eye was drawn to the sweeping views of the wild sea, which was lit by the dazzling afternoon sun. It was as pretty as had been described to him once.

"Thought we would never get here," Gabriel Jennings, former captain of HMS *Persephone,* grumbled sleepily from his spot across the carriage.

Felix spared a brief glance at the shabbily dressed man and had to wonder if he was finally sober enough to make any sense. "You could have stayed behind in London. My rooms at Fladong's Hotel are paid for until the end of the month, and I had a man there to tend to your shaving and such."

Jennings scratched at the scraggy dark stubble gracing his jaw. "London's become a bore. What else was there for a friend to do but make sure you found a modicum of pleasure during your shore leave."

"I do not think you have shorted yourself any pleasure since I saw you last," Felix said, slightly disapproving of his friend's past behavior but willing to overlook it. Jennings looked like he'd been to hell and back and had to have had a fine time on the journey. Getting him back in the good graces of the admiralty might take a miracle at this rate, but he would do his best when they returned to London together.

The man shoved the blanket he had slept under away and stretched like a cat—the kind who felt at home wherever they might be, no matter the conditions. "Who knows what sort of mischief can be had in the country, eh? And we are in your beloved admiral's neck of the woods too," Jennings said with a devious smile, an expression Felix knew well enough to worry about.

It was mischief that had put Jennings out of favor with another admiral, Greer, and therefore with the admiralty some months back. Harmless mischief to some perhaps, but few at the war office had a sense of humor these days. A mistimed jest had cost the man command of his ship.

Jennings had been having one hell of a time in London when Felix had caught up with him before dragging him home with him to sleep off his latest bought of intoxication. He had intended to sober him up and resolve the issue of his future in the navy. Unfortunately, things had not gone as planned, and here they were at the end of a hundred-mile journey into Essex instead.

He shook his head. The first sign that the man had moved on from the loss of his wife, had led to him being punished for it. Felix hoped to hell he could save his friend from further mischief and misery by speaking up on his behalf. "I am sure to be sent away as soon as the admiral states his business. Then we will pay our respects to Admiral Greer in London and see what can be done to get your command reinstated."

"Greer is a first-class piss prophet." Gabriel composed his face into that of an angelic man. "However, I will be the soul of discretion and swear not to make trouble for you. You are a better friend than I deserve."

"Utter rubbish, but your discretion would be appreciated while we are here. I do not like the tone of this summons." Felix allowed the curtain to fall over the view and rubbed the sleep from his eyes. He had been traveling since last night to answer Admiral Lord Templeton's urgent request for a meeting far from London and the admiralty, with only Jennings' drunken snores for company. Felix had faced countless battles, defeated, and claimed a score of French ships in his career, and it was essential to present himself to his admiral with his wits about him.

As the carriage finally drew to a halt, he adjusted his best gloves and collected his bicorn from the facing seat, brushing any dust from the fading felt. Urgent summons or not, it was important he make a good impression and appear calm and utterly in command. He had dressed for the occasion, stopping a few miles back to change into his formal uniform. "There was an inn in the last village we passed. If I have not returned to the carriage in the next hour, have the driver take you there and wait for me. I will send word by nightfall if this affair will be protracted."

Jennings tugged the blanket back over himself and hunched against the squabs. "Have you ever known Templeton to be short of speech?"

He gritted his teeth a moment, considering his chances of making a swift escape. Unlikely. "Not once. I will see you soon."

"Good luck," Jennings whispered. "And remember to mind your manners. You're among the aristocracy now."

Once on firm ground, Felix swayed. Land was a foreign environment for him now. After spending most of his life at sea, he was more accustomed to the rolling deck of his ship than stability of earth. He would much rather remain in the moving carriage or even planted on deck at the wheel of his warship, giving orders to his crew as they sailed into the fiercest of gales than be here.

Blue-liveried servants rushed out to greet his carriage; one older man introduced himself as Mr. Morgan, the great house's butler.

"Sir," Hastings murmured, giving due courtesy easily to the most important servant employed on the estate.

Morgan gestured toward the towering double oak doors with an urgent sweep of his hand. "This way, please."

The situation must indeed be dire, given the rush. He glanced over his shoulder toward the carriage and Jennings and was astonished to see his entire luggage being removed from the conveyance by the duke's servants. He halted the butler. "I thought the matter was urgent and my visit was to be brief."

He had hoped it would be over almost immediately actually, but Jennings was right—Templeton never did cut to the chase in conversation when he had center stage.

"Indeed, it is urgent," Morgan claimed. "His Grace will explain everything soon, Captain."

"His Grace?" Felix and the Duke of Rutherford had an agreement that he keep a distance from the Ford family at all costs, save for his immediate superior's orders. "My orders were to present myself to the admiral."

The butler winced. "Please, the Duke of Rutherford will explain. He must never be kept waiting."

CHAPTER THREE

HOW COULD a man in Felix's position refuse a powerful duke like Rutherford a moment of his time? He could not unless he wished to become a captain without a ship and crew to command. Felix just hoped their meeting could be brief—very brief indeed. "Very well."

Once inside the entrance hall, he tucked his hat under his arm and glanced around, eyes widening. He had known from gossip that the Duke of Rutherford's Newberry Park estate was impressive, but such riches were beyond his wildest dreams. Four marble columns ascended two floors to support a domed ceiling that sparkled with gold. The man had surely spent enough on this chamber alone to build a dozen ships for the Royal Navy, or perhaps even his own personal fleet. No wonder the family had such influence in society. They could buy anyone and anything they wanted.

Felix's advancement to command the *Selfridge* as post captain at three and twenty years was ample proof of that.

"This way," Morgan said as he gestured to a side doorway.

Felix moved through a deserted sitting room, and then into a large, cluttered book room. Finely bound volumes in floor-to-ceiling oak cases covered every wall, maps lay strewn haphazardly across tables, and at the far end of the room sat a small man, almost unseen due to the surrounding chaos.

"Captain Hastings, Your Grace," Morgan announced and then departed, snapping the doors shut firmly behind him.

"Ah, Hastings. At last, you have come to Newberry. You are late." Despite the appearance of small stature, the duke's powerful voice boomed through the room. He had not changed.

"Your Grace." Felix bowed and strode forward, unsure of his reception but determined to meet the challenge. "I came as soon as the admiral's message reached me."

The duke waved his hand toward a chair. "Please take a seat."

"Thank you." He did and then studied the man before him properly once the room settled into a slow drift from side to side. Rutherford might be small, and his gray hair might signify considerable age, but it was easy to conclude the duke was not a man to cross from the direct manner he was being scrutinized in return.

"I trust your journey was uneventful and the weather fair?" the duke murmured.

"Yes, I covered the miles without incident," Felix assured him, growing puzzled by the duke's affable tone. "I have not been to this part of the countryside before. 'Tis breathtaking."

"It is indeed." The duke regarded him with one brow raised. "You have become the best hound in the Royal Navy. You have achieved everything you promised me you would and more."

"I trust you are satisfied with our arrangement, Your Grace," Felix said, shifting in his chair at the memory of their prior meetings. A meeting where he had agreed to give up half the captain's portion of the prize for the duke's political backing and the ship beneath his feet. He might answer to Admiral Lord Templeton, but he was the duke's man till he breathed his last breath. It was in his best interests to be accommodating and humble, too. "I am well aware I could not have achieved so much without your continued support. You have my gratitude."

The duke smiled. "Our bargain was a mutually beneficial arrangement. I asked you not to meddle in family affairs, but it seems inevitable that you cannot help yourself."

Felix stilled. Last year, Laurence Ford, the duke's grandson, and a lieutenant aboard his ship, had eloped with a girl. The Earl of Rothwell, another grandson of the Duke of Rutherford, had helped Laurence just for the fun of tweaking his family's nose since they largely disapproved of him. "I have done everything in my power to protect Laurence without the appearance of favoritism that would set him apart from the other officers. I can hardly be held responsible for his actions whilst on leave from his duties aboard my ship. If his own cousin conspires..."

The duke scowled fiercely, and Felix held his tongue over saying more.

Felix had known about the elopement *as* Laurence and Lady Cecily were fleeing for Scotland. He had to tread carefully about what secrets he kept, ensuring he remained in the duke's good graces was vital. In retrospect, he might have been able to stop the marriage if he had gone to Rutherford with the news immediately. But he had not actually thought it his place to tell tales. "I did not know he had married until his return to ship."

"Is that right?"

"Yes, Your Grace." There had always been a chance the wedding would not take place. The family might have caught wind of the matter, or Laurence himself might have changed his mind. Felix waited, biding his time to see if the duke absolved him of collusion in the scheme.

The duke pursed his lips and then let out a deep breath. "I have no concerns about your treatment of Laurence. A little hardship now and then builds character in a man. I suppose I will have to settle a small estate on him close to London and remove his wife there after the war. Laurence must live with his choice of bride on his return and rue the day he acted so rashly."

Felix sighed in relief and said nothing to that. He was not acquainted with the woman Laurence had married and did not ever pass judgment on anyone declaring themselves in love.

Rutherford, though, must have ambitions for his grandchildren that outweighed everything else. Especially love.

The door creaked open nearby, and he turned, expecting Admiral Templeton to have come to end this awkward conversation. However, three servants bearing loaded trays moved about in the adjoining room and began laying a table with silverware and fine white linen. There was no sign of the admiral, so he resumed his seat.

"Thank you, Swift," His grace called as the servants bowed out of the room. When they were gone, the duke speared him with a hard glance. "Captain, I do not normally eat with the family at this hour. They fuss. But I would have you join me."

Dining with the duke had not crossed his mind, but he could not refuse. It was a great honor that Jennings would undoubtedly laugh uproariously over later if he were still sober by then. And Felix was starved. He had not eaten since yesterday, moments before he had thrown himself into the carriage to reach this meeting place. Hunger or not, generous offer or not, he would have to keep his wits about him still. "It would be a privilege."

The duke stood, collecting two canes for support as he shambled across the carpeted floor. That was new. The movement appeared to pain him, and the man noticed Felix watching. "Wounds from my own stupidity on a horse years ago have begun to plague me. No doubt when you reach my age, your bones will ache like the devil too when a change of the weather is coming."

"I have a midshipman on board whose predictions are accurate enough to set my sails by." He waited until the duke sat, allowed the servants to fuss over him, and surveyed the meal they uncovered. Steak and eggs; pie too. Plus, a great many dishes Felix had not sampled since he had become a captain. A meal fit for a king, or a member of the Duke of Rutherford's large family. He saw a coffeepot and smiled as his cup was filled with the strong, rich liquid.

The footmen then served him a generous portion of everything and stepped back to wait in the shadows. Felix followed the duke's example to eat in silence, ignoring the tension of being under scrutiny of one who would judge him by his manners at table and probably find them lacking. It had been a long time since he had eaten in exalted company.

Months since he had been ashore.

When the plates were eventually cleared away and the footmen had returned to their other duties, the duke patted his stomach. "I like a man who values peace."

"I have been at war my whole life." He chuckled, finding Rutherford not as intimidating as he'd first feared he would be. Rutherford had good reason to be angry with him once. Felix *had* supposedly broken his granddaughter's heart, and the duke was fiercely protective of his family. Perhaps he had mellowed as his age had increased and forgiven him. "I would not know what to do with peace."

"Peace will come, sir, and you should be ready." The duke's stare pinned him in place. "It is only a matter of time before that bloody French prig is given his due, and then what will become of you?"

"Defeating Napoleon and France has been my mission for all the days of my service. I can barely imagine a time without war, and until the day comes when I can pass a Frenchman without being fired upon, I will keep up my guard."

"Very wise, Captain." The duke nodded. "But you must prepare for change."

He frowned at that. Why talk of peace when he had come to speak of war with the admiral? "Yes, Your Grace."

"Now, on to the business at hand. My son begged my leave today as he is engaged in another urgent matter," the duke said. "The family, what there is of it at home, has gathered for the spring, and our attention has been diverted by the excitement of having guests."

The admiral would not see him today? What the devil was going on? Had he not rushed all the way from London for this? Felix clenched his jaw at the unexpected delay that would keep him at Newberry longer than he liked. The messenger had claimed his presence was urgently required. That was the reason he had packed in a rush and departed London with all possible haste. "I am sorry to hear it. When will he see me?"

"Not until tomorrow, or the next day at the latest. He did not say exactly when he'd return, but I expect he will explain himself in due time."

"Tomorrow or the day after?" Damn this nonsense. He set his napkin aside. "Forgive me, Your Grace, but I am needed for the war. My men and my ship are sitting idly at anchor."

"I know exactly what you are needed for and not needed for at this time, sir," the duke barked, as if delaying his return to his command made not the slightest scrap of difference. "A room has been prepared for you. Morgan will arrange a man to attend you. You will make yourself at home, *Captain* Hastings."

To anyone else the invitation to stay at the ducal residence would be a boon to a career, but to Felix it was likely to be torture. He did not want to stay here, but he owed this man his ship. "Your Grace, I should not like to intrude on a family gathering. There seemed a serviceable inn a short distance away. I would be happy to wait there until the admiral has time to see me."

The duke stared at him harder than ever. "Resign yourself to your visit, Captain."

"Yes, of course." He had to wonder why the duke insisted he stay, and stay within these walls, while he waited for the admiral.

The duke smiled suddenly. "You would not want to miss the opportunity of renewing your acquaintance with the family."

Felix gulped.

Was this to be a torment, further punishment for him for past indiscretions.

The duke's family was large and of all ages. He knew the part that belonged to the navy well, and the rest he knew to avoid socially if he could. That was the bargain he had made with the duke years ago, and he intended to keep up his end.

His sole consolation was that if he was here, the duke's grand-daughter Sally Ford, the woman he had almost married six years ago, was undoubtedly elsewhere in the country—perhaps enjoying the delights of back in London.

Meeting his former intended would be awkward indeed since he had it on good authority that she had forbidden the very mention of his name in her presence.

The admiral gestured with his cane. "Pull that bell over there."

Felix stood and tugged on the bell, reining in his frustration as best he could. He must cool his heels in a gilded palace, reminded of all he'd foolishly lost. He had no choice in the matter, not if he wanted the duke's continued support. But at least he had left orders for enough repairs to keep the men occupied while they were at anchor. His second-in-command would keep the men in line well enough until he returned. And when he could return to London, act quickly to assist Jennings in reclaiming a command before he set sail again.

Morgan appeared very quickly. "How might I serve?"

"Escort Captain Hastings to his chambers and assign him a servant for the duration of his visit. And find out where my grand-daughter has gotten to. Sally should have been here to greet the captain."

Felix pivoted to face the duke, an awful sense of dread descending over him. "Sally is here?"

The duke's eyes glittered with dreadful anticipation. "Oh, did not I mention it?"

"No."

"This has always been her principal residence." The duke's expression soured. "She returned from London and brought guests who require entertaining. Undoubtedly, Lord Ellicott has tried to steal her away for yet another private tête-à-tête. I suspect a marriage is in the wind."

Every part of Felix's body screamed out in violent protest at the news that Sally was being courted, but he did not dare show any reaction in front of the duke. Felix had had his chance to win Sally for himself, and lost it through his own stupidity and bad timing. He had known this day would come. Marriage was undoubtedly in Sally's best interests and even more so for her family's connections within the *ton*. It was a surprise to him that she wasn't wed long ago. "I must stay in the village."

"Nonsense. The past is water under the bridge." The duke raised a brow. "It has been six years since the debacle. I am assured she has forgotten all about you."

The duke's words were meant to hurt him, and he supposed he deserved the pain. Debacle was an interesting way to describe how he had walked right into her father's scheming and lost the love of the only woman he had ever wanted. He had been a fool and Sally a stubborn wench who would not listen to his side of the story. She had broken their engagement and sworn to run him through if they ever met again.

Since her brother's had tutored her in fencing and Felix had seen Sally's proficiency with his own eyes, he had believed her utterly capable of it, too. As to whether she would regret it later or not, he was unsure, so he had kept a distance. At times several thousand miles and continents had lain between them.

He swallowed the bitter lump of misery that formed in his throat and pretended to be unaffected by the news. "I am sure she never thought of me again."

"Yes, yes," the duke said, eyes narrowing. "The family has agreed that your past connection with my granddaughter will not be spoken of before our esteemed guests though. It will be as if it never happened."

So, he was to be swept under the rug. How typical of the noble born to wave away the unpleasant with a flick of a perfumed wrist, as if Sally's lost innocence could be restored as easily and their perfect world would remain unsullied.

He smiled tightly and nodded once.

The duke's gaze left him. "Morgan, take the captain to his quarters and provide him with anything he needs for a comfortable stay. I am sure he is greatly fatigued by his journey."

"Of course." Morgan nodded. "Forgive the impertinence, Your Grace, but I would be remiss not to remind you of the promise you made last night at dinner."

The duke's face lit up with uncharacteristic amusement as he met Felix's gaze. "My youngest granddaughter has the whole family under her tiny thumb but has the patience of the ferocious kittens Sally keeps about the place. Barely sixteen and every young man in the district is singling Evelyn out for attention already."

"We met in Southampton a few years ago, and I remember

thinking the same," Felix confessed. The duke appeared startled by his observation. "She was with her brother inspecting the ships, and I was unable to avoid the introduction."

The duke grunted. "She is a curious creature at heart and utterly without guile."

"I thought so too. Very much like..." He broke off that thought and straightened his shoulders. He had been about to mention Sally. And he was not allowed to think of her anymore.

The duke's attention slid away to the butler. "You might tell Evelyn that the carriage will be made ready in good time, and we can spend a pleasant hour in the village."

The butler nodded and led Felix to the door.

"Until the dinner hour, Captain Hastings," Rutherford called out. "You will be joining the family for all meals."

His calm faltered at that news. He would see Sally, be forced to meet her gaze, breathe the same air, perhaps even speak to her, while every Ford looked on knowing what he'd done. Would those that remembered their almost engagement believe the lie that he had meant to use her to advance his career, or that he had loved her so much he had been willing to agree to anything her father had asked of him?

Sally should have believed in him, and her furious accusations had fired his blood to prove he deserved his command. He had paid highly for his success. Since he had the opportunity, he should set the record straight about her father's actions. He smiled, imagining the pleasure of what he might do and say to her when they did meet. He intended the event to be very memorable indeed.

He bowed deeply to the duke. "I will look forward to it."

CHAPTER FOUR

HOW DID one fall in love a second time and know it would last? It was a question Sally had asked herself many times in the past years and especially today. She still had no answer that comforted her.

"You are so beautiful, sister," Louisa enthused, fiddling with the delicate lace on the capped sleeve of the gown Sally would wear for her wedding at the end of the month.

"Thank you, my dear," Sally murmured, twisting a little before her mirror. The little touches made after the gown's creation made her apparel so dear to her heart. Each relative, whether skilled or clumsy, had embroidered in white a small motif upon the garment. The abundance of anchors and other seafaring signals made her smile.

Sally had been preparing for marriage all her life, as had her sister and three female cousins. At five and twenty, Sally and her family too had begun to despair of her spinster state. But the fit of the gown was exquisite, and her future husband was all she required in a gentleman. She would marry a very distinguished earl—and have the life she'd been born to live.

She smoothed her gloved hands down the embroidered silk,

admiring her reflection in the cheval mirror, and pondered her future as Lord Ellicott's wife.

Ellicott was possessed of great wit and conversation. They had a great many things in common—mutual friends, a love of London, and other amusements. He had a face to make many a debutant utterly flustered. She could not do better.

Even her sweet old grandfather, the Duke of Rutherford, had agreed with her there was no better man in England when she had shared her hopes of a proposal from Ellicott with him. He had taken the news very seriously and then told her if the right man were to propose no expense would be spared for her wedding this time around. He would give her and her future husband free use of Torre Cottage, the little-used dower house she admired so much on the edge of the estate, as a wedding gift if she would live there for most of the year.

She turned away from the mirror, well pleased with her appearance and the future laid out before her.

A wistful sigh escaped Evelyn. "I will not have to wait as long as you to find a man worthy of my regard. Love is a surety for me."

Evelyn's come-out might be a year away still, but the girl never doubted she would marry for love and only that. Sally remembered being so optimistic at sixteen, but that feeling had not survived past her eighteenth year. Sally's reasons for delay in choosing a husband had been a private indecision on her part. "Well, whatever happens, the wait will seem like nothing once you settle on the right man."

"I would rather not settle," Evelyn said before sticking her nose into her book again. Evelyn was not impressed by Sally's news she was to marry, and certainly not by Lord Ellicott. Not even the fact he was titled, an earl, swayed her into a more understanding frame of mind. "I will only marry a man who loves me madly," she proclaimed.

Her youngest cousin was decidedly against the match, but she would have to accept it. They might be cousins, but having lived together under the same roof in their grandfather's homes their entire lives, they were as close as sisters. It was unthinkable that they would be at odds over such a silly thing as her choice of husband, and Sally hoped Evelyn could accept her decision and be happy for her.

"I am sure you will find someone when the time is right." She turned her back to Louisa. "Unbutton me so I might put the gown away in readiness for my wedding day."

"I cannot believe how soon that day will come," Louisa whispered as she slipped buttons from their moorings. "Are you really so sure of him?"

Louisa was twenty and unmarried, a fact that didn't seem to concern her. However, she had been unusually interested in Sally's reasons for singling out Ellicott for notice during the season.

"I'm sure enough." Sally stepped from the frothy white pile of fabric and stood in her unmentionables, rubbing a sudden chill from her arms. "Is that thunder or a carriage?"

Both women flew to the windows in excitement. "Is it William?"

They peered out and then slumped.

"That is not one of our carriages," Evelyn whispered sadly, then flung herself onto the bed. "It is leaving anyway."

Louisa cheered up first. "Oh, do say you will wear Grandmother's star coronet with the gown when you marry Ellicott," she pleaded, slipping open a dresser drawer and removing the beloved family heirloom to hold it up to the light. The piece, fine silver wire and stunning blue gems, had been Sally's to wear on special occasions since her come out eight years ago but now mocked her with its purity.

"That would be too much for the simple wedding I will have now." She took the coronet and regretfully placed it back into the drawer where mementos of her younger days rested. She had agreed to a short engagement and a ceremony without fuss instead of the grand affair she had envisaged. Ellicott's extended relations could not arrive in time for the ceremony either.

Sally crossed to the bed, nudged Evelyn so she would make room, and curled up at her side against the headboard. Her cousin's mind was miles away, and Sally was concerned enough to grasp her hands. "I am sorry William has not come home yet."

William, Evelyn's older brother and Sally's cousin, had been injured in an engagement against a French warship; however, no one would explain the extent of his injuries or why they could not see him.

"It has been so long since he came ashore," Evelyn whispered as her eyes grew glassy with unshed tears. "Why does Grandfather prevent us from going to London to see him? He is being so unreasonable."

"We will hear something soon, I am sure. He is alive and we must have faith in him." Sally was worried though. It had been too long since they had had any news of William. Sally longed to comfort the girl and threw an arm around her shoulders to pull her close. She had hoped news of her marriage might cheer everyone, and it had to a degree. Yet she did wonder at the prudence of considering a wedding when for all she knew one member of the family might be on the brink of death at that moment. "Take comfort that he is on English soil and not aboard ship for his recovery."

"We should be with him, tending him," Evelyn protested. "It is our right. We are his sisters. It is not our fault he and Father do not get along and would not be wanted. William should not be alone."

Sally sighed. "He is not alone. Grandfather promised he was in the best possible hands to aid his recovery."

"We do not even know what is wrong with him." Evelyn sobbed suddenly, thumping her fist on the bed. Sally rubbed Evelyn's shoulder; aware this might not be the last time her young cousin threw a fit of temper over a situation they could not control.

The men of the family refused to speak of very much to do with William within their hearing no matter how much they begged for information.

"I am sure they only wish to spare us the details. You know how our mothers will carry on. William never did like anyone fussing over him. I am sure when the worst is over, we will be allowed to see him, or he will come home to Newberry Park."

She did not tell her cousin, but the first thing Sally would do as a married woman would be to visit William in London. Her grandfather could not stop her then.

Sally went to her wardrobe to hide her determination from her cousins and considered what to wear for dinner. She had to choose the perfect gown for such a special occasion as her wedding announcement. She fingered a delicate blue silk gown she had ignored for a while, considering if she could bear to wear the color again.

The door opened behind her. "You really are dragging your feet tonight, young lady," Aunt Penelope Ford chided as she swept into the room. "Lady Ellicott was just remarking about not having seen you as yet."

Sally would not apologize—no Ford worth their salt would ever admit they were at fault—but Aunt Penelope was Sally's favorite relation, unmarried and undeterred from speaking her mind on any subject she was interested in and deserved an explanation. Sally released the blue gown and pulled a lovely pale green muslin trimmed with ribbons from the closet and held it up to the light. "Evelyn wanted to see the wedding gown now that it is almost finished. Everyone has left their mark except for you."

"There is plenty of time," Aunt Pen said. "I will attend to it directly, but first our guests are most anxious to see you."

Her aunt had guided Sally through society's murky waters and comforted her when her parents were at war, which had been often in recent years. She owed her so much. "I will be there soon."

Sally stepped into the green gown, and Louisa fastened her at the back as Aunt Pen examined the wedding gown that had been left lying across the bed.

"A white flag. A flag of surrender?" Her aunt glanced at Evelyn, frowning severely. "Only you could have done that."

"Maitland stitched a hangman's noose on his last visit home," Evelyn protested, speaking of Sally's elder brother. "I was just following his example."

"How many times must I warn you that following in your elder cousin's footsteps will only cause you pain?" Aunt Pen caught Evelyn's face gently and pressed a sweet kiss to her brow. "Maitland and I had words about his attitude to marriage before he left for his new assignment. The example he sets is appalling. He should already be setting up his nursery."

Despite the topic, Sally smiled at the mild bickering. Her family was noisy, bossy, and opinionated in private. She would not have them any other way. She caught Evelyn's eye. "Never admit fault."

Evelyn smirked and sat up a little straighter. "Always repay in kind," the girl replied, reciting the second line of the family motto before she kissed Aunt Pen's wrinkled cheek.

"Family first," Aunt Pen replied with a rueful smile, completing the trilogy as she moved away from the bed. "And soon you will have a new family to please, Sally. I would suggest you make your way to the saloon very soon. Lady Ellicott is rather obviously impatient."

"I am coming now." Sally winced though. As much as she liked Ellicott, his mother's impatience could give her a megrim. She would have to learn how to bear that, too.

Aunt Pen turned in the opposite direction as they reached the hall.

Sally stopped her. "Are you not coming with me, Aunt?"

Aunt Pen brushed her cheek with her knuckles, a fleeting gesture of affection. "There is something I must do this evening. But I am told there is to be an additional gentleman for dinner, so you will not lack for company."

"I am sorry you cannot join us." She smiled though, anticipating another of her grandfather's staid acquaintances had dropped by to talk about the war and been convinced to spend the night. It kept Rutherford happy to pounce on anyone with an interest in the topic. He was forever poring over war reports and speculating where the fighting would happen next. It would be nice to have another man at dinner to even the numbers.

When Aunt Pen was out of sight, Evelyn shook her head. "Is it strange to anyone else but me that she is busy tonight of all nights?"

"Not really. She is always busy with something for the duke. Why do you ask?"

Evelyn hesitated a moment. "I do not think Aunt Pen likes that you are to marry."

"Of course, she is happy about the marriage." Sally shook her head, unable to fathom such a response. "They all get along famously together."

"Evelyn," Louisa said in warning, "do not gossip about the family."

Evelyn set her hands on her hips. "Well, she should know."

"Know what?"

Louisa groaned. "Evelyn has this ridiculous idea in her head that Aunt Pen is not pleased you chose Lord Ellicott as a husband, despite the fact she has said absolutely nothing against the idea."

"You should only marry a man you are madly in love with," Evelyn said. "I am sure Aunt Pen agrees with me. She is not married."

Sally addressed her cousin calmly. "I do care for Ellicott."

"But that is not love," Evelyn said and then moved a few paces away as Louisa shushed her. "Not the way you loved *him*."

Sally reeled back a step. *Him* could only refer to one man, and her family had promised never to remind her of Felix Hastings. "Do not dare spoil today of all days by mentioning that devil."

"But you loved him," Evelyn cried passionately.

"And what a fool that made me." Sally stiffened at the memory of her humiliation at the hands of a fortune hunter. The fortune had not even been money. It had been the early advancement of his career to captain years before he deserved the post.

"Ignore her." Louisa caught her arm and squeezed. "She has become a blithering idiot when it comes to romance and the male of the species. She even suggested that funny old man, Sir Henley Jackson, was trying to court Aunt Pen once, so that says a lot about her state of mind."

Sally laughed to shake off the memory of Felix's betrayal, but the pain was always there. "Aunt Pen will never marry. She could never stand to be away from Newberry Park for long. She rarely goes anywhere these days except to visit with Arabella and Rothwell now they have patched up their differences. She is happy as she is, so do not talk foolishness."

"I agree." Louisa nodded. "You cannot count on love at first sight or otherwise. That is just a delusion."

"Not every love is the same." Sally was well aware her feelings for Ellicott fell short by a wide margin from those she had once held dear. She had grown up a lot since those foolish, impulsive days. She had made mistakes and almost paid the price, but she knew Ellicott's character and had no doubts about what sort of husband he would make. It was not a grand passion she had with the earl, but it was enough for her to begin with.

Tonight's dinner and the announcement of her engagement would be an event she would remember for the rest of her life.

CHAPTER FIVE

FELIX HAD BEEN INFORMED that the Duke of Rutherford dined formally every night and kept to a strict schedule worthy of a naval captain running drills on His Majesty's fastest frigate. As he slipped his arms into his dress uniform and straightened the gold epaulets, he cursed Admiral Templeton yet again for keeping him waiting. He should not be here. He should be in London pleading Jennings's case, not dressing to impress a family that denied any connection beyond the navy.

Besides, what should he say when he came face-to-face with Sally Ford? Especially now that someone else was courting her. *Did you miss me* seemed wildly inappropriate, but it was the question he had wondered most of all over the years.

He had missed her.

He cursed and stepped into the hall only to come upon a liveried servant outside his door.

The slightly built man with a shock of ginger hair bowed formally. "Mr. Morgan sent me to fetch you to dinner, Captain Hastings."

Felix pulled closed the door to his chamber, somewhat relieved, to be honest, at having an escort. Newberry Park was a large, sprawling home, and he did not want to blunder about like a ship without sails.

"Lead the way," he murmured. After a few steps, he glanced at the man escorting him. "Your face is familiar. What is your name?"

"Rodmell, sir."

He recognized the name only vaguely. "Captain Lord Maitland's valet?"

Captain Maitland was Sally's elder brother, a viscount, and not his particular friend of late.

"Yes, sir." The man nodded, smiling proudly. "While he is away at sea, I am charged with attending to the duke's guests. If you are in agreement, I'll be assigned to you from tomorrow morning to act as your valet."

"I would appreciate that very much." Maitland's man knew the ropes and could be depended upon to look after his uniform properly. "I am surprised he did not take you on board."

"He felt his interests were better served with me remaining behind to keep him apprised of family developments." The valet glanced over his shoulder. "If you do not mind my saying so, you look better than last time I saw you."

Felix could not recall the fellow with any clarity or where their paths might have crossed in recent years. "When was that again?"

The valet winced. "Your nose was bloody from Lord Rothwell's fists."

"Ah," he said carefully, any comfortable feelings around this man fading fast. Six years ago, that had been. A time he could not forget for the injustice done to him.

He wisely clamped his mouth shut for the remainder of the journey downstairs. There was no sense revisiting the past, especially not when he had allowed his ignorance of navy politics to lead him into trouble and regretted it to this day.

At the bottom of the stairs, Rodmell paused. "The family and guests gather in the white drawing room before dinner every evening. Walk through that doorway and turn to the right. A dozen yards will bring you there. I hope you can find something in the evening to enjoy. Good luck."

"Thank you," he said but thought Rodmell's remark odd.

Then the man bowed and fled through a servant's doorway and toward the rear of the property as if the devil chased him.

Left to his own devices for a moment, Felix took a breath and then squared his shoulders before strolling forward. How bad could seeing Sally again possibly be? He paused on the threshold of the room, surveying the scene before him. Little groupings had sprung up already. A trio of gentlemen, including Lord Ellicott, stood drinking on one side of the room, a half-dozen women seated and gossiping on the other.

Sally stood in the center of the room with her back to him.

He did not need to see her face to recognize her.

He knew the curve of her neck and the blemish behind her ear very well.

Felix remembered the softness of her skin against his lips as if it were yesterday. He craved the strength of her fingers in his hair as he brought her to release with his tongue and mouth. His heart raced at the thought of her skin pressed against his once more.

His body tensed at the memory.

"Hastings," the duke called, appearing from Sally's shadow suddenly. He must have been there the whole time Felix had lingered at the door burning from within.

"Your Grace." Felix swiftly buried the longing as Sally's grandfather approached, reminding himself to keep his feelings private.

Rutherford hobbled closer, using his canes for support. "So glad you could join us."

As if he could refuse. "A pleasure, Your Grace."

Admiral Templeton, Earl of Templeton and Sally's father, was the duke's heir. He approached. His face was red, and he had a drink clutched in one hand. "Thank you for coming at such short notice. Sorry about this nonsense interfering with business."

"I understand completely." He nodded, noticing that Sally's spine had stiffened as he spoke. It pleased him to know she recognized his voice after so long apart, because she had always had that effect on him. As a young man, he had been head over heels for her. Hopelessly drawn to her despite their differences in background and her being his commanding officer's eldest daughter, and therefore untouchable.

She turned slowly and their eyes met across the room. The dark of the churning winter sea before a storm offered a friendlier welcome. Her eyes narrowed farther the longer she looked at him. Her expression became even more severe, and more beautiful to him as he dragged in a deep breath. It was clear how she felt, and the disappointment cut deep. Perhaps he had expected too much of Sally to have seen the error in her assumptions about him while he'd been away. Her father's intrigues ran deep even now. Felix wished to avoid further entanglements.

He bowed and took a step in her direct. "My lady."

The courtesy, a formality to everyone else, rang true as he spoke the words. Sally had been his once, and he still considered her the star about which his world turned. Everything he had done in his career since they'd parted was to support her. To prove himself worthy of winning her back.

The lady at Sally's side took in his dress uniform with exaggerated slowness. "I don't believe we are acquainted. Captain?"

A tense undercurrent swept the room when Sally made no immediate response.

He had not hoped for much of a welcome, but refusing to identify him was a cruel blow to his pride. Especially after what they had done together that last night. He faced the stranger and bowed. "Captain Felix Hastings at your service."

The lady cast a startled glance at Sally but recovered her composure quickly, smiling with a fierceness he could not mistake for anything else but protectiveness toward Sally. "Oh, I have long wanted to meet you, sir. Lady Duckworth, Arianna to my dearest friends, of Lofton Downs."

The name Arianna was somewhat familiar, but not the title. There had been a woman, a connection of Sally's, who had been spoken of frequently if he recalled correctly. Time and circumstance had kept them from meeting when they had been younger.

He bowed politely. "A pleasure to make your acquaintance," he murmured, keeping watch on Sally's face because she was near, and he was uncertain of this other woman.

Lady Duckworth beamed a smile at him that was insincere. "Sally, have you been introduced to the captain?"

"I cannot recall." She smiled, but her eyes flashed with irritation at the question.

"Yes, I think we have met before," Felix suggested. "In Portsmouth, six years ago it must have been now and in the company of your father. I was a lieutenant aboard the admiral's ship in those days."

Her eyes narrowed to slits, and he strangely enjoying her discomfort.

Young and foolish.

Sally cleared her throat. "Laurence, my younger brother, serves aboard the captain's ship now."

Oh, yes, she remembered him. She just did not want to be reminded of the past or their aborted engagement. Just like everyone else in her family preferred. "Indeed, I do command him. He is a fine officer and a good man."

Sally wore a smile that lacked warmth despite her next words. "Welcome to Newberry Park."

"Thank you. It is a dream come true to be here."

That startled her enough that she licked her lips, a sure sign of nervousness. "I hope you enjoy your brief respite and can return to your ship soon to continue the war against the French."

Felix wanted her nervous. He wanted to get her alone too and rail at her, but not when there were witnesses, and most of them her relations.

When she linked arms with Lady Duckworth and smiled dismissively, he saw it as a sign he had gotten under her skin. She wanted him to go away, and he would eventually because his yearning for her had been hopeless then and still was. But first he would set the record straight about his intentions six years ago. "As soon as the admiral gives me leave, I will go," he assured her. "I keep my promises."

She glanced away at his words and Felix took the time to drink in her profile, her elegance. Something he had known deep in his heart from the beginning that he had not deserved. A sudden smile lit up her face, and he turned to see what had pleased her.

Lord Ellicott.

He had noticed the man in London. In the few weeks he'd managed to come ashore they had attended some of the same society events. A popular fellow, he had a wide circle of friends who did extraordinarily little with their time and wasted their funds on all sorts of gambling. Ellicott had danced with Sally often and an acquaintance—a woman who had not known their tangled history— had remarked that the pair was made for each other. Felix had trouble believing the overdressed popinjay sauntering toward them could possibly be accepted by a family of rough-and-tumble naval men.

When introduced, Ellicott exclaimed rudely, "Good God, I had heard you were dead."

"Now where might that rumor have started?" He glanced at Sally for an answer, and she blushed. "Not yet, my lord, but the French are a determined lot, so who knows when my time on Earth will end."

Sally laughed, a brittle, false laugh he did not recognize or like. He looked her over again, noticing her elegance was as restrained as her laughter. She was entirely proper, and it hurt his eyes to see her gloriously curly hair had been tamed.

She only had eyes for Ellicott though as he stopped at her side. As if to prove her point that she had forgotten him, she claimed Ellicott's arm too and drew him and Lady Duckworth away as if he were unworthy of standing in her presence.

Chastened by her indifference to a time that was still important to him, he turned his attention back to his commander. "Your message said it was urgent."

"Later Hastings," Templeton insisted, waving aside the matter as the duke had done earlier that day. His eyes narrowed on his daughter. "Tomorrow is soon enough for what we have to talk about. Perhaps the day after."

The duke cleared his throat and Templeton hurried off. "Now then, Captain, who do you not know?"

CHAPTER SIX

RUTHERFORD REACQUAINTED Felix with those closest as if the genial host of a long-lost friend, but then a gong sounded, and dinner was announced.

Lady Templeton drew close, her expression openly curious and transparently delighted to see him. "You are with me tonight, Captain."

The duke raised a brow. "I trust you recall Lady Templeton, my daughter by marriage."

"How could I forget?" He bowed deeply to Sally's mother, a woman he had genuinely liked. Lady Templeton was nothing like her husband. She was warm and jolly and very quick with a laugh at no one's expense. "A pleasure to see you again, my lady. You are as radiant as ever."

"I see you have become even more handsome and incorrigible than ever before." She smiled fondly, and he caught a glimpse of that former friendship in her expression. As she looked beyond him to the far side of the room where Sally and her friends had gathered, that spark dimmed. But with a toss of her head, she shook off whatever bothered her. "It is good to have you back onshore."

"Thank you." He held out his arm to the countess and escorted her in to dinner, saw her seated, and took his place at her side. Across the table was a woman who very much resembled Sally but must have been years younger. After a moment she smiled, and he realized it could only be Louisa Ford, his lieutenant's twin sister, given the feeling of familiarity he experienced when she smiled. They had not been introduced as yet.

The countess touched his arm lightly, claiming his attention. "Have you seen my boys?"

He grinned, imagining the reaction of the three six-foot-and-more-tall giants on hearing themselves described as mere boys at the ages of thirty, three and twenty, and twenty respectively. "I would hardly call them boys, but my ship passed within shouting distance of *Reckless Hope* not two weeks ago. Maitland saluted and appeared in high spirits as we traded assignments. The ship looked to be in excellent condition."

The countess heaved a relieved sigh. "And my poor Freddie?"

Freddie was the second son, the spare to the earldom of Templeton. "He is somewhat further afield; the *Newberry* being assigned to the southern oceans at present. I have not met with him or his ship in recent years."

The countess nibbled her bottom lip and stared at her plate, not even looking up when a servant moved to place a napkin in her lap. She said not a word of thanks as the man moved on to attend to him in a similar fashion. The countess was miles away, no doubt worrying unnecessarily about her grown children as all mothers were prone to do.

"Laurence was well when I saw him Thursday last."

"I am glad to know my baby is under your protection," she said. "He is too gentle to be at war, but he could not be stopped."

That so-called baby had dispatched dozens of French during his career, but Felix did not correct the countess at the dinner table. His tongue burned to break the silence though. "Newberry Park exceeds young Laurence's description by a fair margin, my lady."

"Thank you." She sighed deeply and took a sip of her wine.

Felix noticed her animation at seeing him had left with the talk of her sons. Sally had hinted her mother was prone to fits of melancholy once, but he had thought it an idle exaggeration of a daughter frustrated by the confines of her life. However, judging by the countess's current expression, he could easily believe Lady Templeton a troubled soul.

Uncertain of what to do about it, or if he should try to cheer her up, he glanced around at the other guests as the first course was served. What could he say to lift Lady Templeton out of her mopes?

The duke stared, a frown on his face as he watched his daughter-in-law fiddle with her wineglass. Templeton was engaged in conversation with Lady Ellicott and never noticed his wife's low mood.

Sally was seated beside Ellicott, her suitor, and spoke only with him. Lady Duckworth was across the table and stared pointedly, clearly a hostile presence toward him. He noticed how few young men sat down to dinner that night. For a family of this size, the lack of men was telling of their profession. He turned his attention back to Sally's mother. "It must be a difficult task to manage an estate of this size with the younger men away at war."

The countess lifted her chin proudly. "We manage without them. My girls have shouldered the responsibilities well, and Newberry thrives."

"So, the Earl of Rothwell mentioned with the greatest respect the last time I spoke with him." He smiled at the countess's praise for her daughters' achievements and the ever-ready spark of Ford pride she displayed. "I doubt I would do half as well when I come ashore. I know so little of the land and homes that it would be safer for all concerned if I kept only an apartment in Town," he said, laughing. "And hardly any staff."

That caught her interest immediately. "You have been at sea so long."

"Needs must, my lady." He nodded. "I followed my father to sea when I was but thirteen years old if you recall."

"I do remember your mentioning that." The countess sighed, pressing her hand to her breast. "You must have broken your poor mother's heart."

He bowed his head. "I did, to my shame, and I can never make it up to her. She passed away while I was at sea a year after I earned the rank of captain."

"Oh, I had not heard." The countess gave his hand a motherly squeeze. "My eldest could not wait for glory and left me at only eleven to join the navy, but I had Freddie and Laurence still at home then and that comforted me."

He glanced across the table at the unknown young woman. He judged her about twenty years, which would definitely make her the right age to be Laurence's twin. "And you have your daughters too, do not forget them."

Her face lit up as he had hoped, and she smiled fondly at the young woman across the table, claiming her as her own child. "They are beauties, are they not? Sally and Louisa are my comfort and my joy. I suppose you have a wife of your own now. A sweetheart?"

He shook his head. "Who would have me?"

"I might be old, but I am not blind." She glanced around the table, her eyes assessing those present. "You have aged remarkably well for a man already possessed with good looks in your earlier days. A great many women would see much in you that they would want if you were to offer encouragement."

He laughed at that. "With only a brother for my connections and a passing distinction as a captain. Your praise is quite far off the mark indeed."

"Scoff all you like, but I like what I see and that is all that matters." She grinned and with a toss of her head looked him over. "We never had much of a chance to speak candidly before, and I do not mean to pry, but you mentioned a brother? You must miss each other terribly as my children do."

"I have a brother." A useless, worthless gambler. He had never been close to his family, save for loving his mother. Some of his favorite moments with the Fords had been time spent with the countess although that time had been brief. "But we have been estranged since I joined the navy."

The countess frowned at that. "Perhaps when the war is over, you will have a chance to begin again. I could not be without my family about me."

He smiled but doubted he would ever want to see his brother very much. By all accounts, Neville had bled his mother dry of funds while he and his father had been away at sea earning a living to support them. He could never forgive Neville for gambling away everything he had scraped together in the first years of his service, or for leaving their mother at the mercy of charity as she faded away from loneliness and despair. If he ever saw his brother again, he would probably kick him all the way to the next county or do worse if no one stopped him.

However, there was no point in burdening the countess with his sad history when he wanted to lift her spirits. "Perhaps we will."

They talked of London's amusements and of inconsequential matters until she said, "You mentioned property earlier, sir. Do you own very much in London?"

"None at all." He sighed as she struck upon another dream that would go unfulfilled. "I have been at sea too long to have a home and have never had the opportunity to settle in one place for long."

"I highly recommend Essex. There is no better place." Her gaze drifted down the table and a frown pulled at her brow. "All the best families make their home here."

He followed the direction of her gaze, noticing she watched Sally and Ellicott as they chatted. There was an undeniable intimacy between them. He was riveted when Ellicott stroked his finger along the back of Sally's gloved hand where it rested on the edge of the table.

Felix did not like the brazen flirtation in front of her family, and he forced his attention back to his dining companion. "I am unfamiliar with the Ellicott holdings. Are they local landowners?"

"No, unfortunately. When they marry, he will take my daughter away to Shropshire and I will probably not see her more than once a year." The countess whispered the last very, very quietly, for his ears alone he suspected.

Dread settled in the pit of his stomach, and he took a moment to quiet his disappointment. "They are to be married?"

"I should not have said anything, especially not to you before the announcement is made. It is a private agreement and will be announced on my husband's return from London in a week's time. Before the month is out, I expect her gone from me too."

He could understand her low mood a little more than perhaps he should. He had felt something similar when he had been dragged away from Sally six years ago, and still did.

At times he had thought their estrangement a blessing for her though. Those moments when he had been required to pen letters home to the family and spouses of fallen officers had brought into clarity how it would have been for Sally to receive such a letter at his eventual demise.

He had not wanted to hurt her. Not any more than he apparently had.

The object of his thoughts suddenly met his gaze. They stared at each other along the table, and the pull of attraction caught him unexpectedly. He steadied his balance on the table edge, determined to control his feelings. Sally was beyond him. She would be another man's wife soon.

And yet he wanted her with a fierceness that had never abated.

He wrenched his gaze away, cursing under his breath. "I doubt your daughter would ever allow an estrangement to happen, my lady. She is dedicated to her family, as all Fords are known to be."

"That is true." The countess sighed softly. "She is so strong a character, so much braver than me. I could not be prouder of the choices she has made for her life."

His contentment in the evening dimmed. Of course, Ellicott would be popular with Lady Templeton. He was as rich as Rutherford and almost as titled. Sally would remain a lady and not an inferior Mrs. Hastings, as she would have become upon their marriage. "An excellent connection," he murmured with an agreement he did not feel.

"Oh, but you must think it odd to be talking of this now." The lady smiled quickly. "Forgive a mother's vanity that her daughter will have a home of her own."

"There is nothing to forgive you for, my lady. I cannot say the same for my own behavior." Felix glanced at the Duke of Rutherford. The old man was watching his granddaughter with a puzzled expression on his face. "She seems happy, and that is all that matters, is it not?"

Lady Templeton nodded. "It is what Sally wants, and so we let her have her way. What better outcome is there for a woman but to make a respectable match?"

There was love.

Sally might have been wild with him, but he had not thought her indiscriminate in her passion at that time. He had thought they had been falling deeply in love and that the reason they had behaved so shamelessly together was a binding connection. Sally would only have agreed to marry Ellicott if she loved the man. Which meant she could not possibly love Felix anymore. Not even a little.

He had to give her up or he would only be torturing himself needlessly. When the women excused themselves for tea in the drawing room, Felix escaped to the terrace to rage in private under the stars.

CHAPTER SEVEN

SALLY SLIPPED FROM THE HOUSE, heart pounding with panic, and ran far into the garden and away from her family and guests.

Panic. Shock. Anger. Hunger. Her skin practically vibrated with sensations she had thought she had given up.

Felix was at Newberry, not fifty yards away. Smiling and laughing as if he had not a care in the world, as if the heart he had shattered six years ago did not matter in the slightest.

She kept running.

He was supposed to be aboard his ship, not breathing the same air she did. His precious *Selfridge*, the command and promotion he had valued more than her love. She did not know how he had managed an invitation to Newberry Park, but she would ensure it was the last one the blackguard ever received. *Bollocks!*

And if her reaction to seeing him again after so long was any indication, she might not recover at all. She could not seem to catch her breath, and suffering through the interminable meal with her family around them had been almost beyond her capability.

Her eyes had been drawn to him all through dinner, though he barely looked her way again after being presented to her. He had charmed her mother, she could tell, which annoyed her to the ends of the earth and back again. Her mother was supposed to despise him, as was all of her family, for the fool he had made of her.

She did not want Felix to be here.

She stopped at her favorite place, a small pond full of fishes that no one else came to, and lifted her knuckle to her mouth. She bit down on the scream she wanted to let out as a seafaring curse filled her mind. She savaged her finger until it ached and then let it go. "Damn you, Felix."

All she had wanted, for the rest of her life, was to forget him.

"It is lovely to see you too," he remarked from the darkness.

She whipped around, searching the shadows of the gardens, attempting to locate where he stood.

Felix came forward slowly, large, and dangerous as he skirted the pond. Her pounding heart probably gave her away and her cheeks grew hot as he neared. Could he not have changed? A limp, a scar to mar that handsome face? Was it too much to ask that he be as wounded on the outside as she was within?

For a moment she wavered between running toward him or away. Not that she was afraid of him, but what he represented was hazardous to her carefully made plans for a proper marriage. "What are you doing?"

"Strolling the decks of Newberry Park beneath the stars and asking myself the very same thing." His deep voice rumbled over her, and she shivered.

She had thought she had forgotten that voice, but when he had spoken behind her in the white drawing room, she had known who it was without turning around. She had desperately wished to be wrong.

"I mean what are you doing at Newberry." Sally turned away in an effort to gather her scattered wits. She hated him. She truly did for the mockery he had made of her young love. "Are you looking for a way to advance to admiral now?"

He growled, a dark and dangerous warning. Something he had never done around her as a young man. "I have never wanted the distinction because it means playing games with people's lives the way your father has with mine."

She spun about and advanced on him, doing little to hide her fury. "Do not say a word against my family!"

"Against your family, no, but against the admiral I will say what I like to you. I will not pretend he did not ruin my life."

"Ruin your life? That is rich, coming from you," she shouted. "You were the one who made the fool of me, not him. You ruined me, or have you forgotten?"

"I have not forgotten. How could I?" He stopped a foot away and drew in a deep breath.

In the dark she was reminded of their last night together, and her knees went weak. "Do not come any closer, or, or..."

"I was here first," he complained, and then he looked her up and down. "I have it on good authority from several reliable sources you still want me dead, but it seems you forgot to bring a sword with which to run me through. So sorry the French could not oblige you during battle, but I will wait if you would like to arm yourself now."

She took a pace back. "I never expected to see you again."

"Neither did I." He crossed his arms over his chest and glared. "If you are going to kill me, please start now."

She took another step back. "I hate you."

"Yes." He glanced around. "Well, if you are not ready to commit murder upon me, you should go back inside before your mother or sister comes looking for you."

"Do not dare tell me what to do," Sally hissed, furious that he appeared so untouched by her presence. "The days when your good opinion means something have long since passed."

He smiled and took a pace toward her. "I see you have nurtured your temper nicely."

"Oh, shut up and wipe that bloody smirk off your face." Sally gritted her teeth at the language she had used. She should not lose her temper with him so much that the thoughts in her head slipped out. In a moderate tone she continued, "You were always too certain of your appeal."

"I am angry with you too." He cocked his head to the side but kept a distance. "How could you think I could take you to bed and care so little for your future happiness?"

Oh, this was too much. She threw up her hands. "You would take anyone to bed if they helped advance your cause or career, and we both know it."

He laughed then, full voiced and heartily, as if she had told the most outrageous joke he had ever heard. "And who do you think might have held more sway over my career than your own blessed family?"

"Lady Heathcote. Lady Windermere now," she ground out. What man did not know the name of whom he was consorting with? "Or do you not care that she is a married woman?"

Felix advanced on her suddenly until he towered over her. "Say one word against my friend and you will regret it."

She blinked at the venom in his voice. "Everyone knows you call on her and why."

"Esme had a great number of acquaintances in London, and before her marriage received many callers, your grandfather included when he was younger and spry." He sighed. "Are you suggesting she entertained them all just to advance my career? What utter rubbish."

She shook her head quickly. Her complaints were only against Felix. "I never meant to disparage her reputation."

"Well, I know for a fact thanks to her last letter that she is deliriously happy being married to Windermere."

"She wrote to you?" Sally had heard enough. "One of your many letters from paramours, I am sure."

She spun on her heel, but Felix wrapped his fingers around her upper arm and tugged her to his side. "There is no need to be jealous, sweetheart."

Fury spun round and round her head. "I am not jealous, you grasping libertine."

His fingers flexed around her arm. "Esme last wrote to give me her new directions and to share the news she was expecting a babe. Who the devil has been filling your head with nonsense about Esme anyway? I am hardly ever on land to have done as much as you have already claimed."

"My connections in society keep me well informed." She wrenched her arm from his grip but continued to feel where he had held her.

He swore roundly, showing little care that his coarse words were offensive to a proper lady's ears. "I hate to burst your delusions, but your so-called friends are damned liars." Felix shook his head. "About so many things that do not matter to anyone but your father."

Her father was many things, but she could not believe he would deliberately mislead her. He protected her and had rebuilt her tattered trust. "Leave my father out of this."

"Blinded by loyalty to family still," he growled. "I do not know why I should have cared what you thought of me all these years. It is clear you are the only one who cannot see what he does to further his own purse and ambition."

He turned away and stalked off into the darkness.

"Do not walk away from me," Sally cried out. She followed and caught his dark navy coat by the tails and dug her heels into the soft garden lawn. "Damn you. We are not finished."

He stopped, turned slowly, and then bore down on her again

until she felt ridiculously small beside him. He did not touch her anywhere, but she was aware of every inch of him.

He sighed softly and her knees went weak all over again at the sound.

"It is either gag you or kiss you until you see reason," he confessed. He lifted a hand as if to touch her hair but left it poised in midair beside her face. "I think walking away is the safer option all round, because despite your belief—incorrect I might add—it never was my intention to break your heart or mine."

She gasped, and when he stepped back from her, she let him increase the distance between them. He had not a heart to break. He was cold and calculating. When he spun about and strode for the house, she hugged herself. She wanted to hurt him. "She had a son. Lady Windermere delivered a son," she called. "Robert."

Felix returned quickly. "I had not heard that. Is she well?"

"As far as I know, yes, though she remains in Gloucestershire at the family estate," she told him with a smug smile. It was said that Lord Windermere never left his wife's side, but she kept that warning to herself. If Felix was involved with Esme, despite his claim not to be, he would have to find out on his own that the lady's affections had been thoroughly claimed.

"That is a relief. She has always spoken fondly of that part of the world and the Windermere estate. I would hate for anything to have happened to her during the birth." His shoulders relaxed. "I will have to write her a letter and offer my congratulations by post before I return to sea. I do not think I will have time or opportunity to visit them and extend my congratulations in person. Thank you for telling me."

Sally squirmed that her ploy to hurt him had failed, but she seethed with a dozen questions about their association still. When they had been about to wed, Felix had not known very many women in society. Since those days, he had made his name as captain and built a fierce reputation, leading him to become included on many hostesses' guest lists. It had always worried her that they might be invited to the same dinners when he was ashore, but they had avoided meeting for six long years.

But she knew his first visit on returning to London had always been to the former Lady Heathcote's address. "She is important to you."

"She is like a wicked aunt with a compassionate ear. Good night, sweetheart," he called out. "Do not forget you have important guests to entertain inside."

Sally glanced at the brightly lit manor in the distance and blinked rapidly. Dear God, she had forgotten Ellicott. How could she have forgotten she was engaged to marry so suddenly?

Sally patted her blazing cheeks as Felix strode away, heading for the open dining room doors. She checked her hair had not escaped its moorings and hurried for the closest private entrance to the manor and quietly let herself inside. She would make her way to the drawing room, and no one would ever know she had just engaged in a blazing row with one of England's finest captains.

Her far-too-distracting former betrothed.

A gruff male voice called to her, "Is that you, niece?"

Sally ground to a halt again, hand poised on the latch to her grandfather's study. She turned quickly, aware of how her behavior might look and the likely chances of where she had just come from being discovered. "Uncle George?"

"Indeed." He hefted himself up, balancing precariously on his wooden foot before advancing to her side. "Thought you might give an old man your arm."

She quickly linked arms with him. "Of course."

He stared at her a long moment. "It is a funny thing how I am nothing like my brother."

"I do not know what you mean."

"Don't you?" He gave her an odd look, then glanced around the room. "I like it here. I like being around the family and watching you all grow and make your own mistakes."

She gripped his arm tightly. "You are my favorite uncle."

"I am your only uncle living." He sighed, and the scent of brandy hung thick about him. He drank when his foot ached, which seemed often of late. "I am lucky to have married for love, you know. My siblings were not so lucky in that respect."

Sally was not sure how to answer that. Her parents were famously *not* in love.

He chuckled softly. "There is nothing better than a blazing row to reveal how deep feelings run between two people."

"I was not arguing."

"Were you not? Could have sworn I heard a commotion on the lawn as I was taking a stroll. Perhaps not..." He frowned. "Never go to bed angry, Sally. Remember that in the years to come."

She could not imagine arguing with Ellicott the way she had just done with Felix Hastings, so it was utterly unnecessary advice. "I will remember."

He patted her hand. "You were always such a wonderfully unorthodox child. Always wanting to do what the boys could, no matter what was considered proper. You used to make me laugh at your antics."

Her cheeks heated as she was chastened by the reminder of her former hapless ways. "The days of making mistakes are far behind me."

"A pity. I have missed that impulsive young woman." He met her gaze as they walked along. "Everyone makes bad decisions and can be forgiven. Sometimes you do not even have to say the apology to convey that you are sorry indeed for a grievous mistake. Think on that tonight."

He led her into the drawing room where the other women of her family waited and took a chair nearest the doors without another word. The other men were still taking port, so Uncle George lapped up the attention of her mother and aunt as was his due as the only gentleman in the room.

Sally thought long and hard about his advice. In her endeavors to act a lady, had she been too good at it and lost something of herself in the bargain? She had tried to be so well behaved until Felix's arrival had loosened her tongue. The contrast was striking. She rubbed her temple as she took a chair.

She had been so very aware that everything she did in the past years reflected on her character and her sister's good reputation. She had been determined to hide her fiery nature from everyone, believing at heart that with her past behavior she had set herself up for disappointment.

And yet one moment alone with Felix and she was right back where she started, wearing her heart on her sleeve, demanding her voice be listened to. Her emotions had been barely contained as they flowed from her along with her harsh words.

Ellicott had no idea who she was. She was not going to be the perfect bride he might expect on their wedding night, and she realized she had to reveal some of her true nature to him soon. She also had to tell him about Felix before someone else mentioned her former betrothal. She did not want to embarrass Ellicott, but she also did not want to lose his good opinion.

A daunting precipice to negotiate. Unfortunately, she had no notion of how to reveal her sad history to her future husband without appearing shockingly fast.

But what could Ellicott say about it now that the date was set?

He might wish to call off their engagement, but only a woman could do that. Her reasons for marrying were still the same. She wanted a home, and one day she wanted children.

Sally bit her lip and glanced around. Everyone said she could not do better than Ellicott at her age, and they might be right. But if Ellicott was the right man, surely he would understand she was only human and had made mistakes.

But the small voice inside her heart that had waited six years in vain for Felix to come back to her laughed. The hope that refused to lie down and die no matter how much she tried or how good she acted rejoiced. She had enjoyed arguing with Felix in the dark garden.

She had relished the fact that she had spoken her mind and he had not been shocked or offended. It had felt good to let loose her emotions with him.

Liberating.

She could have the future she wanted with Ellicott only if she could find a way to be herself more often and not lose his good opinion by the end.

CHAPTER EIGHT

THE ONE BRIGHT star on his horizon that always led him back to England had been Sally.

And Sally had made it abundantly clear she did not want him anymore.

Felix did not need to be fired upon to know the battle was lost. All he needed to do now was to make a graceful exit and try to forget her. That he had not in the past six years did not bode well for his future success. He would try as he had always tried to no avail before.

If only the admiral would only let him go, he might have a chance to begin again.

If only he was not stuck here.

Felix glanced around the dining room where a thick pall of cigar smoke drifted over the heads of Lord Ellicott, Rutherford, and Admiral Templeton, who had remained gathered around the large mahogany dining table while he had walked the dark gardens.

The duke sat closest to the open door, engaged in a fierce debate with Lord Ellicott over taxes. Felix tried to follow along, but of course with no home of his own or property, he had little interest in or understanding of the complexities of the topic.

"A port, Captain?" Morgan asked as he stopped at Felix's elbow.

"Never touch the stuff. Whiskey, please."

He supposed one day he would have to learn to live upon the land, manage a house and servants, and pay unfamiliar taxes. He would probably run aground at first while he found his bearing, but he would survive. He always did somehow.

It occurred to him he had no real notion of what he would do with himself when his naval career ended and a victory against France was assured. He had always thought that somehow Sally and the Fords would be part of his life. Since that was not to be the case now, he had better consider his options.

He took his drink and stood back to observe the gathering. Lord Ellicott had moved on from the injustice of the tax laws for landed gentry but seemed able to talk on almost any subject to the point where Felix could not remember what the starting point had been. Owning a home and land sounded damned annoying and time consuming. Not to mention utterly boring.

Perhaps I will live in town. An apartment might best suit a bachelor.

Jennings seemed to like London living although he spent most of his nights inebriated.

"Penny for your thoughts, Captain," the duke asked suddenly. "You look like you have bitten into a lemon."

He looked up and forced a smile to his face. "Nothing worth mentioning, Your Grace."

Admiral Templeton and Lord Ellicott departed for the drawing room and the ladies without a backward glance. When they were gone, the duke shook his head.

"Come now, surely your stroll outside did you some good." The duke raised one brow, daring him to deny it. He did not feel better, but he was not suffering anymore.

The duke had nothing to fear. He had accepted tonight that Sally was lost to him and all the reasons he would never win her back. He could not change her mind, nor did he want to turn her against her father. She loved the man, but she could not see the shades of gray he cloaked his world in. "It did indeed. Blew the cobwebs from my mind, in fact."

The duke hauled himself upright. "How do you like your room?"

"It has a pleasant aspect facing the sea," he said. "Quite an improvement from the captain's quarters aboard the *Selfridge,* as you can imagine. A man *can* have too much splintered wood hanging over his head at times."

"Indeed, he can." Rutherford turned toward the fire and tossed his unfinished cigar into the flames.

Felix's attention was drawn to the wide mantel the duke leaned against. A single ivory elephant, no larger than his fist, marched toward the nearest window, trunk upraised. Felix remembered trading for it on the streets of India on his first voyage after he had lost Sally. The merchant had bartered hard and been paid fairly well for the trinket. But it was only one of a pair. He had sent this one home to Newberry to fulfill the duke's bargain and the other he had kept in his quarters on board, wrapped in a shawl he had kept of Sally's.

He almost laughed now at his foolish sentimentality. Had he really imagined the piece would one day find its way into Sally's hands after leaving his own?

"Would it surprise you to learn that the best views are from a currently neglected dower house half a mile away?"

He frowned. He had caught a glimpse of a house distant from the estate, beyond the well-trimmed gardens, but had not realized it was abandoned. "Was it the original manor house for the estate?"

The duke nodded and headed for the doorway. "They built Torre Cottage before my grandfather made his fortune. Later generations have lived there at various times, but because of the cottage's smaller size, Newberry was built to accommodate the growing family."

"Newberry is impressive."

"Torre Cottage is a favorite of mine. I lived there when my wife and I were first married for a time. Mary found the family a touch overwhelming at first." He grinned impishly. "And there are benefits to privacy when you are madly in love."

He was surprised the duke had married for love and made mention of it. Most lords did not speak kindly of their wives, or so he had noticed. "I feel I should already know the answer to this, but were you ever in the service?"

"No, an older brother of mine was a lieutenant, but he died at twenty when the ship ran afoul of a reef, and I became the heir. I had already been married a few years by then, and if not for Mary's steadfast love, I would have been miserable as head of the family when I inherited from my father a few years later."

He was surprised by the duke's candor yet again. Felix had always imagined Rutherford had been born a duke. That made him a little less intimidating in Felix's eyes.

"Love is the one thing that can make a long and demanding life worthwhile," the duke continued. "Do not plan to live without it, Captain, or you will suffer the consequences."

Rutherford took a step and wobbled. Felix grabbed his elbow quickly to steady the man before he fell.

"Damn hands," the duke grumbled. "Next thing you know, I will have to endure the indignity of being pushed around in those rolling contraptions."

"I am sure it will never happen," Felix murmured to reassure the older man, but he too could see that day coming. Everyone got old eventually. Everyone died in the end.

Rutherford thumped his canes on the floor, loosening Felix's grip, and his lips pursed tightly together a moment. He turned slightly toward Felix. "You know, I miss my Mary on days like this. I always thought we would grow old together. She would have let me fall and then joined me on the floor, laughing about my not keeping my own feet beneath me."

Felix shook his head. He could imagine Sally doing exactly the same thing when they reached their dotage, but such a moment was not in his future now. "She must have been a wonderful woman."

"She was my world. It would have been her birthday today," the duke mused and then shuffled off toward the drawing room.

Felix hurried to catch up in case the duke teetered again.

The dark terrace was perfect for some serious contemplation. Unfortunately, Lady Duckworth had forced Sally's face around so she could not be alone with her thoughts.

"You never told me he was so devilishly handsome."

She had never wanted to mention Felix again after their engagement had ended, but the description still fit him. "He appears the same as he ever was."

Sally walked into the darkest corner and set her hand over her churning stomach.

Too tall, too handsome, and too distracting in his naval dress uniform, just as he had been all those years ago when she had been swayed by his charm. She had not quite recovered her composure after their altercation in the garden earlier. Arianna had insisted on talking, so they had escaped to the terrace before Lady Ellicott over-heard their conversation.

"Well, I must say your description of his looks fell far short of the mark. It is always the handsome devils that bring a lady's emotions undone," Arianna exclaimed as she adjusted her gloves higher up her slender arms. The countess paused a moment and then smiled broadly. "I cannot bear the sight of him of course, but my word, his arrival is perfectly timed."

Sally frowned, thinking his arrival could not have come at a worse time. Ellicott had no idea she had been engaged before. No one outside the family and a few trusted servants did. And Arianna, of course. She knew how far Sally had fallen in embarrassing detail. "I do not understand why you would think that."

Having Felix at Newberry Park was terribly timed as far as she was concerned. She had moved on; she had accepted Lord Ellicott's hand in marriage. She would be a bride soon. A wife. A countess.

It was cruel to be forced to remember, to face again the man you almost married, especially on the cusp of her wedding another.

"But surely you knew he had been invited. How sly of you to surprise me, though I do wish you had mentioned him earlier." Arianna rubbed her hands together as she paced. "We would have had time to confer and put together a plan to put him in his place at last. After the pain he put you through, he deserves a thorough set down."

Sally rubbed her arms, chilled by Arianna's glee at seeing Felix in their midst. She had just given him a perfectly good set down and felt no better for it. Arianna knew all about his attempt to use her to gain command of his own ship. The fact he had still been promoted despite their broken engagement had caused her to scream and rage to her in the privacy of her parlor when she had learned of it. "I would rather not be reminded of the past."

"He shall not get away with hurting you a day longer. He

must be made to suffer as you have suffered in silence." Arianna leaned close and whispered, "If you ask me, your marriage to Lord Ellicott is just the thing to make him regret his entire existence. Having him forced to watch you find happiness with a better man, and an earl besides, ranks as the best choice for revenge, although that should only be our first step."

Could she hurt him as he had hurt her? He deserved to be punished for the fool he had made of her, but she truly doubted the past troubled him. With or without her hand in marriage, he had somehow kept his promotion and his ship. He had done very well without her. "Grandfather does not want the marriage to be acknowledged until Ellicott returns in a few days."

"Well..." Arianna glanced around swiftly. "Then someone will have to make sure the captain has heard of it before morning comes, don't you think? That should do to begin with."

"No. I will not use my marriage to Ellicott that way," Sally insisted. "One has nothing to do with the other. It was a long time ago, and I am well over the disappointment. Promise me you will not stir up trouble."

She was over the disappointment, but not the longing to change the past. The loss of her innocence, the damage done to her heart and trust, those could never be fully repaired.

"I promise, and I do understand. I do not like to be reminded of my husband, and we live in the same house a quarter of the year. Oh, if only he would stay away, I could pretend I was a widow very happily." Arianna laughed, then peered at Sally. "So, you are over him entirely?"

"Of course, I am. It has been six years since we have met. It was just a shock seeing him today after so much time has passed, but now the surprise has ended," she said, but truthfully the shock had not left her. It had subsided enough to allow her to think and see how she must act. She needed to ignore Felix and deal honestly with Ellicott from now on.

"Well, I must say I am glad. I would not have you hurt again. Let us speak no more of what he did." Arianna faced the drawing room, her gaze speculative. She lifted her fingers to her hair, and twirled an artfully fallen lock around her finger. "I will find another way to get under his skin."

In the drawing room beyond the terrace, the gentlemen were returning from the dining room. Her father and Ellicott were jolly tonight, teasing the women as they burst through the doors, laughing as they found seats to claim for another long evening. Laughter was a rare thing in these troubled times, and she was pleased to see so many were lifted in spirits thanks to her happy news.

Ellicott went to his mother first, as usual, to see if her teacup needed refilling, and when that was done, he peered around the room as if looking for someone. For her? As his intended, should she have rushed inside to greet him and let him refill her own teacup? Sally needed a moment longer alone. Something held her back from happiness. Something that had nothing to do with Ellicott's nature but her own fickle emotions.

The earl was a good man, kind to his mother in a way many lords of his age often were not. A man she could learn to love the way she had once loved Felix given enough time. She shook her head quickly, annoyed to have that wretched man feature in her thoughts again. "Where is Duckworth, by the way? I have not seen him in months."

Arianna shrugged. "Oh, he is probably tucked away with his latest mistress in that little hovel he keeps for them in London."

"How do you bear it?"

"Easily." Arianna faced her, her expression puzzled. "I am not in love with him, and he does not love me either. As long as he does not interfere too much with our children, I am content enough for him to do as he pleases. Lofton Downs is as much my home as his now."

"Don't you ever wish for his love?"

"I did once. Before our children were born, we spent more time together, but that ended when our second son came along. I learned he did not really need me, and accepting that as a fact made all the difference to our relationship. Few women find what they need in marriage these days that I am not alarmed by the lack of his attention. But enough of me." Arianna frowned at her. "You do not love Ellicott, and do not bother to deny it because I have known you long enough to see the truth in your eyes, so you will understand the advantages."

"I want to love him," Sally whispered, meaning every word. "And I will one day."

"He is a fine man as far as it goes. When you have been married for a while, you will appreciate the freedom a marriage built on mutual respect grants you. No possessiveness, no jealousy." Arianna smiled brightly. "Without love in a marriage, all those foolish emotions remain at bay, and a woman can concentrate on what matters most. Enjoying her own life and her own interests without interruption."

She shook her head sadly at the picture Arianna painted. "No happy moments together? None at all?"

Arianna put her arm around her shoulder and squeezed. "The best day I ever experienced as Duckworth's wife was the day our first son came into the world. We might even have kissed to celebrate the happy event now I think on it."

That did not seem enough to Sally. To live without the love of a man you were bound to for the rest of her life seemed a waste. She had to try harder to fall for Lord Ellicott. Starting tonight, she would make him the center of her world. "I should go in and join him."

Sally relaxed her face into a contented smile for Ellicott in order to further her intentions. The past did not matter, only the future did, and hers was with a good man.

She took a pace forward just as Felix Hastings stepped into the room. She came to a halt in the shadows, breath catching at the sight of the handsome devil. He was late arriving, prowling beside her grandfather who was always somewhat slower when walking with his canes than everyone else. Felix towered over Rutherford, a picture of rude health and vitality, a stark contrast to the frailer man he walked beside. Sally could not stand men who toadied up to titled gentlemen that way; seeking favor by keeping older men company was damn shoddy in her opinion.

Sally bit her lip as further foul language filled her head. Years of living with family who went to sea had broadened her knowledge and vocabulary, but not always in a good direction. She had been working hard to suppress one curse after another since meeting Felix again tonight, and apparently the danger had not passed. Her inner monologue had grown as coarse as a fishwife's diction at the end of a long day without a single customer.

Felix had once fallen into a fit of laughter when she had spoken her mind. He had claimed at the time to have enjoyed her insults immensely and had even committed some of her more elaborate curses to paper.

Felix scanned the room and immediately found her in the shadows of the doorway, sending her emotions tumbling again in another direction as his pale blue eyes studied her. When they had argued in the garden, she had been spared the full effect of his presence, but she felt it now, all the way to the soles of her feet. The corner of his mouth lifted in a half smile, and then he shook his head, moving his attention elsewhere in the room.

He stood back as the duke found a place to sit and then accepted a drink from a servant with a polite word of thanks before downing the glass and requesting another. He only drank when he was nervous, and a brief thought that a kind word might set him at ease teased her conscience.

Dicked in the nob, Sally girl!

She was not over the shock of seeing him if her first thought ran to helping him feel at home among her family.

Not by a long shot.

"Let's do our best to ignore the captain tonight," Arianna whispered in her ear. "Tomorrow is soon enough to make him regret that he lost you."

Would he even be here tomorrow, and why did the idea that he would be gone affect her so badly? *Blast him to hell and back with his own cannon.* It was not fair. How could he still disturb her so much after so long apart?

CHAPTER NINE

LORD ELLICOTT BOASTED of his lands over breakfast and his plans for the future improvements Sally's dowry would afford him until Felix wished to run him through with his gleaming silverware.

Several times would not be enough.

"I have already begun plans to tear up the southeast gardens to build new stables twice the size of what I currently have," Ellicott enthused between bites of poached salmon. "It will be magnificent."

The earl clearly could not wait for the ceremony that would see him wedded to Sally's fortune, and his remarks were the last of an extensive list of expensive improvements intended for his estate. The man openly laughed about his good luck in finding Sally eager for a union with him to anyone who cared to listen.

Those nearest lapped up his enthusiasm while they sipped from the finest porcelain cups and dined with the most elegant silver in their hands, making plans to visit them at the distant estate.

Felix turned his face away in disgust. That Sally could be happy to promise her hand in marriage to such an obvious fortune hunter was beyond his understanding and made no sense. And so much for the private agreement to marry that Lady Templeton had claimed it to be. Everyone at breakfast knew about it. And talked of nothing else but how well suited the pair was.

All the while, Felix's stomach churned with loathing for the man who had a claim on Sally's affections.

He pushed his chair back a little from the table and took in the view while he sipped what remained of his coffee. The duke's wealth was apparent in every nook and cranny of every room. The doors to the pretty morning room were open, and he had a full view of what looked to be a ladies' sanctuary. The feminine room was currently unoccupied, but scattered pillows made from blue and red Indian silk rested on the long chaise for the ladies' comfort, and rugs made of the finest quality were scattered beneath.

He tore his gaze away when he imagined Sally in the space.

Sally herself sat as far away as it was possible to be at the breakfast table, looking lovelier in lemon muslin than his mind could accept was still possible. But her posture was rigid with barely concealed tension. He dropped his eyes, and his attention caught on a dark feline moving into the room. The dark-as-soot cat stopped and sniffed around the polished floorboards near the table, obviously looking for tidbits to scavenge for its breakfast. It hissed at those gathered with ill-concealed contempt and especially whenever a servant's foot came its way. Had the duke mentioned Sally keeping cats yesterday?

Sally lifted her gaze along the table, and their eyes met again. His heartbeat quickened as he remembered her fiery outburst last night, but she soon looked away and gave her attention to Ellicott. Demure, polite, and so different from the woman he had fallen in love with that he had trouble reconciling that the two could be the same female. She hardly ever smiled.

At least last night she had been passionate, even if the emotion was anger. In fact, he had almost leaned down to kiss her. He had always enjoyed her private outbursts of temper and did not know where he had found the strength to hold back his attraction.

"Does something amuse you, Captain?"

He met the curious stare of Louisa Ford and tipped his head. "Yes. The cat."

"That is Sally's wild one, Horace. He cannot stand to be held and will scratch if you try to pet him."

"I will make sure to avoid the surly fellow." He set aside his empty cup.

"Oh, he is not surly, he just likes to do as he pleases." She laughed and glanced down. "Do you like cats, Captain?"

"I do not dislike them." He smiled, deciding that Louisa was very much like Sally. Certainly pretty, direct too, but she had a slight hesitance in her bearing that Sally had lacked when they first met.

Before he could say anything else, Louisa bent down to pick up a tiny, mottled ball of fluff that had been previously hidden from view by the folds of her skirts. "This is Arturo."

"Charming," he murmured before reaching out to scratch the small head with his fingertips. The cat licked at his fingers, then bit him. "He is quite small and just a bit ferocious for his size, is he not?"

"He is Sally's newest and is always hungry." Louisa collected her plate, which he noticed held finely chopped scraps of her breakfast, and slipped from the room to the terrace outside. When she stopped at the balustrade, Felix decided to join her in the sun.

Louisa smiled as he walked over. "He had a terrible start in life. Sally rescued him from a dog in the village and brought him home in her pocket to live with her others. The hunting dogs do not bother any of them, I am happy to report. In fact, I think they are a bit afraid of being scratched."

She fed the cat from her own hand and, when the animal had fed enough, placed him gently on the flagstone pavement. He scampered away into the low shrubbery.

"He is a lucky fellow then to have found a place to belong." Felix glanced around once more. Unlike the stray cats Sally took in, Felix did not belong here. "Some of us never do."

He had to end his obsession with Sally before he made a complete fool of himself. Louisa appeared startled by his remark, so he shrugged.

Revealing how much he had longed for Sally during the past six years would do him no good. Her love was gone, and it was high time he accepted it for a fact and got back to his real life as captain of the *Selfridge*. "Would you excuse me? I need to speak with your father."

"Of course." She smiled sadly but caught his arm to prevent him going immediately. "Perhaps later today or tomorrow if you are free, you might like to walk with me in the gardens. I would love to hear more of your life and of Laurence especially."

The wistfulness of her tone blunted his immediate denial, and he phrased his response more carefully. "I am not sure if I will have an opportunity. It all depends on the admiral."

"Forgive me. I miss my twin, but he does not write to me anymore. He only cares to share his adventures with his wife. Cecily reads me parts of his correspondence, but it is not the same as receiving his confidences directly."

He understood something of the bonds between siblings even if he was not close to his own. He nodded. "If there is time, I will seek you out before I depart the estate and share all that I can."

With that intention in mind, arranging his departure, he said good-bye and reentered the breakfast room. The admiral had already excused himself, so he ventured out into the hall in search of him, or a footman to ask for directions.

He found Admiral Templeton in the Newberry Park great library, but he was not alone. A stranger, likely a messenger, dressed all in black had his attention. Felix hung back a moment to give them privacy, and after a hushed, whispered conversation, Admiral

Templeton turned away with a furious scowl. He stormed off toward the duke's study, and Felix trailed behind. The door banged shut loudly, cutting off any chance of hearing the conversation. After a few moments, the door reopened, only it was the butler leaving instead of the admiral.

Felix peeked inside and discovered the duke standing alone at a window that overlooked the drive.

Behind Felix, the sound of harness and carriage moving off drifted into the hall.

"Good morning, Captain." Rutherford gestured Felix into the room with an impatient wave of his hand. "I trust you slept well last night."

"I did, and thank you."

The duke cleared his throat. "My son has just now received an urgent message and been recalled to London. He will not be able to meet with you as he would have liked. He will not return for several days in fact."

"I will go and pack and follow him to London. Perhaps there he will have time to see me."

"No!" the duke exclaimed, thumping his canes on the floor to forestall his exit. "My son insisted you wait here for his return."

Damnation!

The duke shuffled to his desk and sat with a groan before he continued, "Since the timing of his return is uncertain, his place will be taken by others."

Felix moved to stand before the table. "I was given to believe the matter that brought me here was urgent."

"And it is," the duke barked. "Absolutely vital."

"Then what is this about?" Felix folded his arms across his chest, belligerence heating his blood at the unnecessary delay. "The admiral has told me nothing of my purpose in being here."

The duke appeared amused rather than intimidated by his

posture. "This is about your career, Captain. Your very future as commander of the *Selfridge*."

"Why now of all times?" he asked, incredulous. "We have almost won the day. I have made you extraordinarily rich, and surely you can have no complaints."

"Watch your tone!" The duke straightened up, brows lifting. "Do you not think I am owed an accounting? Until I am satisfied with your conduct, you are ordered to remain at Newberry Park to answer an inquiry into your command."

Felix jutted out his jaw, furious that his career could hang in the balance because of the duke's whim. But then had it not always depended on someone else? He was also now suspicious that Admiral Templeton was not the driving force behind his presence at Newberry Park. Was he here only because the Duke of Rutherford wished to see him squirm and to torture him with Sally's outstanding match? "Am I accused of misuse of your support and funds?"

"Of a sort." The duke smiled in a way that did not comfort. "We will meet at precisely eleven o'clock to discuss the situation. Rodmell will come for you. I expect the process to take several days to complete. Perhaps even weeks."

More than a week and he might be here to witness Sally marry. He could not be present for that. Surely Rutherford would not be so cruel.

The duke's brow rose, challenging him to argue over the length of his stay.

Yes, Rutherford *could* be that cruel. Declining to accept the breach-of-promise payment when Sally had broken with him had not excused him in the duke's eyes. It had only made Felix less of a fortune hunter in his own mind. A distinction the duke clearly did not share. He should have taken the money and been done with the lot of them. "As you wish," he ground out.

"Splendid. I will see you soon then." Satisfied, the old man shuffled away to the window, leaving Felix seething. The Duke of Rutherford truly was a menace, and there was not a damn thing to do about it. He had to stay and clear his name of whatever slur had been cast upon his reputation. He had to keep his ship and his command.

If he did not, he had nothing else to live for.

Not even the hope of Sally.

CHAPTER TEN

SALLY PACED past Ellicott and surveyed the bare chamber full of hope for the future. It was still early in the day, and on impulse she had stolen Ellicott away to Torre Cottage to put forward her proposal that they spend half a year at his estate and half a year in Essex visiting her family. She wanted him to think about her ideas while he was away on his business trip. When he returned, they could negotiate terms in earnest, and he would discover for himself that she was not quite as meek and mild as she had let him believe. "This was my grandmother's favorite room in the whole house."

"Yes, charming," Ellicott drawled, clearly unimpressed by a room that had no furnishings of any kind.

Time and a loving hand would bring this house back to life. If only Ellicott could see the possibilities and imagine it as a summer home by the sea for them.

She glanced out the window, and her breath caught at the spectacular view of the estate and choppy waters beyond. "We could live here a few months to half a year and be very comfortable."

"Why on earth would I want to live in a little cottage on your grandfather's estate when he has ample guest rooms?"

Sally bit her lip, trying not to show her frustration at Ellicott's lack of understanding of her dream. Of what great boon her grandfather offered them by giving her this place if she wanted it. To have a place that was just for them, few servants but close enough to her family that seeing them was no great obstacle. "From here you can see the mansion and the arrival of any visitors who come. My grandmother used to say she could never be surprised when she lived here."

Ellicott's arm slipped around her waist, and he pulled her against him. "It is a very pretty view. But I thought we were to spend the morning getting better acquainted rather than discussing dilapidated houses and long-dead relatives of yours."

They were without a chaperone for the moment, and it felt strange to be in his arms. Louisa had come with them but had claimed to be entranced by the garden's wild beauty. Her sly smile hinted she would stay there for a while too, so they had some privacy to discuss her plans for them.

Ellicott dropped a kiss to her brow and slowly kissed down the side of her face. For a moment the sensation stirred her emotions, but it was a remembrance of someone else who had done exactly the same thing once upon a time.

"I wanted to talk about our living arrangements before we marry, but since time is short, I must be blunt," she whispered as Captain Hastings's handsome face at breakfast this morning taunted her. She could not imagine why he dared to show his face. Her father rarely invited officers under his command to stay, and then only in London. He had promised Felix would never darken her door again.

By the light of day, Felix had been exactly as she remembered him. A little sterner perhaps in his expression, a little more aged and his skin tanned. His nose had been broken she suspected, and there was a small cut on his jaw which was new.

Simpleton! She should not be thinking of Felix. Not now. Not anymore. Not when her future husband's arms were tightening about her body.

Ellicott laughed against her throat. "What is there to discuss? Summers are the busiest time at home, and now we are to marry we have no need to bend to society's expectations. We can do whatever the hell we want and please ourselves first."

"I want to see my family." Her breath caught as Ellicott moved his hands up her torso until they rested just beneath her bust. "Louisa is to return to London for a second season soon, and my cousins too are of an age when they will need me. I cannot let the sole responsibility of bringing them out and chaperoning them in their first season fall on my aunt's shoulders. My mother needs me."

"My dear, your devotion to your family is unnecessary now. They ask too much of you. You must learn to live your own life." He frowned and his hands slid down to encircle her waist. He tightened his grip slowly until his fingers met around her middle. "If the situation is warranted, of course you can go to London any time you like. I do not intend to be a tyrant, but I will need you more than they do."

He moved his hands lower. Sally told herself that Ellicott's possessive tone was no more serious than a fear of being separated. He cupped her bottom and squeezed each globe.

Sally tried to relax. "And I should not like to be parted from you so soon after we marry. But I am sure there will be times when you will have no time for me."

"True, and you will be busy with your own concerns." He groped her flesh with growing enthusiasm. "There will be our children to bring into the world and raise."

"Yes, I hope so," she choked out around her shock.

He spun her around and met her gaze seriously. "If that is not enough excitement, you can always take a discreet lover once I have an heir and a spare to succeed me."

She blinked as he brought his mouth crashing down on hers.

It was a hard kiss and without gentleness. Ellicott backed her into the nearest wall and pressed his body against hers. His tongue prodded her lips, and she parted them, too surprised to refuse.

He thrust his tongue into her mouth a few times, mimicking the act of lovemaking. This kiss had purpose, a definite intent to claim her body despite his suggestion she would take another man to her bed. He cupped her face and deepened the kiss, revealing a hunger she had not known he possessed. He stroked his tongue into the depths of her mouth again until she squirmed. He drew back but grasped one of her wrists to hold it against the wall. "Sweet Sally, you can stop pretending to be modest now."

He slid one hand down her side and grasped her gown, his intent clear to lift it. Did he mean to have her here and now? Against a wall? Sally stopped him. "I am not pretending. I am modest."

"Come now. We have avoided the topic for months, but I have known for some time that you are not as you would have others believe." He raised a brow, challenging her to deny his accusation. Arousal heated his eyes. "I happen to like adventurous women. That is why I think you and I suit for marriage very well. What do you say we visit a bedchamber and practice at being man and wife in earnest?"

Sally was astonished he would suggest it. He had never given any hint he was less than a proper gentleman. "We should not."

"Why not? You are not as other women are, and believe me, I do not hold that against you. In fact, I wholeheartedly approve of a lady developing a broad palate before marriage." His brow lifted. "A woman of your beauty and intelligence attracts attention, and you have all of mine for the present." He licked his top lip, staring at hers so hard she could not possibly misunderstand that his thoughts had turned lascivious. He leaned into her a little, and she felt the hardness of his erection pressing against her stomach. "You will make me the happiest of men if you agree."

"Not now. Not here," she whispered softly, overwhelmed by his proposition and his recognition of her scandalous past. "Why would you ask me to marry you if I am unlike other women?"

"The better question to ask is why would I not." He drew back and cupped her cheek. "You know things about men and have realistic expectations. You have experienced a man's desire before, and I like that about you. You are open-minded and not as prudish as many spinsters who failed to make a match in their first four seasons. Many things you have said and done over the past year convinced me we are of the same mind on many subjects. Pleasure does not need to be contained neatly into a marriage." He smiled suddenly. "I am glad we had this little talk. Now we can be honest with each other and our expectations of married life."

Her heart battered her ribs wildly. She did not agree with his assessment of her character, but she could not deny it. "What are your expectations?"

"Our marriage accomplishes two important goals—a secure future for you and an heir and spare for me at the very least. I desire you but do not expect fidelity, nor do I think you expect it from me. Marriage is a delicate trade of allowances." Ellicott blew out a breath. "I had hoped you would seek me out so many times in the past week. I would have you now if I could sway your mind to mutual exploration."

The blunt discussion about intimacy was something very new from Ellicott and startling. Up till now he had only ever been witty and charming. She had thought she knew everything about him, but he had hidden his rakish streak well. In addition, he had seen through her charade to the wickedness of her soul. She thought about intimacy a lot more than she could ever admit to anyone. Sally drew back from him. She needed time to process what he had said to her and decide how much to confirm. "My sister is outside at this very moment," she reminded him, with an anxious glance at the door. What if Louisa had overheard this conversation? What if she had come into the cottage?

"I can be quiet, but are you the type to scream the house down?" He grinned when she did not immediately deny it. "How decadent of you. I once bedded a woman who screamed out in Russian. To this day I have no clue whether she was calling out for her husband or me."

Sally blinked. "That must have been troubling."

He laughed suddenly. "Then there was this charming little maid we had once. She made me chase her round and round the bed and then giggled through the entire event, the saucy minx."

Sally gulped, thinking hard of ways to delay any more discussion of his former conquests. She had no desire to be compared to other women or know he had bedded a servant in the past. "What sort of example do I set if I am suspected of allowing you liberties merely a day after you ask for my hand?"

Clearly, she needed time to prepare for her marriage to Ellicott. It would be a little more complicated than she had imagined.

He shrugged. "A wicked one. But I suppose you are wise to be cautious. A girl of Louisa's nature would be shocked and never recover. But my door will be unlocked upon my return if you are able to get away from your family for a romp."

She smiled carefully and blushed, trying not to seem as relieved as she felt that she had time apart from him. In London there had not been a chance of dalliance or such frank talk, but here at Newberry Park there would be many more opportunities to be alone with him before they wed. "We should go back. My grandfather expects me at eleven."

Ellicott glanced at his pocket watch. "Eleven o'clock has come and gone while we were kissing. I must be going too. The horses will be restless by now. Have you ever made love in a carriage?"

"We should go." She seized on the opportunity to end the discussion and fled the house, assuming he would follow along behind her. She gathered Louisa from the neglected gardens where she had been collecting wildflowers and hurried toward the distant mansion.

"Why are you rushing?" Louisa whispered as she struggled to securely hold her basket of scented flowers that she had picked at Torre Cottage.

"Later," Sally promised, casting a glance over her shoulder at her grinning betrothed.

Later? What was she thinking? Try never! Louisa was an innocent, incredibly ignorant about men and desire, and she could not be confided in without humiliating them both. The only woman she could talk to about Ellicott was Lady Duckworth, and she was an exceptionally long walk away.

Sally normally enjoyed the stroll from Torre to Newberry, but at a fast walk it left her out of breath.

When they reached the curved garden walks of home and spotted her mother waiting at the drawing room door, she kissed her sister's cheek. "I have to go. Would you please make sure Ellicott's departure goes smoothly?"

Louisa smiled somewhat ruefully at the request and then nodded. She offered a smile toward Lord Ellicott as he drew near. "Say good morning to Grandfather for me."

"I will." To Ellicott she said, "Journey safely, my lord, and I will count the days till your return."

"As will I, my dear. As will I." His voice dropped to a seductive pitch as he leaned close to kiss her cheek. Louisa thankfully missed his intent completely and led him toward her mother.

CHAPTER ELEVEN

SALLY TOOK the most direct path that would bring her to her grandfather's study, trampling across a bare garden bed in her haste. She paused outside the garden door a moment, stomped her feet, smoothed her gown, and checked her hair before entering without knocking as if nothing unsettling had occurred that morning.

"I am sorry I am late." She hurried forward. "Ellicott wanted to see Torre Cottage with Louisa and me, and we lost track of time."

What she had not expected when she took in the room was to come face-to-face with Felix Hastings. She had been trying to forget him all over again, and his presence rooted her to the spot. He unwound from his chair and stood at his full height of six feet three inches, and her heart slammed into her ribs rather painfully as he bowed.

His dark hair was just as unruly as it had been the night before, and she longed to run her fingers through the curls to tame them. His pale blue eyes widened as she stared, and his lips pressed together, reminding her of where they had last kissed her skin. Oh, how those wicked lips had corrupted her.

She tore her eyes away from him, blushing fiercely, and gave her attention to the duke. "Forgive me. I thought you wanted to see me, but if you are otherwise engaged, I can come back another time."

"We were waiting for you. Please." Her grandfather gestured to the writing desk placed beside his own. "You must take notes."

She blushed and quickly took her usual place. Grandfather disliked sharing family matters with servants, and for the past five years when her aunt was engaged elsewhere, Sally acted as secretary to him. She wrote most of his correspondence and recorded his thoughts in a journal he kept. His hands, weary from walking with canes, often refused to cooperate for even the simplest of writing tasks on most days.

She noticed a fresh journal had been placed on her table, and she turned to the first page. "A record of Captain Felix Hastings's actions at sea" had been penned on the front along with his date of birth and dates of his promotions in the service. He had advanced very quickly, she noticed. She recognized her aunt's penmanship, so she did not doubt the accuracy of the record.

She took up a quill, checked the inkpot was plentiful before meeting her grandfather's gaze. "I am ready."

"Very well." Her grandfather sat back, drink in hand despite the early hour, and pierced Felix with a direct stare that would make many men squirm. "I am told quick thinking saved my grandson's life and that of every man on board the *Adelaide*."

Felix shrugged, crossing his long legs at the ankles, and her eyes were unwillingly drawn to the movement of his limbs. Time had only improved his physique, and warmth crept up her cheeks and heated parts of her body that should now be silent. "I did my duty, Your Grace."

"Come now, sir. Modesty will do you no favors in this enquiry."

"Enquiry?" Sally asked, forgetting her role as silent observer in the surprise of hearing why Felix was at Newberry. He must have done something terrible to have been dragged from his command.

She dropped her eyes to the notebook when the duke cast a stern look in her direction, cautioning silence. Her grandfather might indulge her in many matters, but he did not ever like to be interrupted.

Felix let out a long sigh. "The *Adelaide* was well engaged when we were close enough for guns. However, since Captain Ford would undoubtedly wish to claim the prize, I ordered my men to board after the first round rather than repeatedly fire on them and risk sinking either ship."

"You led the boarding party, I am told."

"Yes, Your Grace. Lieutenant Laurence Ford took command of the *Selfridge* during the encounter and did an exemplary job of it."

"You saw my grandson fall?"

"Captain Ford did not fall," Felix corrected. "He stood his ground despite his injury and fought until the battle was won."

Sally sat forward, eager for news of her cousin. She had not known the *Selfridge* had been part of that action. "You saw what happened to William?"

Felix faced only her grandfather, but his jaw clenched at her question. "I made a full report to the admiralty and left nothing out of the telling."

"That is not good enough," she bit out when he did not elaborate or look at her. She would not be ignored.

He turned toward her slowly, frowning. "Injuries obtained in war are not fit to be spoken of around a lady."

"You will tell me," she demanded with uncharacteristic heat. He must understand their need. "You will tell me so his sisters and cousins can know what has happened to him."

His brow creased and he glanced toward the duke as if puzzled. "Forgive me, Your Grace, but surely Admiral Templeton has relayed the relevant particulars to the family."

"Somewhat," Rutherford murmured. "However, a firsthand

account is better than a fifth person's retelling. Do explain in detail for my granddaughter's edification before she uses that quill to cause you bodily harm."

Sally blushed and quickly set aside the implement she had been writing with. She should not have lost her temper, but Felix provoked her.

Felix sat up a little straighter. "You will need to read Captain Ford's report for the battle's beginnings. We were some distance away when the guns rang out and made haste to join the fray. As I said, it was my decision to not risk sinking either ship but to engage hand to hand and support the *Adelaide's* crew. We split our boarding party between fore and aft, crossed the French vessel without encountering much resistance. I engaged those at the stern of the *Adelaide* and fought forward. By that time Captain Ford was heavily pressed and against the main mast." He paused a moment too long and Sally feared he would stop. "He was struck by a saber across the face. I immediately feared it a mortal injury and doubled my efforts to reach him. It caught his mouth and split his skin from the corner almost to his ear. I had never seen anyone survive such a wound, but he fought on regardless. In pain and bleeding."

Sally covered her mouth to hold in a cry. It was no wonder the male family members refused to discuss William. How terrifying for him. All was silent for a while except for the dull tap of Hastings's foot upon the carpeted floor. Sally clung to that sound as she strove for calm. She would have all the answers she wanted today. She would not allow Captain Hastings to deny her. "Go on. What happened after William was wounded?"

"Slaughter. The crew of the French vessel would not yield, and we were forced to put them down to the last man." Felix shook his head, his expression bleak. He swallowed and a look of pure revulsion swept his face. "Once the enemy ship was ours, I took command of the situation and assessed the damage. The French vessel's rudder had been shot away in the battle, which accounted for their zeal in attempting to take the *Adelaide*. I ordered repairs made and advanced Captain Ford's officers to their temporary posts while the surgeons attended the captain's injuries."

"What do you mean, *injuries*," Sally asked, pressing her hand to her chest in dread.

"Aside from his cut face, he was sheeted in blood and his right hand had been smashed to a bloody pulp," Felix continued. "The captain had fought left-handed as we dispatched his assailant together. I fear his right hand might have suffered irreparable harm."

Sally almost swooned.

Felix though, ignored her reaction and kept his eyes on the duke. "We made sail together for several days and saw the *Adelaide* and her prize back to the safety of port for repair."

The duke shifted a letter. "Where you also put Laurence ashore with orders to dispatch an urgent message to Newberry."

"Yes, Your Grace. I felt certain you would wish to know of Captain Ford's situation immediately and to oversee his recovery. The admiralty has many other concerns at present, and despite William's stubborn streak, I feared for his life under less respected hands. Lieutenant Ford, Laurence, was positive that a courier was best to reach Newberry Park, and I felt it reasonable to accommodate his wishes."

"But the final say was yours, was it not?" Grandfather shifted in his chair, his expression piercing. "Your quick thinking ensured William's survival, but it also went against your direct orders, which were to make haste to rejoin the channel fleet. Some in the admiralty are less than pleased by your show of favoritism."

"Yes, Your Grace." He lifted his chin defiantly. "I do not regret my actions, although William curses me now."

Sally leaned forward, surprised by his words. "Why would William curse you? You saved him."

"When you see the wound, the state of his fist and face, you will have an inkling of the suffering he has endured these last months," Felix said softly.

Her eyes widened. "You saw William before coming here?"

"Only long enough to assure myself that he survives." His gaze was steady. "He was not happy to see me, but I could never hold his anger against him. I am certain he suffered a great deal to be saved."

The clock struck the hour and she shivered. They were all silent until the chimes quieted once more.

"Never admit fault," the duke said, a wry smile curving his lips as he quoted the first line of the Ford Family motto. Rutherford turned to his granddaughter. "Will that satisfy you and your cousins and end the tears?"

"Yes." She hurried to scratch out the past few minutes of the captain's statement, although her eyes were full of tears at the thought of William's pain and suffering. She was grateful to Felix for doing so much to save her cousin. He had gone beyond what was necessary for the sake of a fellow officer, putting his own good standing in peril to ensure a member of her family lived to come home.

"Hastings, pull the bell for me. You will now tell my three youngest granddaughters, William's sisters, anything you deem fit to give them peace with their brother's condition. I will allow you to be the judge of what they need to know about the extent of William's injuries."

Felix stood slowly, pulled the bell, and then resumed his spot before the duke's table, his expression grave. The way the captain moved kept her attention fixed to him yet again. In his youth he had been an energetic man, but in maturity he possessed a caged power that lured her thoughts into scandalous territory of when they'd been alone together. She was as much attracted to him now as she'd ever been.

Sally rubbed her temple. Appalled by her traitorous thoughts. Why could she not think these thoughts around Ellicott? When Ellicott had kissed her that morning, she had been waiting for the moment he would stop kissing her.

It was disconcerting.

When the door opened, her younger cousins filed inside quietly.

"William!" The youngest shrieked and ran the length of the room as if to embrace the captain but pulled up short on seeing his face. "What are you doing here?"

"Miss Evelyn." He glanced past her head and smiled warmly at the other two more composed of her cousins. "Miss Ford and Miss Audrey. How much you have grown since I saw you last."

The other pair seemed at a loss and all glanced Sally's way quickly with wide eyes. They knew Felix had almost been her husband once, but she had not known they had met him often enough for him to become so fond of each other.

"Captain." Evelyn stared up at him, then at their grandfather. "You sent for us?"

"Captain Hastings has news of your brother."

The girls crowded Felix immediately, and Sally had to commend the captain on holding his ground in the face of their youthful eagerness. "You have seen our brother?"

"Yes. Not too long ago, in fact." He glanced at the duke. "Perhaps you would allow me to walk outside with the captain's sisters while we speak."

"That would be appreciated." The duke rubbed his brow. "Sally will go with you as chaperone."

Felix raised a brow at the suggestion but agreed readily enough. "As you wish."

CHAPTER TWELVE

CAPTAIN WILLIAM FORD'S sisters took the news of his injury as well as expected, even when he left out most of the gruesome details. Evelyn's arms tightened around his waist as she sobbed brokenly over the ruin that was her brother's face. "He was so handsome."

He was shocked the youngest sought comfort from him. Felix was more or less a stranger to them, though they had met several times over the years of his service, and he was a man they should have kept a distance from given his past relationship with Sally. "He survives, poppet," he murmured gently, hoping his assurances would ease her pain.

"But you said he would not smile at us," she whispered brokenly against his dress jacket.

He tried to lift her face from the fabric, but she resisted. "He would if he could, but to smile pulls at the stitches and that is not a good thing for now."

He secured enough freedom to move and led them along the curving paths toward the sea, away from the prying eyes of any who might try to curb their sorrow. He'd had no idea the girls would be so emotional, or that Sally would not prevent them from clinging to him. However, he had to admit it would be better for Captain Ford if their distress had eased before they met each other. Ford was bitter enough as it was without his family having hysterics when they saw his face the first time. He could not be called handsome anymore.

"Is he cross?" the middle girl, Audrey, asked, struggling to hide her distress.

"Sometimes they say." Felix eased Evelyn away from his side and set her on her own two feet. He liked Captain Ford's sisters, but he should not encourage them to be too familiar. The duke would not like it. "Brothers are often cross creatures, are they not?"

Audrey burst into fresh tears and turned away. As Sally's arm crept around the girl's shoulder, it dawned on him that these cousins were terribly important to her. They had a mother somewhere, he assumed the woman still lived, but they looked to Sally for the guidance and comfort a mother could bring them.

The elder girl chewed her lip, her tears ended, as the shock passed to be replaced by curiosity. "Is he in pain?"

"Not as much now, but I do think he finds the situation frustrating. He cannot express what he feels easily for fear of slowing his recovery and tearing the wound open again. The mouth is a delicate area to heal. The risk of infection is great. That is why he remains in London, in seclusion from others. When he speaks it is very softly and not for many words at a time."

He did not mention that Ford likely hid his injuries in darkness too and that he had driven away all but the bravest of servants with his endless pacing of the house. During his short visit, Felix had longed to tell the man to be still more than once.

The middle sister found her voice. "How were you able to speak to him? We were told he would not see anyone."

He pointed to his epaulets on his shoulders, a decoration of his uniform that signified his rank as captain. "These and determination not to be turned away from the door. His nurse agreed I had a right

to see him, though I believe Captain Ford disagreed with her decision fairly strenuously at first."

Sally glanced around at the girls. "That is everything he knows,
my dears."

The girls held hands and then curtsied to him. "Thank you,
captain."

"You are welcome. I am sorry I do not have better news." He felt
a pang of sadness at their long, tear-stained faces. "Your brother will
come to see you as soon as he feels himself well enough for travel, I
am sure."

Evelyn and Audrey stared at him with large doe eyes, clearly
hopeful that day would be soon. The eldest appeared lost in thought,
no doubt caught up in imagining the difficulties her brother faced in
his recovery and the future. Felix wanted to make things right for the
girls, tell them exactly when they could expect a reunion, but there
was nothing more he could do or say. William had complained to
him that his recovery had slowed. He hoped the girls understood
that fretting over their elder brother would do them no good.

"You said he had a nurse."

"I did." He thought a moment, recalling the brief encounter. "I
do not think William called her by name, but she seemed a capable
woman, a bit younger than your cousin."

"Did she seem intelligent? Could she read or write correspondence?"

"I assume so."

The girls began to whisper in each other's ears, and then they
turned to him, smiling broadly. "Thank you again, Captain. You
have eased our minds greatly."

They hurried away, leaving him alone in the garden with Sally.
"I feel I have just landed that poor woman in the center of an
ambush."

"Most likely," Sally said, brushing aside a tendril of fallen hair from her cheek. When it failed to stay back behind her ear, he clenched his fist to prevent himself from reaching for it. He had once wrapped his fingers in her wild curls while they had kissed the night away.

The girls were some distance away before Felix realized that once they passed through the arch ahead, he and Sally would be utterly secluded from casual view. Alone.

The girls left his line of sight, and with no witnesses to hide his real feelings from, he slowly turned to face the woman he had yearned for all his life.

Time stood still for him, as it did whenever he saw her. Only this time she saw him too, and unlike last night or earlier that day, she was not the least bit composed.

Now that the girls were gone, tears flowed down her cheeks, and she hastened to wipe them away. "Thank you for your candor. We have worried so much for William, but the men of my family would never share the details with us."

He glanced back along the path. The girls were gone, and he did not like to see Sally in distress over something that could not be changed. He eased closer to her, wondering if he could take her hand and offer any comfort. "My only hope now is that they do not suffer nightmares from the telling."

She was so close he could inhale the delicate perfume she wore, a hint of rose and spice that matched her personality to perfection, and see the fine lines of tiredness around her eyes. He caught her hand and squeezed. "The details of the battle were not meant for delicate ears."

"You told them enough." She wiped her cheek again with her free hand. "Not knowing and falling prey to imagination has been worse for them."

"And for you too it seems," he said as he caressed the back of her tiny hand with his thumb and let out a shuddering breath. They were finally touching, and he did not want to let her go. "I am glad to see you have not changed beyond the surface view."

"Of course, I am not changed," she protested indignantly.

"I see a difference. You have lost your trust." He shrugged. "But you still carry the worry for your family on your slender shoulders."

She glared at that. "I love my family."

"I remember." He sighed and released her hand when she tugged on it. "There are worse people to love."

She stiffened, eyes accusing. "Yes, there are."

He looked deep into her eyes. The hurt he had inflicted when he had chosen to continue his career was still there in her exquisite green eyes. But he had chosen to accept the promotion and Rutherford's offer of financial and political support, anything to have a chance to deserve her. He had not even been allowed to say goodbye, and now it was too late to do anything but that.

Before he considered the wisdom of his actions, he leaned down, pressed his lips to her cheek in a soft kiss, intending one last tender moment to hold dear for what remained of his life.

He would never forget her.

Sally turned her face toward his suddenly, and their lips brushed.

As they stood in the warmth of the sun, the scent of Sally's perfume brought his desire rushing to the surface. He deepened the kiss immediately, running the tip of his tongue across the seam of her lips until she opened to accept him.

The next heady moments kissing Sally were everything he had held dear and dreamed of during the lonely nights of his command. He dragged her into his embrace, and she came, unresisting, and eagerly wrapped her arms about his neck as she had done when they had been courting. She tasted sweet, of desire and of unbearable innocence. Her lips and body were warm and soft against him.

His bright star. The place he wanted to call home but could not claim now because she had given her heart to another.

He released her swiftly when it dawned on him the risk he had taken with her reputation. She was engaged, and he should not forget that. He had made a mistake in being with her despite that it felt so right. "Good-bye, Sally."

He turned away before she could berate him, protest at the liberties he had taken. He should not have kissed her. She was not free. She was not his.

"Wait," Sally called urgently.

He swung around and met her gaze. Desire had brightened her eyes. Hope rocked him. "Yes?"

"The duke will expect us to return to his study," Sally said calmly, reminding him of the reason he was at Newberry Park. Even though her chest rose and fell from heightened desire, she would never forget that duty to her family always came first.

Felix took a deep breath and let it out slowly. Of course, she would not want him to stay for selfish reasons. Why would she give up her perfect future for the man who she believed had taken advantage of her untutored desire all those years ago? "Yes, of course. The duke. After you, my lady."

They strolled slowly toward the house, a new tension between them. Awareness of Sally strong and sharp, and painful. And still he wished to take her hand and press it over his thundering heart. He had done that the last night they had made love, tangled in the sheets of her bed, and drunk on desire.

Sally cleared her throat. "Why are you here?"

Not to seduce you. Though he wanted that and more.

"You could have more of an idea than I know myself." He shrugged. "Your father summoned me from London. The note said it was urgent and I came immediately. I still have no idea what is going on."

"My father returned to London and the admiralty this morning," Sally confessed, her expression puzzled. "He did not say when he would return."

"I am sure it will be soon." He winced, cursing the lost time, and experiencing discomfort. The admiral would undoubtedly return to marry off his eldest daughter. "You are to be married, and I do not believe your father would miss the occasion."

"No, he would not." Sally nibbled the tip of her glove as they stepped through the arch and proceeded down the wisteria-covered walk. The scent was sweet, and the hum of bees droned in the air above his head. "Have you been accused of something untoward?"

"Not so far." He glanced at Sally's face for some sign of what she was thinking. She appeared not the slightest bit angry he had kissed her. Did nothing he did affect her now? It was as if that kiss had not even happened. "The duke insists that a reckoning of my past service is in order."

He did not feel it wise to confess to her that the Duke of Rutherford had quietly funded his rise through the ranks at this time. The duke had made sure he was not denied his promotion to the rank of captain six years ago, despite their aborted wedding and the admiral's strenuous disagreement.

All the duke had asked in return for his support was half share of Felix's portion of any prize he took. Felix had been successful and made himself a comfortable fortune and the duke an even richer man. He had given his agreement willingly and without coercion, though knowing he would never have another chance at command if he refused Rutherford's lifeline.

The admiral, however, had insisted he stay far away from Sally, which made his summons here at this time inconceivable.

He had worked toward his own secret mission over the years though: to make Sally proud of him again and give him another chance one day.

That second chance would forever be denied him now.

The doorway to the mansion loomed. The duke waited, balanced on his canes.

"I guess I will have to answer all his questions to find out what I have done wrong," he muttered as he took a deep breath.

The only wrong Felix had ever done was touching Sally before they became man and wife. The best nights of his life were also the ones he regretted most. Sally's innocence had been lost, along with his chances of ever deserving her. He could not change their past, but he could quietly disappear from Sally's future when the duke let him go.

CHAPTER THIRTEEN

AS SALLY SAT down to tea after dinner that night, she fought back her embarrassment and kept her eyes on those seated closest to her. What a stupid mistake to have made—kissing Felix just to prove she felt nothing for him. Thankfully, Felix stood some distance away and at an angle that made it hard for them to see one another. She was grateful because she did not know what to do.

She had allowed Felix to kiss her without one word of complaint or protest of his presumption, purely on a whim. And she had enjoyed it far more than the kisses Ellicott had bestowed on her.

So much more.

During their brief kiss, her whole body had lit up with a surge of desire and an undeniable ache that she had had trouble controlling. Even now she was on edge because of that kiss and could not stop thinking of Felix's whispered good-bye.

But that kiss had brought into sharp relief what she had with Ellicott.

A distinct lack of passion.

The realization was lowering. She was bound for bedlam if she did not sort herself out soon.

"Captain Hastings," her mother called. "Do come and join us."

Sally kept her eyes on her teacup as Felix excused himself from conversation with Lord Cameron, an earl, neighbor, and close friend. Marrying Ellicott was a sensible plan, a good match. She knew it to be true. But was that all there could be to their union—a meeting of great fortunes and family connections? She had hoped time and familiarity would remedy the lack of response with Ellicott, and yet six years apart from Felix had done nothing to dim her response to *him*.

The situation troubled her. She intended to be a good wife, and even though Ellicott expected her to take lovers when their interest in each other waned, she had never intended to. She should have been content enough with the life she had planned for—if only she had not kissed Felix Hastings again.

Eventually she lifted her chin. Felix had a pleasant smile on his lips as he bowed over her mother's hand. At Mother's urging, he took a place at Sally's side on the chaise. Sally folded her hands in her lap and tried not to look at him or remember how much she had enjoyed being in his arms again.

He talked of her elder brother's success against the French, of Laurence's aptitude for command, and he was introduced to Laurence's wife, Cecily. "A pleasure to make your acquaintance," he said in a firm voice that tied her insides in knots.

"And you. My dearest husband thinks so highly of you," Cecily insisted, primping a little under the captain's gaze. "He is so fortunate to sail with so distinguished a captain."

Cecily had no idea that Sally and Felix had almost married, so her praise was undoubtedly intended to make the sort of impression that helped her husband advance.

Felix accepted the compliment with a curt nod. "He is a fine officer."

Her brother's praise for Felix bordered on blind devotion. His letters home to his wife always mentioned the man in glowing terms, and she had endured each reading in stoic silence.

Cecily fluttered her lashes. "When might he return to shore next do you think?"

His jaw firmed a moment as his gaze shifted to stare at her grandfather, who sat across the room. "That I am afraid I cannot say."

"I have not seen him since we married, and he writes so infrequently," Cecily said to him.

Such a bald-faced lie. Sally had heard Cecily's complaint many times before and knew how lucky the woman was. Sometimes as many as six letters arrived at once. Laurence was an exceptional correspondent.

Her brother's wife was not the only one inconvenienced by the war. There were mothers of sons, sisters too that longed for news of loved ones.

"I begin to think he has forgotten all about me," Cecily said next.

Felix frowned. "Lieutenant Ford speaks of you often."

Her eyes lit up like a fire on a dark night. "What does he say?"

"I, well," he mumbled then frowned, clearly perturbed by the question and how best to answer.

"Now my dear, do not pester the captain," her mother interrupted before Felix was further pestered for particulars. "He has orders to follow, just as all sons do."

Felix smiled at her mother gratefully. "Indeed."

Sally almost laughed at the relief he attached to just one word. Cecily's need for reassurance was a constant thorn in her side. Her fear that she was forgotten by her absent husband tried her patience. Sally knew what it was like to truly be forgotten. Cecily at least received letters at irregular intervals.

She glanced at Felix again, annoyed. She could not fault him for his manners tonight, but six years of silence was difficult to forget.

He was polite and charming to her family, though he never looked her way more than common courtesy demanded. That hot desire that had filled his eyes after their kiss was gone. He did nothing to remind her that she had been in his arms.

He took his lip between his teeth, then licked it with the tip of his tongue. All of Sally's wicked remembrances of Felix struck her at once.

Dear God, she had sucked his tongue into her mouth.

She had not wanted to stop kissing him either, which made no sense if she claimed to hate him.

Her mother laughed suddenly, and Sally wrenched her attention back to the here and now. "I had forgotten how witty you can be. My dears, I told Captain Hastings during his first dinner at Newberry that when he is of a mind to settle down, he should make his home in Essex, and I swear I almost have him convinced. He would be a very welcome addition to Newberry society, would he not, ladies?"

The captain laughed. "My ship and men need me back, but if it were possible, I could live in this part of the country very comfortably, I am sure."

Bitterness twisted her lips. She was getting married and would move away when Felix was finally settling down. The talk was that the war would soon be over. Once peace was assured, Felix would come ashore, make a home, and make a life. Her chest tightened. He would make that life with another woman.

The others began to talk amongst themselves, so she turned to him, "Have you seen so much of the district you could make your mind up so easily to live in Essex?"

He faced her. "Not very much at all. Your mother knows better than to believe my interest in Essex anything beyond idle speculation."

"I am sure it is nothing more."

"I do like what I have seen though. The duke has assured me I am not a prisoner, so I have been considering where I might venture when he is done with me for the day. Where are your favorite places on the estate? Somewhere within easy walking distance would make for a pleasant outing in the afternoon."

His following grin was as warm and irresistible as she remembered. He had always made her smile with his curiosity about her preferences. He had been the first man she had met among the naval set who had not flattered her family excessively to curry favor, and his attention had gone straight to her head. He had been clear and direct from the start. He had told her he was ambitious. Sally just had not understood those ambitions meant more to him than she ever could.

Reminded of the past once more, she strengthened her resolve to fight nostalgia. That was all she was feeling when they were together. They could not ever be friends, so there was no point encouraging familiarity. She shrugged off his question rather than offering her opinion on the best vantage points on the estate and asked instead, "Would it really be possible for you to be happy so far from your ship?"

"Most likely you will never find out." He sighed deeply. "I do intend to visit the village as soon as the duke is finished with me tomorrow, and after that I will find my own way around since you cannot bear to offer advice."

"You must be anxious to return to your ship."

"I hope I can leave soon."

Sally's breath hitched in irrational distress at the thought of a carriage taking him so far away that she would never see him again. But when the duke finished with him, Felix would undoubtedly run back to his ship as quickly as possible. They *were* a country at war. Of course, he must wish to return to his men.

"Yes, it is pointless growing accustomed to your being ashore."

His jaw clenched as her younger sister and cousins took their leave in search of their beds for the night. Her mother left them to follow Louisa to the door.

After the room had settled again, a footman brought over a tray filled with drinks, stronger beverages of a kind she preferred to have late at night. However, when she saw a glass of sherry and a tumbler of whiskey perched on a silver tray, she felt a pang of irritation. She did not drink sherry and the footmen knew it. "With the duke's compliments, Captain. My lady."

Sally took perverse delight in taking the whiskey, leaving Felix to claim the sherry, which she remembered he had once confessed to disliking.

It was strange that she could recall so much of his preferences when she could not say the same about the man she was to marry.

"To your happy future," Felix toasted and then downed the sherry, only to grimace at the sweet aftertaste.

Lady Duckworth strolled across the room; her eyes fixed on Felix. "I have never seen a navy man willingly consume sherry. Are you as daring in everything you do?"

Sally groaned. She did not need her friend involving herself in this affair. Not that she was having an affair with the captain. *One kiss did not make a tryst.* She knew exactly how this would end anyway.

"Needs must," he replied with an easy shrug, crossing his long legs, and reclining somewhat in his seat. He spread his arm along the back of the chaise as if he owned it. "A humble captain takes what's on offer and makes do."

Arianna inserted herself between them on the chaise and turned slightly to give him her full attention. "Then I insist you visit Lofton Downs and take full advantage of your country holiday."

Hastings withdrew his arm and sat up properly. "I have never heard of the estate. Is it close?"

"Never heard of it?" Arianna laughed and glanced around to see who was paying attention. She skimmed her low-cut bodice with her fingertips. "Oh, my word. Lofton Downs is my husband's ancestral home, though he is seldom there. Less than a mile away, in fact. A place of beauty said to rival Newberry Park's grand vistas."

Sally's mother bustled over and plopped down in her seat. "Now, where were we?"

"Lady Duckworth has extended an invitation to visit Lofton Downs." Felix leaned toward Sally's mother. "Should I believe her claim and give Lofton Downs the same distinction as this great estate?"

The countess patted his hand as if they were the best of friends and laughed. "As in everything, a gentleman must make up his own mind about whom to flatter and the timing of it."

Sally's stomach turned at the idea that Felix would offer false flattery.

He shifted again to look at Lady Duckworth. "I have my doubts a better place exists or the wisdom in agreeing to such a thing without confirmation. But I must warn you after so many years with hardwood boards beneath my feet and the roiling seas pitching me about, Newberry Park is heaven on earth to me."

Sally was impressed he had managed to flatter Newberry without slighting Lofton Downs. Clearly, he had learned something in the past six years.

"I will convince you that heaven can be found anywhere a man cares to set down his cap," Arianna purred in a lower tone that Sally could only describe as an attempt to be seductive.

It took all her strength of will not to reveal her dismay and she darted a glance at her mother to see if she had misheard. Her mother nodded and smiled as she glanced between the pair as if seeing a match in the making. Sally *was* over the disappointment of Felix, but how could Arianna flirt with the man she had almost married right in front of her? And in front of her mother too!

Lord Cameron strolled over. "Do excuse the interruption, Lady Duckworth, but my mother wishes to take her leave and retire to Braden Park. Are you ready to come with us?"

"Yes, indeed." Arianna held out her hand to Felix. "Until next time, Captain."

"I look forward to it, Lady Duckworth," he murmured as he stood and then helped her rise. He dropped her hand immediately.

Arianna turned to Sally. Her eyes were alight with feverish excitement. "Do not be a stranger, and if you have time before the wedding, bring this handsome devil along with you."

Dread filled Sally at the open mention of her impending marriage before Felix. Although Felix knew she had promised her hand to Ellicott, she was uncomfortable hearing the matter discussed before him. Especially after she had allowed him to kiss her.

She buried her embarrassment again as she said her good-byes to Arianna. "I doubt there will be time."

"Make time," Arianna whispered. "Remember what we discussed."

With a flirtatious wave of her fingers, Arianna swept from the room on Lord Cameron's arm. Only then did Sally remember that Arianna wanted to punish Felix for breaking her heart. Did Arianna intend to tempt him and then turn away from him? Oh, she hoped not.

Felix relaxed, stretching out his arm along the chaise once more, and drew in a deep breath. "She is not how I recall you describing her," he said so quietly her mother could not hear the remark. An impressive feat.

"She is married now."

"Ah." Felix shook his head. "And bored of being so, I suspect."

There was disapproval in his tone, and Sally straightened,

noticing belatedly that she had not consumed one drop of the whiskey that should have been his. No matter what Arianna had in mind for Felix, Sally was no good at holding a grudge. She would take her friend aside and insist she leave the captain alone.

"Take it," she whispered as she passed him the glass. "I recall you prefer it."

"And so do you, which is why I suffered the sherry," Felix remarked dryly, keeping his hands in his lap. "I never could deny you anything you wanted, though I think you should return the glass to your lap. Our conversation has caught the attention of a certain older lady across the room."

Sally slowly scanned the room and met Lady Ellicott's hard gaze. Her heart thudded at the woman's obvious disapproval of her talking with Felix. "Oh dear."

"Trouble?"

"Hopefully not." Sally licked her lips. "Lady Ellicott has opinions."

"And so do you," Felix said. "I have always been of the opinion you should not have to change to please the ones you love."

When they had first met, they had been at a small dinner, and he had caught her sneaking sips from her father's whiskey glass. He had smiled and said nothing. When he had begun to aid her by passing her his untouched glass the following nights, she had fallen a little bit in love with him each time. Together they had skirted the boundaries of propriety in public and laughed about it afterward whenever they could snatch a private moment. She had had so little time to know Felix, but those innocent days had not lasted. Their interest in each other had quickly strayed into passion.

"You certainly did not." Sally sucked in a breath at how quickly resentment flared in her. Felix was a dangerous man. Ambitious and charming, he made her forget the way she should behave. She should not be sitting next to him unless she had no choice. He had used her to feather his own nest. "You should leave."

"I think you are correct." A few moments later, Felix excused himself from her mother and retired for the night without looking back.

CHAPTER FOURTEEN

"MY WORD, THAT MAN HAS A PRESENCE," her mother gushed as she collapsed at Sally's side in quite a state. "I know you still think meanly toward the captain, but I think he would do for one of your cousins, or perhaps for Louisa. He has aged very well indeed. Can you imagine how handsome his children would be?"

Sally had imagined that many times, but the thought of Felix as a potential suitor or husband to any of her female relations was appalling. She glanced sharply at her mother. "Mother, I do not think you should play matchmaker."

Lady Ellicott joined them, her eyes fixed on Sally. Her lips pressed together in a tight, disapproving line.

"Well, I know I should not play matchmaker, but," Mama continued, oblivious to Lady Ellicott's growing scowl, "when we dined together last night, I could swear that man is terribly lonely. No family but a brother. I suspect there is bad blood between them. No home but his wretched ship. If Victoria or Audrey can cheer him, then who am I to stand in the way of a second betrothal for him?"

"Felix knows how to look after himself perfectly well." Sally bit her lip at her use of his first name. If she wanted to hide her past from Lady Ellicott, she had to stop thinking of him in such informal terms.

The countess frowned. "Felix?"

Sally floundered a moment, but her mother spoke up before she could. "Captain Hastings, of course. He has had such a long acquaintance with our family and was once engaged to be married to someone I knew well. Such a dear man, and so polite to me. I would have him happy once more."

Lady Ellicott's eyes lit up as she scented a scandal worth hearing. "Was it his profession that turned the connection sour?"

Her mother smiled. "In a way, although I think an outside influence had more to do with the break than anything."

"Mother, we should not talk about his past," Sally whispered, frantic that her past betrothal to Felix was not revealed to Lady Ellicott.

Mama took no notice of her distress. "It is such a shame. Many parents have ambitions for their children that conflict with what's truly best for them. And he was in love too, I think. The poor man has never looked at another woman the same way."

The countess stiffened in her chair. "How inconvenient, but I am sure he will easily find another. He has means, I understand."

"He does, but it is so tragic I can barely speak of what he has suffered. I have hope now that he is finally ready to put the past behind him and love again. He has made his name and a tidy fortune and will surely catch the notice of some deserving woman." Mama smiled serenely, leaving Sally with the distinct impression she was goading Lady Ellicott on purpose.

But why? Her parents' arranged marriage had never been much of an example of wedded bliss, and everyone in society knew they lived separate lives. Even so, Mama always claimed a love match would best suit her own daughters when their turn came to marry.

She wanted her children to be happy, and yet lasting love had eluded both Sally and Louisa.

"I am sure Captain Hastings will find someone." *Else.*

"I would not be too sure," Mama murmured.

"Please, not tonight," Sally whispered.

"Soon then."

Sally nodded, knowing she could not escape a lengthy debate about Felix forever. In a way it was odd that her mother had barely mentioned him in the past years, except to occasionally say his name when sharing news of him in her letters from Laurence.

Mama was going to be disappointed once she discovered Sally had not agreed to marry Ellicott because she had fallen in love with him. And after her little talk with Ellicott, it seemed highly likely she might have committed herself to a union similar to her parents' marriage. Unless she could make Ellicott love her.

But love was a fleeting and fickle companion and never a certainty. Sally had to embrace whatever opportunities came her way and accept what she could not change. She could marry without love and be content with that outcome. It would enable her to live the life she was always meant to have.

Last season she had felt the odd one out among her married friends. This year she could not help but notice that others made plans for house parties that she could not accept invitations to. For one, she would have to take a chaperone, and two, someone had suggested Sally was almost of an age not to need one.

That remark had hurt her feelings more than she had let on at the time. But later, when she was alone, she had decided it was high time for a major change in her life.

Marrying Lord Ellicott was necessary.

Across the room, her grandfather caught her eye. He winked at her, so she winked back and then laughed, allowing her doubts to subside. She had made a responsible decision to marry. She and Ellicott were cut from the same cloth. Things would be different from her initial expectations, but if Sally had learned anything in her five and twenty years, it was to adapt to change.

She would make it a rule with Ellicott that if either one of them took a lover, then the details were not to be shared. "I think I will turn in, Mama."

Mama grasped her hand and squeezed. "But it is so early."

"I have had a long and tiring few days." Her duties often left her exhausted, but today had been particularly taxing on her emotions too.

"Indeed, you have. It is not every day a woman accepts a man as her husband." Her mother nodded sagely. "Rest well, my darling."

CHAPTER FIFTEEN

SALLY CLIMBED the main staircase with no particular destination in mind once she reached the top. She was not really that weary, but she suddenly could not bear to be around her family. And especially not Lady Ellicott.

Uncertainty plagued her. She was still attracted to Felix, and much more so than she was to the man she would marry. As she ascended the stairs, she studied the face of the late Duchess of Rutherford. Her portrait hung at the top of the stairs leading to Sally's bedchamber, and her grandmother's smile had always intrigued her.

She had only vague memories of the woman. Kind, with a laugh like sunlight. Soft.

Sally did not feel she was very much like her, but she wanted, more than anything, the sort of life her grandmother had lived—with a husband's unconditional love supporting her endeavors. Unfortunately, Sally had not the faintest idea of how to make Ellicott fall in love with her.

The swish of skirts and rush of soft footsteps drawing near broke her out of her reverie. Unwilling to face anyone at this hour, Sally ducked into the nearest guest room and quietly closed the door until it was almost completely shut. She held her breath as her future mother-in-law hurried past, her direction leading her toward her own bedchamber at the end of the west wing.

Sally pressed her brow against the cool, solid door and closed it all the way. She did not want to be questioned by Lady Ellicott about the captain, so she would remain here a while and avoid her. She would not be able to offer a satisfactory answer if questioned about the past anyway.

A throat cleared softly behind her, and she spun about.

Felix Hastings, captain of the Royal Navy and her first lover, stood before the open bedroom windows with the sea breeze billowing the curtains around him. Naked as the day he had been born too.

Moonlight played upon the taut skin of his body, making him seem as insubstantial as air and terribly appealing. Sally gulped as her body reacted to the sheer beauty of his form and the unexpected moment. Strong, muscled, big. Sally was blushing before it occurred to her that she had sought safety in the guest quarters.

She lowered her eyes. "Forgive the intrusion."

"Of course." He did not move to cover his nakedness but stood immobile until she lifted her gaze again. "Can I help you, my lady?"

She had not seen him without clothes in such a long time. She bit her lip and struggled to breathe. When she glanced at his body again, his cock thickened and lifted in reaction to her presence. Sally closed her eyes as the desire to skim her fingers over him grew unbearable. "You should not stand about like that."

"Why not? It is my room." He sighed.

"A gentleman would cover himself, and you could catch a chill," she concluded rather lamely.

"A gentleman I have never been. Not the sort that you are used to now. Besides, a proper lady would have done one of three things by now—faint, scream, or leave."

"I *am* a proper lady."

He shook his head. "No, you're not. You are Sally Ford."

"I do not even know what that is supposed to mean."

"It means I like that you are bold. I like always knowing where I stand with you." He said nothing for a long moment. "Tell me you are satisfied with your life."

Had she ever been? Sally was not sure she could describe her life as happy even now. She had always wanted more. She wanted her heart to not feel so conflicted by what was proper and what she needed. Right now, she desperately needed to feel the warmth of Felix's hand on her skin. Her heart sank as she imagined what that would be like once more.

She had never reacted to Ellicott the way she had to Felix—desperate at just a glimpse of his body, needy with barely an ounce of control. She had been happy when first engaged to Felix, but that was the past. She was not the same woman. She had no delusions that he would stay. "No," she whispered. Her knees trembled and she leaned against the door for support. "I am not."

"You should walk out that door," he said. "No good can come from seeking me out."

Sally knew that to be true, but her legs refused to cooperate. The moment she had laid eyes on Felix in the white drawing room, she had apparently lost all sense. She opened her eyes and discovered he had closed the gap between them. He stood just out of reach, magnificent even scarred from his battles. There were old and new marks upon his skin that had not been there when they had lain together. She longed to touch the wound on his thigh that still appeared red, a recent injury she assumed, to assure herself that he suffered no lasting pain.

His chest heaved and her eyes were drawn downward, following the smattering of chest hair that trailed low to his groin. He was fully aroused, and they had not even touched. She had dreamed for so long of what it would have been like to be in his arms that she knew, standing alone with him again, that she could not leave without being intimate with him once more. "I cannot leave. Not yet."

"Did you tell him we were engaged and what we did all those years ago?"

"He does not know about you nor need to."

Felix inched closer until his body could warm hers. He dipped his lips to her ear and his hot breath sent chills racing along her body. "You are breathing so hard, Sally. I can hazard a guess at what you are thinking about tonight. How long has it been since a man pleasured you with his mouth?"

Oh, hell. "Some time ago."

"Is that what you have come for then? A reminder of the pleasure we shared. An affair before your marriage takes place. Before Ellicott returns and takes you away from all that you know?" He braced his hands on the wall beside her head. "Tell me what you want, Sally, and I will do it gladly. My lips kissing your skin? Our bodies entwined on my bed?"

His words made her burn with hunger, and she quickly nodded before she lost her courage and her mind. The memory of such a pleasure had tortured her long after he had left; during the long hours she had lain awake in her bed wondering why her love had not been enough. He had used her, and she wanted to use him tonight. "Yes, all of it," she managed to gasp out. "I want an affair."

His lips hovered beside her ear and then he kissed her neck, exactly on the small mole at her hairline. She shivered as he licked the spot.

"Very well," he said as he straightened, grasping her arms to pull her away from the door. She trembled in his grip, excited and yearning for his kiss. "An affair that ends when you marry. Now get on the bed and do not slap my face afterward when you have regrets. I will not share them."

She had not truly regretted anything Felix had done to her or made her body feel. Her regrets stemmed from disappointment that he had not returned to set things right in six years.

Sally moved toward his bed, shuddering when his palm caressed her lower back and then slid lower to cup her backside. He squeezed and then the pressure eased to gentleness, urging her toward him. Her reaction was so quite different to when Ellicott had touched her that she closed her eyes briefly.

Was she so lost in sin that she could not feel any guilt?

Her legs trembled as she lifted her skirts and set her knee on the thick pile of mattresses on the high bed. Felix slid his hands to her hips and steadied her as she tumbled down on his sheets, breathless with anticipation.

She expected him to stretch out above her as he had that last night together and claim her immediately. It had been so long. However, he remained at the edge of his bed, inching her gown up until her thighs were bare. He stroked her calves and then moved higher, his hands rough and hot.

"So lovely," he whispered as his thumbs traced the inside of her thighs. He met her gaze. "So soft. Such hunger in your eyes too. I can see and hear your desire. It feeds my own for you no matter how wrong that might be."

"The only thing wrong is your delay," she whispered.

"Everything in good time, sweetheart." His grip firmed, then he slowly parted her legs. Her gown, still covering her most intimate place, remained a barrier between them.

He slid down to kneel beside the bed and pulled so her bottom rested at the edge and her legs dangled over the side. Her gown had risen to expose her lower body, and she squirmed in anticipation. Felix hooked one of her legs over his shoulder, and the blistering heat of his skin against the back of her limb made her gasp out loud as disremembered sensations swamped her.

She had forgotten precisely how hot his skin could be and how the texture of it had affected her excitement. What they had done together was scandalous, and she reveled in memories too wicked to repeat aloud.

He pushed her gown up to her waist roughly, exposing as much of her torso as he could. His hand brushed over her corset, then dug beneath, a rumbling sigh filling the room as he caressed her soft stomach.

Sally squirmed, wishing he were not so far away and that she could see him. As the seconds ticked by until he touched her, kissed her, and made her feel again, she held her breath.

But when he slid a finger over the lips of her sex, she jerked so wildly she was surprised by her own reaction. She wanted him to touch her, but her nerves were so overwrought she could not stay still.

He chuckled softly against her thigh and bit her skin lightly. "You were always so sensitive. Are you ready, Sally?"

"Yes." The desperate quality of her voice when she answered him took even her by surprise. "Please."

Heat from his lips on her sex brought a moan bursting from her lips. He kissed her hungrily, and Sally widened her legs, demanding more of that feeling as she lifted her hips into his claiming.

He parted her folds with his tongue, teasing the place he had touched before. She ground her hips into his wicked mouth and lost herself in the sweet torture of a forbidden and missed pleasure.

Her arousal built swiftly, sharp, and raw, and she jerked back from him before she climaxed. "No."

He rose to his feet quickly, his brow furrowed. "Doubts now?"

"No." She sat up and reached out to touch his face, trailing her fingers over his hard jawline and the new scar. "I just did not expect to feel so much so soon."

He pushed her backward and bent to nuzzle between her legs again, "I always liked that quality in you. Trust me. I know what you need better than anyone ever will."

He skimmed her opening lightly with his fingers but then shook his head and instead brushed them over her sensitive nubbin. He glanced beyond her head to the open window and the moonlit night beyond and grinned. "My Sally beneath the stars once more."

He maneuvered to lie with his face between her legs and settled himself to kiss her lower lips fiercely. Sally grasped the bedding as he brought her back to the brink before she was ready. He teased her, loved her until she could barely remember her own name. He moaned against her sex.

Sally touched the top of his head as he lapped at her, threading her fingers into his messy hair. Her sex quivered again with a warning of imminent release that she could not control alone. His arm clamped down on her hips when she tried to move away again to delay the moment. His intent was clear. He would not allow her to put off her release a second time.

He had not changed his bedding habits very much. He had insisted her pleasure come before his own.

Sally fought against her body's need, prolonging the moment for as long as possible. She writhed on his bed, tortured, eager, and when her release burst, her every muscle shuddered violently. She muffled her cries with the back of one hand, fighting to breathe while holding Felix's mouth against her.

Struggling to make sense of why she had just betrayed her own plans for a proper future, she let herself slowly relax. There was no explanation, so she reached for Felix, eager to reciprocate—to have him slide inside her body and gain his own satisfaction.

"No," he murmured and drew back to sit up far away from her on the bed. His cock full, hard, and waiting for her touch.

She fought with her lassitude to rise from the bed and follow him. He evaded her a second time. She sat back on her heels in surprise. "Why not?"

"This is not right." He reached for his trousers. He tugged them on roughly while Sally could only watch in confusion. He turned eventually once they were fastened, but his expression was grim. "Sally, let me make one thing perfectly clear. The next time you seek me out alone, I will have the rest of you too. I will not hold back again; I will not even ask permission. If we are ever alone like this again, I will make you mine and dishonor us both. Do not come back."

Sally scrambled to a sitting position as he stood up. "Felix, you do not understand."

"Oh, I understand all right." He wiped his brow with the back of his hand, scowling. "You always did like the danger of meeting me in secret. An affair will not ever be enough for me, but you know I am willing, so you came anyway."

She gasped at the bitter edge to his voice. "That is not why I am here."

"You are engaged to be married to one of the most eligible bachelors in society. It is a good match for you. For your family. This"—he gestured to the bed—"is nothing more than an adventure for you, like it must be to so many married women who flirt with naval officers with nothing but their years of service to recommend them. I know why Lady Duckworth wants me to visit her at Lofton Downs. I assume I am to be made to look a fool."

Her eyes filled with tears at how he must perceive her intentions. "I have not changed that much. I never expected this when I sought sanctuary in your room. What happened just now was not planned, but I am not sorry."

He seemed taken aback for a moment. "Even so, an engaged woman should not allow another man to bed her before her wedding day. Ellicott will want his own heir."

"He does," she agreed, although in the heat of the moment Sally had forgotten everything but satisfying her own passions. Felix had considered Ellicott far more than she had. As far as he was concerned, they were in the wrong. "And he shall have his own son thanks to your level head. You must not feel concern he will call you out for this though. Ellicott and I have an agreement to marry, but fidelity was not part of it."

Felix growled, a dangerously loud sound that shocked her. "How could you agree to such terms?"

She shrugged. "In many ways I am the same woman you knew, but I have grown up too. I have given up the fantasy you dangled before me, then snatched away. I have given my word to marry Ellicott. He understands what I want from life."

"Then you are not the woman I loved but a veneer of her former glory."

Sally blinked. He had not loved her. Not really. She could not waste any more years on a dream of love *and* marriage too. Felix had already disappointed her once. Sally did not think she had the strength to recover from a second heartbreak. Lust without love was the only experience she wanted now.

At least with Ellicott there would be no disappointments. Their discussion had freed her from guilt and allowed her to do what she wanted with whomever pleased her as long as she remembered to be more careful next time. She jumped from the bed, pushing down her gown. "I am sorry that I disturbed your evening."

He stalked to the window to stand in the cool breeze and said nothing at first. But then he turned around, eyes blazing. "When you were mine, I would never have shared you," he told her bluntly.

"I was never really yours." She rubbed the sudden chill on her arms. "You bargained with my father for my hand and command of the *Selfridge*. You never gave what you did to me a second thought."

"I thought of you," he insisted. "Too damned much."

"Well, not enough to bother to say good-bye or write to apologize for the fool you made of me," she snapped angrily.

"*Never admit fault*," he ground out. "Is that not what you always said you admired in a man? Someone who owned his decisions?"

He ran both hands through his hair roughly, forcing the dark strands to all angles. After a moment he shook his head and gestured to the door. "You got what you came for, my lady. Please be so kind as to let the door smack your pretty backside as you leave."

"Fine," she snapped again. With as much dignity as she could muster, Sally swept from the room and into the hall. She stood in the dark, shaking with frustration and confusion. How could it feel so right to be in his arms and the next moment argue about it? How dare he use the Ford family motto against her too? He was not one of them.

She scowled at the door behind her. "You will be sorry."

"I already am," he replied bitterly from the other side before locking the door.

CHAPTER SIXTEEN

SALLY TOOK A BREATH, startled by Felix's admission, and then decided he could not have meant it. He did not really understand her and would say anything to advance his own cause. Love to him was something he could put aside until he needed it again.

Furious with herself for lingering, she stalked away. A short walk before bed might be required to quiet her temper, and she was very used to navigating Newberry's twisting corridors in utter darkness.

But the walk through deserted, familiar halls did not help very much. She was still too full of salt and vinegar to shake off her irritation with Felix. In desperation, Sally slipped into her sister's room as she often did late at night when Louisa was abed, hoping she was awake and in the mood to talk. Unfortunately, Louisa's soft, even breathing suggested she slept deeply. Disappointed to be denied her good and calming presence, she lay down on the long chaise and stared at the painting of Lord Cameron's neighboring estate that hung above Louisa's hearth.

When she grew chilled, she tossed a blanket over herself.

Louisa stirred in her bed. "I thought you would already be fast asleep."

"I was not sleepy after all," Sally explained. "I have been prowling the house for an hour. I did not want to wake you, but who knows when I will be able to slip into your room again."

"I will miss these nighttime visits of yours. When you marry Ellicott, I will hardly see you, so do not ruin it by snoring." Louisa adjusted the pillow under her head. "We have a lot to do before the wedding takes you away, and I need my beauty sleep."

"I do not snore," Sally protested and clutched the blanket to her breasts. "And you are always beautiful regardless of how much sleep you have had."

"What do you think of Captain Hastings now?"

"He seems unchanged," Sally grumbled, but her heart was thumping wildly at the question. "Why do you ask?"

"Mama is still very taken with him, and he is handsome. She thought he might do for Victoria since you do not want him anymore."

Sally ground her teeth. "He is a career man, like so many others in the navy. I would not wish to have Victoria's heart broken when he leaves her behind."

"Perhaps he could grow to love her enough to resign his commission. Mama believes he has funds enough to make Uncle George accept the match despite your past with him."

Sally had once dreamed Felix would give up everything for her love, but such a dream could never come true. "Go to sleep and stop matchmaking. Victoria will find her own husband, someone other than Felix, when the time is right."

"Well, even fate needs a push now and then." Louisa sighed. "Lady Duckworth enquired about him as well, which I thought was odd."

Sally sat up quickly. "What did she ask?"

"She wanted my assurance that his bedchamber was far from

yours," Louisa grumbled. "I told her Grandfather would not stand for any sort of nonsense under his roof and neither would you."

Sally pressed her hand over her face as her cheeks heated. She and Felix were good at *every* sort of nonsense. Things Louisa did not yet need to understand. "Certainly not."

Louisa fell quiet once more, but Sally was wide awake, watching in total shame as the moonlight cast shadows upon the walls. Thoughts of the changes to come brought no end to her confusion. There was so much she still had to do before she could leave for her new life. The wedding breakfast might be called a small affair, and yet she expected all the neighborhood, tenants, and local aristocracy, to come to celebrate with the family.

Thoughts of Felix and her behavior with him worried her more though. Could she learn to desire Ellicott the way she did Felix?

She certainly had to if she wanted to recover her dignity.

Felix pulled at his cravat to gain some air but to no avail. The duke kept his private study damned hot, and on top of the accursed fever that was building again, he could not concentrate on the conversation. He wished to escape the heat and the endless questions. A cooling ocean breeze was just the thing to help on such a day. Perhaps even a dunking in the nearby sea to cool his body and clear his mind. However, Sally's aunt Penelope was taking notes today with a diligence usually reserved for a court-martial, so he sat and did his best to be cordial.

"Tell me more about the day William was wounded. I understand you took an injury to the leg during the skirmish. The left leg, was not it?"

The duke was uncomfortably well informed. He brushed over the spot. "Yes. A flesh wound that has long since healed. A piece of the ship splintered during cannon fire from the enemy, and I was in the way as so often happens."

"And Laurence was injured in that skirmish too," the duke said. "Explain how that happened."

"A minor cut to his sword arm," he murmured, wishing the duke would make him stop reliving battles in so much detail. "A few of the enemy boarded the *Selfridge,* and he and his men had to defend the ship. He made a full recovery."

At night when he was alone, he could not banish the deaths of his enemy to allow for peaceful sleep. Sometimes not even the memory of Sally could banish them from his waking thoughts.

He had not slept after Sally had left his bed last night. He had been too full of her, too distracted by her passionate response, to settle down for the night. Her ridiculous arrangement with Ellicott infuriated him and remained a source of discomfort even now. Men in love did not willingly share their wives. Felix might have had the opportunity to keep Sally with him till dawn, but the idea that he would have done so with Ellicott's blessing made him ill.

"Yes, so I understand." The duke pursed his lips. "The injury to your leg, was it received before or after William's wounding?"

"Before we had truly engaged." He grimaced as he rubbed his leg, remembering how it had dragged toward the end of the engagement. His boot had filled with blood and his thigh had burned with sensation. He wiped his brow with the back of his hand. "I barely noticed it at the time, which is often the way of things during battle."

The duke sat forward, peering hard at him. "Is something the matter, Captain?"

"No." Felix was only burning from the inside out. He had hoped to hide his affliction, an irregularly recurring fever he could not be cured of, but it seemed the damned fever could not be stopped or delayed enough to protect his career. There would be ample witnesses this time round unless it passed quickly—which it rarely did. There would be no hiding it unless he could get away. Once found out, the duke would tell Admiral Templeton, and then Felix would lose command of the *Selfridge*. After that, his fall from favor was inevitable. Rutherford would withdraw his support, and then he would be like Captain Jennings, a man with a limited future.

"You appear flushed." The duke peered at him. "Do you find talk of war uncomfortable?"

He blinked when Rutherford's image split into two hazy shapes, a warning of what was to come. He was about to lose control of his senses in the worst possible place. "No, of course not. If there is nothing else?"

A door opened behind him. "Luncheon is ready, my lord."

"Ah, excellent. Shall we join the family?" The duke spoke to his daughter, and when she rose, so did Felix. However, with the fever climbing and the inevitable peak soon to follow, his balance was decidedly unsteady, and he intended to cry off from this meal.

He reached for the back of the nearest chair and stood a moment in silence while he got his bearings. Unfortunately, the world continued to tip and sway.

As if through a long tunnel, a woman's voice called his name. "Captain Hastings?"

"Felix!" The duke's voice was nothing more than a wavering bark until the floor pitched and hit him.

CHAPTER SEVENTEEN

FELIX WAS GONE.

Sally had not caught sight of him all day even though he had been closeted with her grandfather since daybreak. Not that she was looking for him precisely, but knowing he was around made her unaccountably anxious that their paths did not cross again. They would only argue, and she did not want that.

"Why so great a sigh?" Louisa asked as she took stock of the contents of the preserve's pantry.

Sally glanced toward the doorway that led upstairs to the entrance hall. This area of the servant's quarters was quiet for the moment. Most of the staff were gathered about the housekeeper's door, discussing the needs of tonight's dinner. "It is nothing."

Her sister frowned and shifted bottles to see into the darkness of each shelf. "Are you impatient to see him?"

She snapped her head around. "Who?"

"Lord Ellicott, silly." Louisa made a note on her papers. "Who else could I have meant?"

Who else indeed? She hadn't thought of Ellicott all day. Upon her return from her duties on the estate, Sally had expected to dodge Felix, but avoidance had not been necessary. "Are you done?"

"Almost," Louisa murmured, shuffling the sheets, and checking each one. "I just need to run this list up to Mother and see what she has to say. We are running a little short of everything. The harvest has been slow to come in because we lack enough manpower."

Sally bit her lip. "I should have helped."

"You had guests to entertain," Louisa reminded her gently with a touch to her hand. "And I would say catching a husband is more important than filling a basket with fruits. You do not have to help with everything you know."

"I know, but I like to." She hugged her sister quickly. "Well, do not let me hold you up. Mama will be waiting, and you know how impatient she can be to see us."

"True." Louisa tilted her head to one side, her expression puzzled. "Are you sure you are all right today? You seem a bit lost."

"It is just nerves about the wedding."

"And the wedding night." Louisa laughed and then hurried out before she could be scolded for teasing her.

Sally was not worried about her wedding night, or any of the nights of her marriage. She knew full well what could happen between a man and a woman. But she was thinking a lot about her life and what she would miss when she left Newberry as a bride. There were ten women at Newberry, and they somehow managed never to get in each other's way. Everyone pulled together. Would she eventually work that well with Lady Ellicott?

Sally made her way to the main staircase, lost in thought, and ascended to the entrance hall. The house was quiet for this time of day, and she prowled the ground floor rooms restlessly, discreetly searching for the captain while also keeping her eye out for her aunt or grandfather who had disappeared too. Aunt Pen had been taking notes for the duke today while Sally dealt with a stock issue. She needed to mention the outcome to either of them, so they were not surprised by her decisions.

Mr. Morgan was not at his post, and the other servants she questioned had no idea where the butler had gone. Felix had not been in the library or the drawing room with Lady Ellicott and Sally's remaining family. Her grandfather's study door was open, and the captain was not there either, seated before the large table talking war with the duke.

There was only one conclusion she could reach: he'd left her.

Had he taken up Arianna's invitation to visit her at Lofton Downs, or had he gone away entirely thanks to their argument? He had claimed to have no desire to see Arianna again, but she could not help but feel after last night that she might have driven him away.

Jealousy, a feeling she hated, seethed beneath her skin at the very idea of another woman touching him, especially Arianna.

She took the west staircase, ascended to the first floor, and slowly approached his bedchamber. If he had gone for good, she wanted to know immediately. The last time, after she had broken off the engagement, he had left England and she had not known for two whole days. She might have been the one to have stopped their wedding, but he had not even tried to win her back. The crushing pain of abandonment was a feeling she never wanted to experience again.

After checking that she was unobserved, she tapped on his door, then tested the handle. Unlocked. Sally let herself inside and glanced around, expecting the worst, and finding it.

His possessions were gone, his bed stripped, and the hearth cold.

So, he had gone without saying good-bye again.

Sally took a long moment to accept it, to acknowledge the end of a young woman's dream of love and desire.

She should be relieved that the temptation of him was gone, but instead the hollow ache of loss, a feeling she was all too familiar with when it came to Felix, returned to pain her. After all this time, she still was not immune to foolishness.

She still cared about Felix, and far too deeply.

She glanced around once more, her gaze lingering on the bed. Memories might be all she could ever have with him, but they were good memories for the most part. Passionate ones. When she married Ellicott, she would devote herself to feeling that way about her husband instead. After all, many women loved more than once in their lifetime.

Sally slipped from the room and pulled the door shut quietly behind her. She was filled with sadness, but had she ever expected better where he was concerned?

A few paces down the hall, she spotted her aunt disappearing into a distant guest room. In need of a distraction, she headed in that direction to see if her aunt needed assistance for anything at all. Keeping busy had always been good for mending her soul, and with a wedding ahead there was much yet to do.

The door had been left slightly ajar. Other voices talking low joined with Aunt Pen's and drifted into the hall. Sally leaned close to listen before blundering inside and interrupting.

"He seems no better or worse," Aunt Penelope said.

"Why did you move him?" her grandfather asked.

"I did not dare take any chances," Aunt Pen replied. "There was no hint of fever on his arrival, but I thought it prudent to have him moved in case it is a serious illness that might spread."

"This is unfortunate," the duke said. "Find out who he has had most contact with and keep a discreet eye on them for signs of similar symptoms."

"If only we knew what they were. He collapsed so suddenly," her aunt said. "Besides us, my nieces have all stood close to him.

Maggie partnered with him at dinner and a valet attended to him morning and night. They could all be at risk."

"He visited William before arriving here too. Send a warning to the nurse to keep a close watch on William's health in the coming weeks and specifically to watch for signs of a fever. His health is still much too delicate to fight off another infection."

"I have already done so," Aunt Pen promised.

The duke thumped his canes on the carpeted rugs inside the room. "Damn it all, I wanted to see what he has made of himself, not bury him. Something must be done."

A throat cleared and Mr. Morgan spoke. "There was a gentleman with him in the carriage on the day of his arrival, Your Grace. The man went on to the inn and intended to remain there, I believe. Could he know the nature and perhaps a cure for this illness?"

"Bring him, by whatever means necessary," the duke demanded. "We must know what we are dealing with and be prepared to contain the spread."

"I am so sorry I could not be more help, Your Grace. No further cases of high fever have been reported so far. However, without particulars from the patient, I am at a loss of what to recommend in this instance. We might have no choice but to wait and see if the captain recovers on his own," Doctor Hobbits advised in a voice devoid of hope.

Sally pushed her way inside the room.

Felix lay on the bed around which they were gathered and was as still as the grave. Her grandfather, aunt, and the doctor and butler observed him, looking as if Felix was about to die.

If not for hearing their remarks, she might have thought him dead too on first glance. But on closer inspection, Felix was so drenched in sweat that his shirt was limp and stuck to his skin. His lips were parted and pale, but it was the shallow quality of his breathing that sent gooseflesh rushing over her skin.

She moved into the room, heart pounding with fear and dread at the state he was in.

He could not die. Not like this.

"Sally, get out," her grandfather growled when he noticed her. "You have no business being in this sickroom. Morgan, take her out and then fetch his friend."

Morgan rushed toward her; arms outstretched as if to hold her back without actually touching her.

"You have to help him," she begged. "Please do something."

Felix sucked in a sharp breath at the sound of her voice, but that was all he managed.

"My lady, there is nothing we can do but wait," the butler advised, still trying his best to herd her toward the door. "You must think of your own health first and foremost."

"I am." She had been intimate with Felix last night. His mouth on her body, his hands on her skin. She had noticed his heat but not realized it had been a fever in the making at the time. If his condition were to spread to others, then she would undoubtedly have the same complaint by now. She should be kept apart from everyone else to prevent the spread of infection.

Sally rolled up her sleeves and avoided Morgan as she scanned the room, looking for a basin of water and a washcloth with which to cool her lover with. "I am staying. We touched yesterday."

"Touched?" her aunt queried, one brow raised high and then she frowned.

The tone of Aunt Pen's question suggested much, but she ignored it. For too long she had suspected her aunt knew she and Felix had shared a bed anyway. Thankfully she could not possibly know how often it had been or that they had been intimate last night. Sally chose the lesser of her indiscretions to confess. "He grasped my bare hand in the garden, so if he is contagious then it might already be too late for me."

"I see." The duke pierced her with a strange look. "Penelope, you can leave since you undoubtedly wore gloves when you were reintroduced to the captain. Please ensure the good health of the rest of the family. Discreetly, mind. Let us not start a panic. It seems we have no choice but to leave the captain in Sally's care for now if we want to contain the situation."

Aunt Pen rushed from the room; the doctor followed.

Sally poured water in a basin and soaked a cloth.

Her grandfather drew close. "Are you sure you will be all right with him?"

"Yes, but I will need a few things. Ice chips, clean sheets, and a fresh cotton mattress for after the fever breaks. I have some beeswax balm for his cracked lips on my dresser. My maid knows the one. Have them delivered as soon as possible."

"The ice was to be set aside for your wedding breakfast. Your mother planned a pair of towering swans for table decoration."

"She can fret about the size of the swans later." Sally stripped away the drenched cravat hanging loosely from Felix's neck. "He must be cooled as quickly as possible."

Her grandfather approached to aid her, but she held her hand palm out to stop him. "Did you touch him?"

"No. But we have spent many an hour together."

"Without knowing what we are dealing with, it is best to limit any further spread." Her grandfather was not a young man and not robust of health anymore. She could not allow him to place himself in harm's way. "Best be safe and stay back."

Her grandfather appeared amused. "Do you plan to undress him entirely, all by yourself?"

"It is necessary." Sally nodded. She had partially undressed him six years before, but the last time he had been standing and very much aware of what she was doing to him. "He cannot stay as he is. I will be as quick as possible and then cover him."

"I forget sometimes that you are braver than I give you credit for." He wavered a moment, then nodded, ceding her the right to decide. "I will leave so you might not be embarrassed. I will send this fellow, this friend of Felix's, up to the door as soon as Morgan returns and arrange the other things you asked for."

"Thank you."

CHAPTER EIGHTEEN

THE DOOR SHUT QUIETLY BEHIND her grandfather, and then Sally took a deep gulping breath, bracing her hands on the bed. She was not brave. She was trembling with fear and equal parts of relief too. Felix had not left her without saying good-bye. He had been moved to protect everyone's safety. She looked into his face and swore to think better of him from now on and not jump to conclusions. She touched his brow gently and discovered him scorching.

"Felix? Can you hear me?" she whispered, soothing his skin with her fingertips. "You have to help me undress you. You might be too heavy for me to lift on my own."

He mumbled something unintelligible she hoped was agreement. She attacked his clothing, removing his pocket watch and a few coins tucked into his pockets, then rolled him to remove his waistcoat, unbuttoned the fall of his trousers, and then forced his shirt up over his head. He did help a little, but his efforts seemed uncoordinated and just a touch confused at what was going on.

When his torso was bare, she worked on his lower portions, peeling his breeches down his hips and legs, and removing the stockings on his feet. His skin, wherever she touched him, was slick with sweat and burning hot all the way to the soles of his long feet.

She tossed the sodden bundle aside and raised the sheet up to his waist just as someone knocked loudly on the door. Startled, she took a moment to compose herself before answering. "Come in," she called.

Her elder brother's valet stuck his face and little else through the door. Despite his reluctance to enter the room, she was relieved to see the man. "You can take the captain's uniform and have it laundered and pressed."

"Begging your pardon, my lady, but His Grace suggested it might need to be burned."

"Burned?" The idea of Felix without his captain's uniform shocked her. "I do not know that you need go that far or so soon. Felix, the captain that is, will need it for when he returns to his ship."

The valet wavered. "I will have to come back for it if he worsens."

Sally swallowed. The idea of Felix in a worse state filled her with utter dread. "Thank you, Rodmell. I do not understand how this could happen. He seemed so healthy last night. So vital."

"And this morning too when I laid out his uniform, if a bit out of sorts and short of temper."

Most likely her fault. She twisted her fingers in the sheet near his hip, feeling guilty and ashamed that their last words to each other had been angry ones. They had once gotten on together so well. Holding a grudge against him now seemed pointless.

"The duke said you wished for chips of ice and other things," Rodmell said as he hefted items through the door. "I have also brought canvas sacks to put the ice into."

"Thank you, Rodmell." Sally nodded. "I did forget to ask for those."

"Are you feeling all right, my lady? No fever in yourself, I trust."

"I am in excellent health as always," she assured the man.

"Good." The man peeked at the half-naked captain quickly, then averted his eyes. "If there is anything else you need, the duke has bid me remain outside the door until his fever passes. Just call for me."

Sally nodded, appreciating the support even if it was simply a lingering presence down the hall that she could depend upon. Her brother's valet was a member of the staff whom she had learned to depend upon over the years, and she would now too. She did not know what she would do if Felix worsened. If he died... She could not bear to consider that outcome. Rodmell departed with a bob of his head, leaving her alone with her former betrothed.

Practicality would help her manage and keep her panic at bay.

Sally marched to the door, grabbed the first heavy pail and small canvas sacks, and hauled them across the room. She dumped enough ice into the washbasin to fill it. Next, she stuffed the sack to halfway and laid it atop Hastings's sweaty head. He flinched. "This will help cool you," she promised him.

She placed several sacks of ice about his body, one beneath the sole of each hot foot under the sheet, another two beside each arm. He hissed when anything touched him at first and then sighed after the shock of the cold lessened. She took a soft cloth and filled that with just enough ice to lay upon his chest without burning his skin. There was also an empty tankard beside the bed, and she filled that with ice before perching at his side on the mattress.

"Felix?" Sally brushed a piece of ice against his dry lips and watched it melt into his mouth. "You must get better. The *Selfridge* needs you. You have a ship to command. A war to fight and win. I will not have your death on my conscience. We should not have argued."

To that he grumbled her name, but then a shuddering sigh left him, and he swallowed down a little of the melted ice. She continued to feed him ice chips, holding them even when he sucked her fingers into his mouth too to get at the moisture.

When he began to shiver, Sally removed the ice packs and drew the sheet up to his chin. She rubbed his body briskly and promised him he would recover soon. Too soon though he thrashed about enough to dislodge the sheet and, entirely nude, began to sweat once more. Sally patted his skin dry and reapplied the ice packs, offering comfort as the afternoon progressed toward evening. She swept the beeswax salve across his lips, lips that had brought her so much pleasure last night, now twisted with pain and misery. Doubt wormed its way into her heart that recovery might be beyond him. She had never known anyone to fever so fast and not die from it.

She was terrified as never before. He might die before they made peace. She eased onto the bed and took his hand in hers. A useless action since he likely did not understand what she was doing. She wished she had not told him she hated him, but she could not forgive him for leaving her alone with her desires.

Desires that had not abated in the intervening years.

"Lover, come back to me," she whispered, brushing his unruly hair from his face. "Do not dare leave me again."

The door opened suddenly, and caught by surprise, Sally bolted up from the bed.

A stranger preceded her grandfather into the room, a rough-looking fellow with gaunt cheeks, unruly black hair, and the bluest eyes she had ever beheld. But they were cold eyes. Hard and unfriendly.

Her grandfather introduced them perfunctorily. "This is the captain's friend, Gabriel Jennings."

She knew him by reputation. A disgraced captain was always much talked about. She nodded to him and wrung her hands. "Can you help him?"

He squinted down at Felix, and the stench of gin reached her nose. She took a closer look at Felix's friend as he swayed and realized he was utterly disguised, hardly in a condition to be fit for proper company let alone a sickroom. The man shrugged. "No need to worry."

She had hoped for so much more. However, Jennings was here, and he had answers Sally needed. "Why do you say that?"

"He has suffered this before." Jennings strolled around restlessly; he leaned right over Felix's face and then shrugged again. "He is not catching."

Sally sagged against the bed, resting her hands over Felix's thighs, and sent up a prayer of thanks. He would live. That was all she needed to hear.

Jennings stopped beside the duke. "Was that all? You interrupted a pleasant afternoon of drinking."

Rutherford's eyes grew flinty. "Not quite."

Jennings heaved a sigh, then strolled away, inspecting the empty decanters on a nearby table. He pushed his hair out of his eyes and turned back to face them. "You know that fellow you sent after me is lucky I was in a good mood today and did not have a sword at hand. What more can I give in the service of my country, Your Grace?"

"Time. I want to hire your services for the day and tonight."

Jennings inspected his fingernails. "It will cost you."

"Insolent pup." Her grandfather barked out a laugh. "Sally, you can leave."

She glanced at Felix's flushed face. She could not leave him. "But Felix..."

"No argument. If the captain is soon to be on the mend, you have no business remaining. Jennings will stay, and Rodmell can take care of them both very well indeed." He came closer, grasped her arm lightly, and turned her toward the door—away from her lover. "Do you want Lady Ellicott to discover you here? I do not think she would agree that your intended sacrifice in caring for the captain is a harmless activity for an unmarried woman. She is already looking for you."

He opened the door and pushed her out so hard she stumbled over her own feet.

Rodmell darted inside, carrying yet more ice chips. He glanced back once, shrugged, and then kicked the door shut with his foot. She straightened her gown and let out a huff, scowling at her treatment.

What was she to do with herself now? She would still worry for Felix until he had recovered his feet. But that begged the question: if she had been so ready to put her life at risk to care for Felix, could it really be over for them?

If he died, she would never have an answer. But if he lived, she had some tough decisions to make, and soon.

CHAPTER NINETEEN

FELIX SMOOTHED his cravat into place, embarrassed and ashamed to have worried so many people unnecessarily. He was seated at the duke's dining table for breakfast again, still pestered by questions, but at least he could answer them now with better clarity. "I do not know what it is, in truth. I was afflicted some years ago with a fever-like malady after shore leave in the West Indies. It comes and goes on its own schedule. This time was the worst it has ever been in a long time."

"You scared us all to death," the duke grumbled, stabbing into his steak with more enthusiasm and even less finesse than a midshipman in the heat of his first battle. "And at my age I do not appreciate the experience."

Jennings pulled a face. "We had our close calls with fevers a time or two on board the *Essex*. Not much can be done but bury your dead when they do not recover."

Jennings and the duke made an odd pair of breakfast companions. They rubbed each other wrong Felix could tell, and yet the duke did not have Jennings removed and Jennings did not seem inclined to leave.

"I should not have been here," he agreed, weary but well once more. He would undoubtedly lose his command, but there was nothing to be done about that. He had fought hard to manage the illness without detection until now, and he could not very well deny a report of incompetence made by a respected and influential duke. Rutherford was sure to tell his son, Felix's admiral, all about the situation upon his eventual return to Newberry Park. "I will pack and leave immediately."

"About time," Jennings exclaimed, throwing down his napkin and standing.

"You can go whenever you want, Jennings. However, I am not finished with Felix, and he must stay." The duke scowled. "What is it with you men in the service? You have not the least bit of patience for the way things must be done."

"But my health is a black mark against me. Am I not unfit for command?"

The duke studied him until his skin prickled with alarm. "By your account, and that of Jennings too, your health is no different than it has been for the past few years when you have captained your ship with outstanding zeal for His Majesty."

Felix was completely confused. "You do not think this illness affects my ability to command? I was insensible for two days."

The duke patted his napkin to his lips. "What do you normally do on board when the fever comes?"

"Weather the storm. Have the officers dunk me over the side in the bosun's chair on occasion. I pretend I need to bathe or deliberately lose a bet."

"Yes," the duke said then pursed his lips a moment. "I recall Laurence mentioning such a lark in one of his first letters under your command. I thought it highly foolish of you at the time and sure to lead to unrest, but my grandson says the crew respects you even more. Next time we will toss you into the sea, although I hate to think how Sally will complain about that sort of treatment."

"Time for me to depart before this gets overly dramatic," Jennings asserted suddenly, collecting his hat from a side table. "I will see you at the village, Hastings, when you are able to escape this lot."

Felix waited until Jennings was gone before he faced the duke. "Why would Sally care?"

The duke sipped his coffee and then added more sugar. "What do you remember of the past few days?"

"Speaking with you, here, with Lady Penelope taking notes. Maitland's valet and Captain Jennings arguing in the adjoining room about the length of his hair as it was being cut. I first thought I dreamed that altercation. My memories during my illness are often jumbled about."

"Jennings had the look of a scoundrel about him on his arrival," the duke remarked indignantly.

He had indeed. "Then waking up alone this morning as Rodmell laid out my uniform."

The duke grunted. "There are some things that should be remembered. Think about the time you have lost again, Captain. Harder."

He had dreamed of Sally, but he could not imagine her bent over his sickbed. Not after he had told her to never come near him again after arguing. Her cool fingers had slipped over his skin in the dream, enthralling him as she stripped off his clothes. She had begged him not to leave her in his dreams.

Her family should not have allowed it, and yet they had been there too.

He glanced at the duke sharply, fearing he remembered not a dream but Sally actually at his bedside. Her cold fingers had slipped between his lips with ice in the dream, and she had told him not to die. Damn, but she was a confusing wench. Had she been in his room and the duke knew about it? "I hope I have not caused problems."

"Eat." Rutherford pointed to Felix's plate with his knife. "I have no more questions for you today, but I do have a favor to ask if you are well enough for a short journey."

"Anything. I am entirely myself again."

"Good." The duke drained his coffee. "My granddaughter acts as my emissary about the estate. I would like you to accompany her on a visit she must make today, but only if you feel up to it."

"Alone?"

"No, of course not alone. She normally takes a pair of servants with her, but I would like someone with a presence that can intimidate. Ensure she remains safe from harm and discourtesy, and you will have my thanks." He gestured to the world outside. "Morgan heard whispers of dissent among the tenants. With my eldest son and grandsons gone so often and so long, it appears some feel courtesy for a nobleman's granddaughter is optional. She wants to call upon the wife of a somewhat difficult tenant."

"I see." The thought of Sally facing open disrespect did not sit well with him. There was no question he would go and protect her, but he had not exactly come prepared to be an armed guard. "I have only one pistol with me."

"That cabinet behind you will have everything you might need."

Felix rose at the duke's urging and surveyed the small arsenal inside.

"Be impressive, Captain," the duke advised.

"Impressive?" Felix took a sword, second pistol, and sufficient shot for the weapon. After a second thought, he took a sheathed dagger to wear at his waist, hoping he would never need to use any of them. He held his arms out wide as he faced the duke. "Will this suffice?"

"Splendid. You appear quite bloodthirsty." The duke chose another slice of ham to add to his plate. "I am trusting you with my granddaughter, Felix. Do not disappoint me."

He frowned when the duke used his first name again, something he had never done before today in their conversations. "I would not dream of it."

"Oh, and one more thing. Whatever you do, do not tell Sally why you are armed to the teeth. She will only deny there is any danger to be found at home."

Felix shook his head. "She is a Ford. She is not afraid of anything."

"No. Not even a little scandalous undressing of an incoherent captain." The duke raised a brow. "I have to wonder where she learned so much about unfastening male attire when, until recently, she has kept all men at arm's length."

Felix cursed under his breath. No wonder the duke was in an odd mood today. "She should not have done that."

"No, she should not have. But she did so after ordering me out and with hardly a blush to her cheeks. Rather interesting, don't you think?"

It was very intriguing from his perspective; he had thought she would only care about him because he could bring her pleasure. Caring for him during an illness was quite unexpected and kind. Why Rutherford was not angry about the impropriety made him worry.

"On your way now," the duke insisted. "My granddaughter rises early with the dawn, and she has been waiting for you long enough."

By the arch of the duke's brow, Felix suspected he knew there was, or had been, something decidedly more between him and Sally than just the broken engagement. He did not understand why the duke was not keeping them apart though. She was marrying another man. A lord everyone in the family openly approved of.

Or had Rutherford a different opinion entirely?

Felix jammed his hat onto his head, nodded, and strode out to the stables without bothering to question his lack of resistance to Rutherford's plans. First, he was forced to keep a distance from Sally by one Ford, and now the head of the family kept throwing them together.

What did the duke mean for him to do about Sally, if anything, or was this just another test of his character? If it was, he had failed that test days ago to act as a proper gentleman.

CHAPTER TWENTY

SALLY GLANCED over her shoulder as footfalls echoed in the cavernous stables. A tall, broad shape with the rolling gait of a naval hero drew near. She ran to him, wrapped her arms around his chest, and squeezed. "Felix," she whispered.

He embraced her in return, his fingers cupping the back of her head gently. He spun her away from the open stable doorway and into a dark corner where they would not be noticed. "I am all right, sweetheart. Everything is all right now," he whispered against her hair.

Sally buried her face in his coat and breathed deep. "You were sick for so long, and they would not let me stay with you."

"So, you *were* there in the beginning?" He kissed the top of her head when she nodded. "I am glad they sent you away. How would it have looked to your family and future mother-in-law if you were found in my bedchamber? The poor old duck would be scandalized. I was well looked after."

Sally let out a shuddering breath and ran her hands up and down his sides. His coat pockets bulged with strange, heavy objects she could not identify at first. "How you were looked after by that pirate, Jennings, hardly bears thinking about."

"He is a good man. He is just not used to being around women anymore."

She pressed her head harder against him. He might have died, and seeing him standing before her, touching her, was all she wanted right now. Dear God, she had worried for him these past days. She wrapped her arms about his body and released the tension she had carried.

Curiosity got the better of her though, and after a moment of much needed reassurance that he was not a product of her imagination she drew back to toy with one of the strange shapes in his coat pocket, discovering what appeared to be the handle and muzzle of a pistol. "Why are you carrying weapons?"

Felix pushed her off his chest, but she caught his coat and held on. She parted his uniform and discovered a dagger sheathed at his waist that she had not known was there.

He glanced down at the weapon and shrugged. "It is a dangerous part of the world I am told."

"Who said that? My grandfather?"

Felix neither confirmed nor denied the accusation but did change the subject. "Gabriel Jennings was married, and when his wife died while he was at sea the news changed him. Please make allowances for his bad temper at the injustice of life. She was a rare woman, and he adored her."

Sally stared up into his face. "I will try, but you did not answer my question."

"Thank you." He stepped back out of reach and glanced around as a groom led her dappled gray mare from the rear of the stables. Jester was her favorite mount, but she could not take him with her as he belonged to her eldest brother. "Are you about to leave the estate?"

"Not exactly. I have an errand for the duke at a distant tenant's home," she told him. An outing she could not delay just because Felix was on his feet, even if she wished to stay with him. She had responsibilities she could not shirk. In the distance she could see two servants headed their way. "Would you like to see more of the estate with me, if my grandfather does not need to see you, that is?"

"He excused me for the day." He studied her a moment and then nodded. "I would love nothing better than to see the estate with you as my guide."

"I can point out my favorite places along the way." She looked him over, and her heart raced. To look at him now, she could not imagine him being so unwell just two evenings ago. If she had not felt his fever, witnessed his condition with her own eyes, she would think he was incapable of change.

There was one thing that had not altered in the intervening years. She could still notice when something weighed heavily on his mind. He was up to something. She was certain of it from the way he shifted his weight from foot to foot. "I will have an extra horse prepared."

Twenty minutes later they were on their way, and she had figured it out. "I cannot believe my grandfather sent you to guard me."

Felix sighed and shook the reins. "He was concerned enough to ask for help, and after my illness I owe him a debt of gratitude I can never repay."

Sally twisted round to view Felix where he sat on the gig. He looked impossibly large on such a small conveyance but seemed happy enough urging the pony along in her wake. She had not expected him to opt for the small carriage when the stable had been so full of horses that required exercise. "Hardly a hero on a noble steed, are you?"

He looked at her, his jaw set firmly. "The gig is all I need to get there and back. The weapons are for the intimidation."

"We had other horses." Horses he had denied he would ride. She had been positive he would choose Zeus, a horse that would form part of her dowry when she wed Lord Ellicott. She would not mind hearing his thoughts on the great beast. Most men coveted the animal. However, Felix had hardly paid him any attention. Every other visitor had drooled over the gelding, but not Felix. He had been more interested in teasing Horace, her wildest cat, when he had crept out of a dark stall. "Are you afraid of them? Horses."

"I am not afraid." He scowled and slapped the reins on Long Peg's rump until she moved at a quicker pace. "I simply do not care to sit upon a mode of transportation that possesses a mind of its own."

"You do realize you have the most stubborn pony at Newberry Park pulling you about, do you not?"

He sighed. "You are not going to let this go, are you?"

"No." She moved her mount closer to his carriage. She refused to shout at him on such a beautiful day. He was well and they were at peace with each other for the first time since meeting again. "I want to understand why one of the finest captains in the Royal Navy chose to follow me about in such inferior transportation."

"Finest captain? High praise, but you had better not let Maitland hear you say that. He claimed the distinction as his birthright years ago." He grinned and then shrugged. "I never learned how to ride, and at my age I am sure there is no reason I need to start."

She laughed at discovering something new about him. "Oh, so there is something you do not do well. That must be rare."

"Aside from the obvious, yes." He glanced toward her servants, frowning at the great distance between them.

Sally was glad they had ridden ahead. It gave her more time to be herself around the captain. "What else don't you do well?"

He tipped his head to the side, his expression serious. "Forget you."

Sally turned her horse away and urged it on, uncomfortable with his answer. His words proclaimed he had missed her, but his actions proved otherwise. If he had deeply missed her, he would have found a way to see her long before this. And he had not even come to Newberry because he wanted her back in his life. He was here because he had been ordered to come. She rode on in silence.

The rumble of the cart increased on the downward slope, and she circled back as Felix whooped out loud. A wide grin split his face as the gig bounced along in the wake of the pony's enthusiastic canter. She had not seen him so happy since they had renewed their acquaintance. Before, during their engagement, he had always possessed high spirits.

He drew on the reins eventually, stopping near her side. "Your brother and I raced donkeys in Port Royal. He beat me by a nose." Felix chuckled, snapping his fingers. The pony started and lunged forward, and he was thrown backward, legs thrown up in the air. He scrambled for the reins and halted the carriage, laughing all the while. He pointed ahead to a nearby house. "Is that where you are going?"

She frowned as she took in the closest building about two hundred yards away. "Yes. Mr. and Mrs. Frazer have lived there over a year, but I have not laid eyes on her in the past three weeks. I want to make sure she is all right. Her husband is an odd fellow."

"Do you think he harmed her?" His eyes widened. "Is he violent?"

"I do not know his temper well, but I used to see her all the time talking with their neighbors. The last time I spoke to Mr. Frazer, I felt a chill from being around him."

Felix checked his pockets where the pistols rested and then urged Long Peg toward the hitching post. He jumped from the gig, lashed Long Peg to the post, and then helped Sally dismount. As his hands slipped from her waist, Sally glanced up into his eyes and leaned into him. Desire flared briefly in his gaze before he stepped back to increase the distance between them.

She swallowed back a protest of disappointment. What good was desire if she was always drawn to the wrong man?

She hurried toward her maid, whose horse had carried a basket of produce from Newberry's kitchen garden and the orchard. This offering was her way inside the cottage to see how Mrs. Frazer fared with her own eyes. She would deal with desire and Felix when they were done.

Mr. Frazer met them at the gate, his body blocking her path to the building beyond. "What do you want?"

"I have a gift for Mrs. Frazer." She displayed the overflowing basket in a manner that she hoped would appeal to him. "Something for your supper."

Frazer's gaze slipped to Felix and grew tense. "Who is this?"

"Mr. Frazer, this is Captain Felix Hastings of the *Selfridge*." Sally introduced the two men. "He is lately come to Newberry Park as the duke's special guest."

A little embellishment never hurt in a potentially tricky situation. Father was not well liked around the estate thanks to his continued absence, but the duke was adored. She had long ago learned to phrase her requests as if they came from her grandfather even when they did not.

"Mr. Frazer, a pleasure." Felix stretched out his hand immediately, and the tenant appeared surprised he would do so.

They shook briefly. "Captain."

Felix took the basket from Sally. "Here, let me carry that for you, my lady."

The ease in Felix's tone seemed to soothe Frazer enough that he opened the gate and invited them inside the small yard. Sally thanked him and made a beeline for the closed front door.

Felix stalked beside her, glancing left and right as if looking for an enemy to fight. "Gently, Sal."

They waited a moment before Frazer, cap in hand, scrubbed his feet and opened the front door. Her servants remained outside and out of the way.

Frazer's home consisted of four large square rooms and a central corridor that ran from front door to back like many of the tenant cottages on the estate. A bedroom and kitchen at the back; a sitting room and second bedroom in the front. It was neat and practical and on the whole well cared for.

Mrs. Frazer was not in the sitting room or front bedroom, which were both as neat and tidy as a lady could hope to find. However, Frazer stood in the hall, indecision clear on his face and in his stance. He did not like her very much she was sure, and if not for Felix's intimidating presence, Sally would not have the courage to speak up. "Well, where is Mrs. Frazer?"

"Gone," he grumbled, his face flushing the hot red of anger.

"Gone? What do you mean, gone?"

He stumbled deeper into the sitting room and took a letter off the mantel. He held it, stared at it, and then shoved it in her direction. "I can guess what it says."

Felix took the letter before she could open it, his eyes locked on Frazer. "Sally, my dear, would you mind stepping outdoors? Actually, I insist you do. I will take care of this."

If Mrs. Frazer was not within the house, Sally had no reason or wish to linger. She had discovered what she needed to know most of all, so she did not mind complying with Felix's request to leave.

In fact, she was relieved. There were days when dealing with rough-and-tumble men like Frazer was difficult, and there was often only her to restore order.

Sally made it as far as the gate before a window shattered behind her back. She spun around as shards of glass rained down on the grass below the little cottage, the victim of a thrown chair. "Felix!" she screamed.

Her maid and footman restrained her when she would have returned to the house. "Stay back, my lady."

An unholy din, splintering wood and breaking China, lasted but a few moments. Then all was silent within. Sally trembled. She had not heard a shot ring out from the pistols Felix carried on his person, but she was still worried. He had carried a knife. Frazer was the larger man and Felix could be hurt even if he was armed. He could need her help. "Let me go."

Felix emerged from the house the moment the words left her mouth. He appeared unscathed, his expression sober and unruffled by the commotion that had just taken place. He joined her at the gate, casting one last look behind him.

"She fell in love with someone else," he said simply, pulling a face. "We have done enough here. He will not starve. Back to the horses, everyone."

When the servants were gone, Sally gripped Felix's arm. "Are you harmed?"

"I was never in any danger, but he has wrecked the place." Felix slid his palm down her spine and held it against her lower back. The touch was comforting after the fright she had just endured, and heat rushed down her limbs and warmed her through and through. He pushed her toward her horse very gently, voice pitched low for her ears only. "He is heartbroken, and it would be best if he was left to grieve in peace. He could not read the letter himself but did not want to ask for your help. He is very embarrassed."

"I understand." Sally faced the house, loathe to go. "But I cannot leave him like this."

"A man like Frazer will not ever ask for your help, and in his current state of mind, a woman would only be a reminder of his disappointment." He sighed, wrapped her arm around his, and drew her away. "I have known men like him before. They would bleed out from a wound rather than admit an enemy bested them."

She stared at him. "Surely not."

"The trick is to ignore the outburst and give them no choice in the decision to fix things." Felix forced her to her horse, helped her mount, but then paused beside her leg. He straightened her gown over the stirrup, frowning at the cloth. He pitched his voice lower still. "I told him someone would visit in a few days to begin repair of the window, but I strongly suggest you do not come without me or someone more important than a pair of slightly built servants. He is very bitter. She had told him she loved him, and her change of heart has robbed him of all civility."

"Oh dear." When Felix had abandoned her, she had wanted to scream and rage even though it was she who had stopped their wedding after learning he was marrying her to advance his career. She envied Frazer his loss of control even if she was terrified of it. "I understand how that feels."

"Hmm, I thought you might say that." He glanced up. "And I deserve your anger and more, I suppose."

Sally pressed her lips together to keep herself from apologizing. She could not say she forgave him, and it was harder still to forget.

CHAPTER TWENTY-ONE

THEY RODE SOLEMNLY BACK to the stables in single file. And although Sally attempted to engage Felix in conversation, he appeared lost in thought and rarely smiled. Her enthusiasm for the journey had dimmed a great deal without his earlier merriment to encourage hers.

He did help her dismount when they reached the stables, but his reserved manner filled her with longing to see his earlier grin return.

She smiled warmly at him. "Next time you, sir, will ride a horse. I think Nero will do for you. He is a sweet and gentle older fellow."

"There is no need to fuss about my lack of horsemanship." He turned away to speak with the stable master who had finally come out to render aid. "Where were you?" he demanded.

"Helping Lady Louisa in the orchard, sir." Dudley took Sally's gray away while the footman led his and the maids' horse toward their stalls.

Felix petted Long Peg fondly and then unhitched her himself. He might not ride a horse, but he seemed familiar enough with the strappings of a gig. Sally watched him in silence for a long while as his capable hands soothed the twitching pony. "When were you in Port Royal?"

"Laurence's first year aboard. I took him ashore out of pity. The first year on a new ship is always the hardest."

"You like him?"

"I do, just do not let him know." Felix detached the long reins and bridle from Long Peg and then scratched her nose. "He is cheeky enough as it is when the other officers are not around."

"That sounds like my brother."

"And every Ford I have ever known." He spoke without bitterness and then glanced around, taking a keen interest in his surroundings in a way he had not before their outing. He seemed in no rush to escort her indoors, and she did not know why he dallied.

She gestured toward the house. "Are you not going inside?"

"The duke does not require me again today, and I do not want to get in your way." He shrugged. "I will be along in a while or perhaps as late as the dinner hour if you do not mind."

She did mind. She needed to figure out what to do about her conflicting feelings. She was about to marry a man she did not love and desired a man she did not entirely trust.

Felix turned away as the stable master returned, as if the matter of them parting ways was settled.

Sally ground her teeth. "I will wait," she insisted. "I should hate for you to become lost on your way there."

"You really have not changed, have you?" He faced her, smiling at last. "You should not feel obliged to keep watch over me. The illness has passed and likely will not return for many months. I do not think it is wise for us to..."

His expression grew shuttered as he looked toward the distant manor house, and he never finished his thought.

"What is it?"

His shoulders slumped. "Ellicott has returned."

When he turned away, she saw disappointment had twisted his smile into a grimace. As if it pained him that she would marry another.

He retreated into the stables and left her to face her future husband alone.

Sally turned to Ellicott, guilt warming her cheeks with uncomfortable sensation. She was sorry to see him returned because she now could not spend any more time with Felix. Her heart grew heavy with each step that brought him closer, but she managed a smile. "You are back early."

"I could not stay away." Ellicott lifted her hands to his mouth, kissed them both, and then planted a brusque kiss on her lips. He drew back, grinning. "And you have been out enjoying the morning without me. How did you entertain yourself while I was gone?"

Calling on a tenant, and one recently upset, was hardly the sort of call to be considered enjoyable. However, she had enjoyed showing off Newberry Park to Felix and her guilt increased. She withdrew her hands. "I had errands to run for the duke."

"Well, remember when you do misbehave that I want all the delightful details." He hooked her arm through his and tugged her toward the empty gardens. "You cannot imagine how much I am looking forward to hearing your every scandalous misdeed in the future."

Sally laughed at his enthusiasm, but her heart was not really engaged in the conversation. She was aware that Felix stood not ten feet away and could be listening to them, watching her live her new life with the earl. "Well, let me see. On Thursday night I did something terribly shocking..." She led Ellicott firmly away from the stable. "I woke my sister up at midnight and we talked for hours."

Ellicott groaned. "Hardly scandalous, though I do admire your bravery in disturbing her rest. That sister of yours has not your sense of humor or sense of fun. Much too severe for my taste. What else did you do?"

"Nothing of significance." Sally did not intend to reveal the details of her tryst with Felix, his illness, or how she had feared for his life. Anything to do with the captain was simply too personal to share. She asked him instead about what he had done while he had been in London, as they walked through the drawing room doors in search of her family.

Felix's temper flared as Sally and his replacement strolled away arm in arm. In the quiet stable yard, their voices had carried quite well enough that he was sickened by their conversation after a few minutes of it. How dare she speak of what they had done together on Thursday night with her future husband? She had told him what they did together would remain a secret between them. He had taken her at her word. He would never have touched her if he had known her tongue was now hinged in the middle, that she would share the details of their tryst with Ellicott as if it meant nothing.

He turned away in disgust, catching the stable master's guilty expression as Sally strolled away. The stable master had eavesdropped too. That annoyed him. "Dudley, is it? Why are there so few grooms to manage the stables and so few horses?"

The older man grimaced. "Most went with the admiral to London and never came back."

"Bloody hell!" He raked his fingers through his hair and took in the rows of empty stalls. The estate was practically abandoned in that case. Trust the admiral to think of himself first and to take the best too. "And the other half?"

"Not too many able bodies left in these parts, truth be told." The man scratched his jaw. "A few of the footmen double as out-of-doors staff unless the estate has extra guests to be waited on inside. We do the best we can with what we have and do not complain."

Felix grunted, unsurprised by the confirmation of the picture he had already formed during the day. Loyalty to the Fords held firm, but Newberry Park had too few men indeed for the tasks to be done around the place. Sally might speak of Newberry Park with immense pride, but the home was falling apart around her, and she could not see it. She could not do anything to stop it either. The duke was right to worry about letting her wander the place unescorted in such an atmosphere of neglect. "Why do you stay?"

Not that this man or his life was any of Felix's business, but he preferred to know who he was dealing with at all times.

"I have lived and worked for the duke since I was just a boy. 'Tis a grand estate the Fords have, and he lets me run the stables as I like."

Grand or not, Felix could not help but feel genuinely concerned by what he had discovered here. An estate was very much like a ship. It required constant attention and maintenance. If left much longer, Newberry Park might fall into disrepair that could take years of hard work and expense to recover from.

The estate needed more able-bodied men and someone to keep them in line. Someone to keep order as tight as a ship's captain required of his men. He could turn this place around in a week with the right help.

He spun away from that thought and glanced over the tired pony. "Dudley, I require a carriage."

The man appeared surprised by his request. "Going far, Captain?"

"The village."

"Happy to drive you, Captain." He glanced toward the manor and shrugged. "It will not take a moment to hitch a better carriage than the gig you used to get around the estate."

He touched his cap and hurried deeper into the stables, shouting for the stable lad to come out and help him. Felix stood aside as the old man and a boy of around nine led out two chestnut horses out and backed them up to a tidy black carriage. They worked well together, but Felix could see the boy struggle with the straps almost beyond his reach.

He glanced away and noticed Louisa and Audrey Ford in the distance, carrying a basket of fresh-picked fruit in from the orchard. The basket looked too heavy for them, and they stopped many times on the way, laughing and talking, but despite their happy mood he could see the strain of their efforts and slow progress.

By the time the conveyance was ready, Felix had seen more than he cared to about how the place was run. Shoddily for all the money the duke had amassed. He was glad to be going away for a while. He might not know much about the land, but there was too much that needed doing, enough that even he, an ignorant seaman, could tell required attention.

Rutherford's growing wealth, thanks to his efforts in the war, was not going to keep this estate from disarray. Admiral Templeton was too wrapped up in the politics of war to care what happened here. Lord George had already admitted he was doing all he could, and it was not anywhere near enough.

When the war was over, there would be so much to do.

What Newberry needed right now was someone with the experience to convince men to do their best in difficult circumstances. Someone to take the burden from the ladies should it be needed. Whomever they hired would have to be someone Sally and her family trusted, since so many of the ladies were unmarried. If the war progressed or Sally's brothers failed to come home soon, they would need help desperately.

He paused beside the horses and glanced at the manor house once more. Sally, Lord Ellicott, and their mothers were visible through the open set of drawing room doors. The sign of such famil-iarity and domesticity caused his heart to pinch in discomfort.

He needed to go.

"Right you are, Captain." Dudley put down the steps of the carriage while the boy held the horses in check.

"Thank you." He climbed inside and let the dark interior soothe him. "What good does it do worrying about them when I am not allowed to care," he whispered to the empty space.

It did him no good at all.

CHAPTER TWENTY-TWO

"I HAVE BROUGHT YOU A PRESENT," Ellicott said, digging into his pocket and removing a stunning diamond-and-ruby ring.

Sally gasped at the beauty of it as he slipped it onto her finger.

"Now we are truly engaged." Regardless of her mother's presence across the room, he brought her into his arms and planted a brief kiss on her lips.

"Indeed, we are," Sally agreed, but that thought brought with it an unexpected animosity toward Ellicott. She had agreed to marry him of her own free will. No one had pressured her or suggested she must. She had all but thrown herself into Ellicott's path with her usual determination and practicality, and she had not missed him one little bit.

Unfortunately, she was not feeling committed to her goals anymore.

He leaned close to her ear. "Come, let me tempt you away somewhere more private."

From the open doorway, she saw a carriage and team of chestnut horses being led out by Dudley and his son. Her heart stopped as Felix climbed inside the dark carriage. As it pulled away from the stables, her heart began to pump blood to her limbs at a fast rate, and she stumbled away from her betrothed and stepped out through the door.

He was leaving now. But why?

Her mouth grew dry as she caught a glimpse of Felix's profile. He did not lift a hand to say good-bye but stared straight ahead, ignoring his surroundings.

He could not leave. Not when they still had so much to resolve. Panic filled her. "Excuse me. I must speak with my grandfather about an estate matter. It simply cannot wait."

Ellicott sighed heavily. "Very well, but the minute his business is concluded you and I are going on a long walk, and we are not telling anyone where we are going. Just the two of us. I would have you alone for once."

"Yes, of course," she murmured, already leaving the room. Sally hurried to her grandfather's study and knocked loudly on the heavy door.

"Come," her grandfather called out when she knocked a second time.

When Ellicott restrained her by grasping her arm, Sally gasped, quite surprised to find he had followed her, and she had not noticed his presence. She was usually much more aware of him. "What are you doing?"

Ellicott slipped his hand around the back of her neck. "Kissing you."

"Not here."

"Why not? We are engaged to be married. The duke can wait a few moments. I cannot."

A troubling need to flee assailed her. "We are in the front hall where my family and any passing servants can see us."

She was making excuses and knew it. She did not want his kiss today.

"That is the point. I want to mark you with my lips. My beautiful bride-to-be."

Sally stepped away. He thought her wanton and she might deserve the stain of the label, but the only man she had enjoyed kissing was the one she could not have. Felix. "We are not married, my lord, and such liberties can wait to be taken until then."

Ellicott frowned. "Has something changed in my absence?"

"No."

"Then you and I need to have a private chat. I will wait on the lawn. Ten minutes, then duke or not, I will come and drag you out."

Taken aback by Ellicott's clipped tone, she shook her head. "I will be as long as my grandfather needs me, and then I insist upon a chaperone until we are married."

Ellicott's jaw firmed and his eyes narrowed. "Is that the way you are going to be when we are married too? Hot and cold?"

"I am not either of those, but I will protect my reputation and set a proper example for my sisters." Sally let herself into her grandfather's study and shut the door in Ellicott's angry face. Gods, what was she doing risking her future with Ellicott? She must have lost her mind when Felix kissed her.

"Sally?" Rutherford was peering out the window. "Was that my carriage going out with Captain Hastings inside?"

Sally hurried across the room in time to catch a last glimpse of the carriage disappearing from view. "I believe so. Did you not know he was leaving?"

"He is not to leave, and I told him so." Her grandfather scowled. "Where the devil is he taking my carriage?"

"He never said a word." She noticed the dining table in the adjoining room had already been set for two. "Are you expecting someone?"

"Yes. Him." Rutherford shuffled around to stare at her. "I require him here. What did you say to him?"

"Nothing. He was extremely helpful this morning." Sally worried at her lip. "You need not concern yourself. I am certain he will return and explain the situation we found ourselves in with Mr. Frazer to your satisfaction."

"He told you I sent him." The duke drew close and peered into her face. The shrewd inspection was remarkably familiar. "You are not angry with me then?"

"The weapons were a little excessive and obvious since he had not carried any before. Are you playing games with him?"

"Hardly." The duke pursed his lips as if he had tasted bitter fruit. "It is your father who plays games, and damn the consequences for everyone else."

Sally raised a brow at that outburst. Father and Rutherford often did not see eye to eye. Rutherford was usually annoyed that her father spent so much of his time with the admiralty and none at all here. "His presence was remarkably helpful actually. It seems Mrs. Frazer has fallen in love with someone else and run off. She left a letter behind that Felix read to him because he could not. The man is terribly upset about it."

The duke grunted. "After you mentioned your concerns about the wife, I sent Morgan out to discover if there was any gossip. They were all so very taciturn that he could not get a hint of the truth. It seems our clever captain made the right sort of impression if he could understand a man like Frazer on first meeting."

Our clever captain? Rutherford hardly ever complimented sailors, so his praise of Felix was noteworthy. "He also promised Frazer he could count on assistance for the repairs he now needs to the cottage from Newberry."

"Oh, did he now?" The duke nodded firmly. "I was right about him then. Always willing to take charge in a difficult situation, but never leaps to take the credit. He would make an exceptional estate manager when peace comes."

"Estate manager? But that has been my role for years."

The duke cupped her cheeks and pressed a kiss to her forehead. "And you are getting married in a few days' time, might I remind you. Who will run the place when you leave, eh? Who will be my legs and eyes and ears when you are far away? Certainly not your sister, and I have already asked far too much of your aunt and mother as it is."

"Louisa would indeed be much too timid to confront the tenants when they are being obstinate." Sally grimaced. "Even I find that difficult."

"Our brave, brave girl. What we need is a man with a presence that can get things done. A competent man who will tolerate no nonsense. Someone who knows our methods would be preferred, but also able to compromise within reason. What do you say you show Felix the ropes while I tempt him to stay on?"

Sally shook her head. "I do not think you will be in luck."

"Oh, I don't know. Until today, he appeared curious about the estate. I wonder what could have prompted him to leave so suddenly though. He was in remarkably good spirits this morning. Has anyone been difficult about your former betrothed being at Newberry?"

"No. Hardly anyone mentions our past relationship even in private, and I still have not mentioned it to Lord Ellicott. He wandered deeper into the stables after Ellicott found me there." Her voice trailed off as understanding dawned. Felix had turned away as soon as his replacement, Lord Ellicott, had reappeared in her life.

The closeness she craved had vanished as soon as he had spotted the earl, and why would he not turn away from them?

"Probably for the best. Dudley and he need to become acquainted if he is to take up duties here," the duke murmured, missing Sally's conclusion entirely. "Felix has made a good effort to restore his friendship with your mother and sister and cousins already, so that is a wonderful start to having him live here. Your mother will be the duchess when my time comes, and given your father's undependable nature and his dislike of country living, I would not rest easy thinking Maggie had no one to depend on."

"Mother does have staff of her own."

"Who mollycoddle her moods just as much as you do." The duke banged the floor with his canes. "She must have more than just blood relations to guide her. She needs someone who will not abuse her trust. Your cousin Rothwell trusts the captain, and we both know how cynical he can be. If Maitland were out of danger, I would not have this worry, but even he will have a lot to do on his return. Oh, if only this wretched war would end soon," Rutherford grumbled with more heat than usual.

"Please, Grandfather. Calm yourself. Maitland will be back. I have no doubt of that nothing could keep my brother away from us for long. And Fredrick and Laurence and William will return one day soon as well." Sally rushed to her grandfather's side and gripped his shoulder, feeling the sharpness of bones rather than the muscle of his younger days. "Felix would look after the family's interests before his own, I am very sure of that. We can always offer him the position and see what he says about it. I do think he likes it here."

And with that, Sally committed herself to securing Felix for Newberry Park's estate manager. It pained her that she would have to see him whenever she returned to visit her family, but that could not be helped. He could be of use to them and be as happy here as Sally had always been.

All she had to do was convince him to accept the position after the war was won. If he survived to see the day come. She glanced out the window and spotted Ellicott passing by the study windows. He was waiting for her to finish talking with her grandfather so he could lure her to a private spot and try to kiss her again. He looked to still be in a bit of a temper too. "Would you like company for luncheon?"

The duke spotted Ellicott too. "Just you? No one else?"

Sally nodded quickly, relieved to her core to have an excuse to avoid Ellicott for a little while longer. "Just me. I am sure Mother will not mind entertaining our guests without the pair of us."

Rutherford studied her long and hard, one brow rising slowly. "Maggie has always been a congenial hostess. I am positive she will not mind at all."

CHAPTER TWENTY-THREE

"NOW THAT IS ONE FIERY WENCH," Gabriel Jennings said as the innkeeper's wife sauntered past their table yet again, juggling a pile of dirty plates and tankards.

"Married woman," Felix reminded Gabriel as he peered across the smoky dark room too. Not that he needed to point out the woman's status. Gabriel had rules about attached women, especially those with large and dangerous husbands like the innkeeper of the Newberry Arms.

Gabriel peered into his tankard. "I can still admire a married woman's fine temper, is that not so, Mr. Wharton?"

The innkeeper drew close with a jug of ale. "That you can, but just remember that her temper often requires an outlet, and she will use whatever object is near to hand."

Felix squinted across the room. He was just a little bit inebriated, and a pleasant lassitude had washed over him some time ago. Several hours or so had passed since leaving Newberry, and although he was no closer to leaving his own bad mood behind, the fresher company and drink had managed to make his problem recede. "I think she is a fine wench too, but Mrs. Wharton also has a fire poker in hand and deserves the utmost respect."

He toasted the woman and earned a laugh from the innkeeper.

"Another drink, Captains?"

Gabriel scowled. "He's the captain, I am just the lone wolf in your midst."

"You need to get yourself a wife to distract you from saying that over and over," the innkeeper said and then scowled at Jennings. "And do stop admiring my wife, sir. Find your own."

"I had a wife. She's dead," Gabriel said bitterly. He drained his tankard and slammed it on the table. "More."

Felix leaned into Gabriel's shoulder in sympathy. "Now, Lizbeth was a fine woman."

"That she was." Gabriel frowned though. "Only I never told her so often enough."

"I am sure she knew how you felt about her," he said. They had had this discussion earlier in the day, and the poor man still did not believe. "She was proud to be your wife."

"You are the only one who thinks that. She married me and I drove her to her death. I should have taken her with me, or better yet have given up my commission. I had enough to live on four years ago, but no, I had to keep fighting, thinking she would be waiting when we won the day." Gabriel stared down at his hands. "They are not like us. Women like, no need, to have men spell out their feelings in the finest of detail. If you think a wench is pretty, say so. If you love her, tell her so every day, not just the once. I did not deserve Lizbeth, so she was taken from me."

There was not much Felix could say to that rant that he had not commented on before, so he pushed Gabriel's refilled mug of ale toward him and hoped he would keep drinking.

The innkeeper topped off both mugs again after Gabriel had taken a long swig. "Are you married, Captain?"

Felix glanced up at the innkeeper's question. "No."

"He almost married once," Gabriel told the innkeeper. "Now, that Sally is a fine wench. Quite the temper, I'll wager."

Felix took a sip of his fresh ale. "She is and she does. My word, she does. Usually directed at me."

The innkeeper's eyes lit up. "I gather you have fallen under her spell."

"Unfortunately," Felix said morosely, considering Sally. She had not been angry with him today. It had been wonderful when she had thrown herself into his arms. Everything had been going so well until Ellicott showed his smug face. And everything had changed for him after that.

The innkeeper drew up a stool. "What happened, Captain? If you do not mind me asking? Did she pass on, too?"

"No, she lives on to haunt me in the flesh." Felix had spent so much time not talking about Sally that he was tempted to share the burden of his mistake. "Her father's political scheming led to her throwing me over. I did not know what her father was doing until it was too late to save us from an argument that did not end well for me."

"She blamed you for her father's schemes. Hard to fight that."

"Impossible, given her loyalty to her family," Felix said and then sighed. "Six years and she has not wavered in her conviction that I was duplicitous. I would have beaten down her door and kidnapped her if I had thought it would do me any good. Too late for that now, of course."

Jennings leaned closer to whisper, "Then if you still love her, you had best prove yourself a better man than her father."

"There is no point. She is to marry another man soon, and he is titled," Felix admitted, depressed by his loss.

"Then you have no time to waste. If she is still angry, she must still care." A customer hailed the innkeeper. "Excuse me."

Felix considered that piece of advice carefully as he watched the innkeeper disappear. There were many reasons to keep his distance from Sally Ford. His career for one, her family for another. He would not like to have a second bloody nose courtesy of Lord Rothwell or whatever tortures her brothers could concoct.

Jennings shook his head. "You are still sitting here?"

"She is not the woman I fell in love with." He took another sip of his ale, pondering all the ways Sally had changed over the years they had been apart. The way she dressed, modest and prim, the way she seemed conscious of every move she made around others— he missed her curses. He missed the wilder Sally of her youth. Her fallen hair and the way she would secretly come to him for a kiss and more.

"And you are not the man who landed in her father's sticky web of political schemes without a clue how to fix things. Kiss and make up. Ask her to wait. What have you got to lose?"

"Everything I have worked so hard to obtain," he said. "My ship, my command."

"Believe me, you can survive without all those. Not happily perhaps, but it is not a death sentence not being a captain." Jennings lowered his voice. "Can you bear to watch her marry someone else, knowing the fellow is rutting with her, and never once try to win her back?"

He gritted his teeth at Jennings's coarse description of Sally and Ellicott sharing a bed. He could not imagine Sally happily married to Lord Ellicott, and he did not want to think of her in the earl's bed, which she probably already was, and that made him ill inside. Ellicott was a smug prick and a fortune hunter. Whenever Felix saw Ellicott near Sally, he wanted to drive his fist into the man's pretty face and never stop.

"It is too late."

Jennings swallowed another mouthful of ale. "It is only too late to change a mistake when one of you is dead. Until that time, there is always a choice."

Felix gritted his teeth. No regrets, no doubts. He had feared and hoped for entanglement with Sally's life for so long, and now he was neck deep in lust and longing once more. How the hell was he supposed to walk away this time?

In Sally's opinion, Lord Ellicott's mother was a puzzling woman. Not given to moving too often or too quickly and certainly not given to theatrics, she did not have much patience with explanations but required that she know everything. She had not much liking for talk of the navy either, which had been a frequent topic during her visit, and Sally hoped that despite their difference of interests they could become friends one day. And yet she felt as if each meeting was a battle. "More tea, Lady Ellicott?"

"I should think two cups are more than enough for the evening."

Sally ignored the urge to agree and had a maid take Lady Ellicott's cup away. She poured another for herself and her mother. "Will it rain tomorrow, Uncle George?"

He glanced down at his absent foot, lost when a dog had mauled him as a child. "No chance of rain, sadly. We will have clear skies for the next few days."

"Wonderful." Uncle George was never wrong about the weather, so Sally made up her mind to enjoy a few pleasant days out of doors while she could. "Might I take your girls for a picnic lunch tomorrow?"

"Indeed, you might. Audrey was hoping to have gone out today, but you were occupied."

She smiled, relieved that she would have family about her

tomorrow and would not have to deal with Ellicott alone. Sally usually spent a number of hours with her younger cousins, but between her work and the Ellicott's visit, and Felix, she had neglected them. "We might go to the lookout this time and take telescopes with us."

"Are you hoping to see a battle underway?" Ellicott asked, his tone still as surly as it had been this morning. She had managed to spend the whole afternoon with her grandfather discussing the estate, and Ellicott was not pleased or the least bit understanding.

"Whales, we like to look for passing whales." Sally sipped her tea and then fondly petted the cat perched on her knees. "Arturo might even come with us."

Ellicott shook his head. "Take the cat walking?"

She scratched Arturo behind his ear until he purred loudly. "Have you ever tried to stop a cat going wherever it pleases?"

"That is what I keep dogs for," Ellicott muttered angrily.

Sally gasped in shock. She glanced at Lady Ellicott, but her expression revealed none of Sally's distress. "You would not."

Ellicott glanced away as Louisa rushed over then and placed Arturo in a wicker basket. Her expression was horrified. "I will keep him now."

Sally struggled with her temper as Louisa hurried from the room, then she turned on Ellicott. "I never thought you could be cruel to a lesser creature. Cats are harmless."

When he shrugged, Sally stiffened. She had never imagined her future husband would be a danger to her cats. She had intended to take them with her to Shropshire, but that did not seem like a wise plan now given his attitude. She would have to leave them behind, along with so much more. Was starting a new life always so difficult, or was it simply that Sally had made a bad choice?

Perhaps there were many other things they should discuss before they wed? Such as what he had been doing in London and why he felt he could not explain his errand to her. Did he think her simple?

"That is a lovely color on you," Lady Ellicott said suddenly, diverting her from quizzing Ellicott immediately. "You are always so elegant and stylish."

Sally glanced toward Lady Ellicott and blinked at her interruption. She had worn a gown from last season tonight. Not her best or most elegant and certainly not worn to impress the Ellicotts, but one that felt right for the night. "Thank you. So are you. Is that another new gown?"

"Indeed, it is. Four yards of lace in the skirt and pure silk all the way from Asia. Ellicott went to London just to fetch it for me."

Sally was rendered speechless, but Uncle George grunted out, "You would look just as well in sackcloth."

Lady Ellicott opened her mouth and then snapped it shut at the insult. Everyone else in the room froze and then started talking at once about other matters.

Sally licked her lips. "You have to forgive Uncle George. He does not think much of current fashion. You have no idea of his resistance to funding a new wardrobe for Victoria and Audrey's come-out."

"Few men have a sense of what's important," Lady Ellicott replied, but it was clear she was annoyed with Uncle George. "Except for my dear Ellicott."

Uncle George's eyebrows rose high, and then he made a show of opening his book with a shake of his head.

Sally's doubts about marriage doubled. To her it was extraordinary that Ellicott should have made a special trip to London just to collect a new gown for his mother.

"That reminds me, how long is Captain Hastings staying at Newberry," Lady Ellicott enquired. "He comes and goes with extraordinary irregularity, but should he not be on his ship somewhere, defending our great nation from the French?"

"I have no idea," Sally answered when no one else replied. How much time could she steal with Felix? "He is my grandfather's guest."

The countess frowned. "And that other fellow, Hennings?"

"Jennings," Sally corrected.

"Now that is a man the duke should not allow anywhere near his estate," Ellicott murmured.

Sally glared. "He is a widower."

The countess sat forward. "All the more reason in my opinion to keep the man from darkening your door again. He is only after one thing when it comes to women."

"He loved his wife." Sally waited for the countess to take back her criticism.

"Love. Posh! Love is only for the very foolish," Lady Ellicott exclaimed.

Utter silence answered her. When the countess finally noticed she held the minority opinion, she straightened her spine. "No one marries for love these days. I am sure you will agree with me, Lady Templeton, that a good match requires only wealth and good connections."

"Then I guess you have never been in love," Uncle George cut in and then cast a questioning glance at Ellicott. "Nor ever plan to be."

"Do not drag me into this nonsense before the wedding," Ellicott grumbled, shoving his glass aside so carelessly it landed half on the table and half off. An observant servant hurried to prevent its fall and set it safely back on the table. Ellicott barely noticed the assistance. "Which reminds me, I thought we might return to Shropshire on Tuesday next week as man and wife instead of waiting."

Sally sat very still, her heart thumping against her ribs at the unexpected request to advance the wedding date. They were marrying by license, so they could marry any morning they liked. However, she did not intend to marry in an unseemly hurry that would result in the worst sort of gossip. Everything was set for their wedding the week after he suggested. "I prefer to leave on the day we discussed when you first proposed."

"I see." He stood suddenly. "Then do excuse me. I have a few letters of apology I must write tonight to my friends."

CHAPTER TWENTY-FOUR

ELLICOTT STRODE FROM THE ROOM, leaving Sally reeling. Was she really going to marry a man who was cruel to cats, uncaring about love, and thought to push her around and into his bed by being a bully?

And what letters of apology did he need to write? They had no plans so far, or at least none she knew of. When was he going to confide in her?

"He is just nervous about getting married," Lady Ellicott explained.

"He does not sound nervous to me," she told the countess with as much dignity as she could. "He was rude."

"Well, what do you expect of him? There is hardly enough to entertain a grown man used to a full social life. He cannot be expected to sit around with us women while we make lace and such. He needs more to amuse him. He's always had his own friends, and now he is trying to accommodate you and your family too. It is hard for men to be idle. Things will be different when we are back at home, and everything returns to normal."

It was hard for Sally now. Always apologizing for being busy with her work on the estate was wearing her down. Always controlling her nature just to please the pair of them so they would accept her into their family. She was not sure she even wanted that life anymore. She shook her head. Everything depended on her being one way when she was being held back from the very things dearest to her heart. She did not know how much more she could bear before she started screaming.

"Everything will be settled soon, and you and I will rub along together as best we can," Lady Ellicott said. "The painters have started on your apartment and promised it will be done by the time we return. Then new drapes will be hung throughout the house to match," Lady Ellicott enthused, little realizing her words were another blow to Sally's contentment.

Perhaps she was bound for spinsterhood after all.

"You have chosen to decorate my bedchamber, and the house, without bothering to consult me about what I might like?"

"My dear, it will be beautiful. I have picked just the right shade of crimson to match the gold thread in the bed hangings."

Gold embroidery too?

Was her dowry to be spent on frivolous decorations she did not want? She could never sleep in a room decorated in red. The color kept her awake at night and always had. Sally set her teacup aside and went to the window, mind tumbling in confusion. The dark drive was empty.

"Where are you, Felix," she whispered. "Tell me this is all a bad dream."

Her reflection gave her no answer and no comfort. Behind her the countess quieted, but none of Sally's doubts did.

"Excuse me, my lady," a footman whispered. "Lady Templeton requests to see you."

Sally glanced about the room, unable to spot her mother, who had been seated with her moments before.

"She has retired for the night," Rodmell murmured.

"Yes, of course. I will go to her immediately. Please ask my sister to offer my excuses to Lady Ellicott."

Sally hurried away gladly, along the dimly lit hall to reach her mother's ground-floor apartment.

At the door, she nodded and then pushed her way inside. "You sent for me, Mama?"

Her mother glanced up from her writing table and the papers she had been reading and smiled. Swathed in lace and white muslin tonight, she appeared adorably pretty and ready for bed. "At last," she remarked in an exasperated tone.

Sally crossed the room and kissed her mother's cheek. "You always say that."

"And I always mean it." Her mother set aside her work. "I miss you the moment you walk out of the room. I will miss you even more when you marry that man."

Sally twisted her engagement ring on her finger. "I have always wanted to marry."

"True. When you were a girl, you used to speak of what your life would be like. The color of your drawing room, the number of guests you could seat at your dining table. You always wanted a blue bedchamber like this one. You made an early start on preparing me for the loss of your company one day."

"Was I really so fixated as all that? I do not remember saying any of it." She thought a moment. "I will still have a blue drawing room and seat sixteen for a dinner party in London. Not a body more or less. There is something to be said for an intimate gathering of friends and family."

"Those were a girl's dreams from one who hasn't the faintest inkling of what marriage will really be about. From what I heard tonight, you might not have a choice in anything so long as Lady Ellicott rules the roost." Her mother frowned down at her robe, pleating a fold of fabric nervously. "Your future mother-in-law has ideas of her own about the sort of impression *her* family must make for their guests. She has made it clear that you will be expected to behave as *she* wishes."

"I am hoping to bring her around to my way of thinking."

"Are you certain you can? You have not been yourself around them. I understand why, but I do not like to see it because you appear so very miserable around her and *him*." She sighed deeply. "I wish you all the luck in the world, you know that. I want you to marry and have children. To have a man to spoil you as you deserve and the protection of his name. When a woman gets to a certain age, she becomes set in her ways. She either likes to sleep late or rise early. Treats her servants well or does not. Believes in love, scorns it, or accepts that love is only for the lucky. *You* believe in love."

Sally took her mother's hand. "I love you."

"I love you too, my darling, but I speak of a different love. I am not loved in return by the man who should have cared for me above all others." With a little toss of her head, Mama's smile returned. "Your father has his amours and ignores me. I have had a long time to accept that, and I doubt he will suddenly decide he loves me at our advanced age."

Sally considered her mother, then decided she would never have a better moment to ask a question that had been on her mind of late. "Mama, how could you have had six children with a man who does not love you?"

"Stubbornness." Her mother looked away. "Each time, I prayed a child would bring us closer, but it did not. When your sister Mary was taken away from us so young, just barely out in society, your father never came to me again. He took her death as a sign that our marriage was over, and I have been alone ever since."

Years without a husband's, albeit fleeting, affection. "Oh Mama,

Mary would never have wanted to be the cause of your pain. She had her own troubles."

"I wish I had known of them before it was too late to save her life." Her mother sniffed. "Do not pity me, Sally. I went into my marriage with my eyes wide open, and I gained so much despite your father. I gained you and your brothers and sisters to love. A home and extended family to protect me. I have been incredibly lucky in my life."

"Except for Father."

Her mother nodded. "I want so much for you to have a good life."

"I do, too."

"And you can love Ellicott?"

Sally swallowed a lump in her throat. "I could."

"That is what I said to myself when I was young." Her mother's hand tightened on hers. "If you have any doubts, do not marry Ellicott. Better to be married for love than never experience it."

Sally chewed her bottom lip. "I loved once."

"Felix?"

Sally nodded and stood, turning her back to her mother and the uncomfortable truth. "And he left me."

"He did." Her mother joined her at the window and put a comforting arm around her back. "And he will leave again to further his ambitions for glory and greater wealth. Did you ever wonder what he wanted it all for? Success and a fortune? He has not used any of it to better his situation. From what I can tell, he owns little more than his possessions aboard his ship."

Sally sighed. "So, it seems."

"On the surface, your father married me for exactly the same reason you feel Felix wanted you. Connections to increase his standing in society and my hefty dowry to better his life." She laughed. "I was described as an incomparable in my day. Pretty enough to turn heads, accomplished, and with a fortune not to be sneezed at. I could have picked anyone at all to marry. I chose with my head rather than my heart."

Sally was doing the very same thing. "Why did you pick Father if you knew he did not care for you?"

"I was not going to. I had half a dozen young men from excellent families contending for my hand and my connections. Unfortunately, there was none that I liked more than the others. My parents pressured me, so I decided to use another method to choose which family I gave my fortune to."

"So, you chose Father, not for himself but for the connection?"

"No, I chose him for his *family*." Her mother grinned. "I knew I would have to spend the rest of my life in this place, live side by side with your aunts. Not to mention their husbands and children too. Rutherford liked to keep everyone close, and of course the duke rules this place. I was young and considered by many to be just another pretty face with a pretty penny to her name. I liked your father's family from the moment we met. They made room for me in their lives, in the running of this place, and never made me feel unwelcome. Over the years I never had to fight to have my way simply because I was to be the next duchess. I wished for a peaceful existence because I understood everyone has needs and ambitions. They have become my family, much more so than your father."

Sally sank into a chair and hugged a pillow. She could not say she would choose to marry Ellicott for his family. She would rather not be around his mother even now. "Not everyone can say that about the family they marry into."

"True," Mama murmured. "I am just lucky that they liked me being around as well, or I would indeed have been miserable. As you will be too if Lady Ellicott's opinions continue to hold sway and conflict with your own. I am not suggesting you must change, but there will be a battle ahead. You are too much like your aunt to back down every time there is opposition. You are used to being heard."

She adjusted the pillow on her lap. "Does it bother you that Aunt Penelope decides so much of what happens here?"

"Never. She has good taste, and we hardly ever disagree."

Sally tossed the pillow aside as her mother joined her. "What do you disagree about?"

"You."

Sally blinked. "Me? What did I do?"

"You and your sisters." Her mother squeezed her hand. "She has always believed I allowed you girls too much freedom."

"I am sorry to be the source of any argument between you."

"Not to worry. We have been discussing your futures for years. I tell her you know your own mind and can easily put a stop to any shenanigans some young men might tempt you with." Her mother rubbed her temple and then smiled. "Then Penelope reminds me that even the smallest flirtation can lead to eventual ruin."

"Yes, she has warned me of that often over the years since I almost married Felix."

"I know. That is why I did not feel the need to bring up the subject of him again. You have heard it all from her. You have already had a close call. But are you sure you do not want to see what sort of man he has become? He seems rather intense whenever we discuss you. The look on his face when I mentioned to him your engagement broke my heart, but it had to be done."

Sally gasped. "You were the one who told him I was to marry?"

Mama nodded. "At dinner the first night. I did not want him to imagine he could walk back into your life and pick up where he had left off. If he wanted you, he had to work for your forgiveness. Do you forgive him?"

"I do not know."

"That is an excellent answer. The very best, in fact." She drew

Sally into her arms and squeezed. "He was not a fortune hunter, darling. He did not keep the breach-of-promise payment your father gave to him. He sent back every penny to your grandfather with a note protesting his innocence."

Sally's head spun. "How did he achieve the rank of captain without funds to buy his way up the ranks?"

"I do not know, but I have a suspicion someone does."

"Who?"

Her mother raised one brow. "Who knows everything that happens in this family?"

"Aunt Penelope." Sally ground her teeth. "And Grandfather."

"Penelope has not said a word." Her mother crossed the room and shook out a length of cloth. "What do you think of the color?"

Sally wrenched her mind back to the moment and studied the weave. "Beautiful. French?"

Her mother nodded.

"That will look lovely. Trust Maitland to send you an early birthday present. I loved the prints in the last shipment."

Her mother shook her head. "Maitland sends nothing back to Newberry. He never has."

"Then where?" Sally blinked, recalling all the carts that had turned up their drive over the years. Goods from far-flung places came at irregular intervals but often enough that she had taken them for granted. "Not from Father, surely?"

"Your father has terrible taste in cloth, and if they were from him, he would have bragged about his generosity to us poor women." Mama pursed her lips. "I think these little luxuries come from another captain, one who might have made a bargain in exchange for something he valued highly."

Sally closed her eyes. "Felix should be very rich."

"But he is not. He does not own very much. I have suspected a share of his prizes has been sent to Newberry for some time, but your grandfather denied it. I have been keeping a close eye on Laurence's accounts of battles fought and goods taken in his letters to Cecily. This"—she held the fabric up—"is undoubtedly the spoils of Captain Hastings's success."

Sally bit her lip. "Grandfather has always given me first choice."

"Indeed, he has. Even Penelope and I know not to set our hearts on anything until you have looked at it all. Your bottom drawer is full of the captain's wealth. He never took more from you than you gave to him freely, but he continues to give to you indirectly, and I think he always will. Do you understand why?"

Sally put her face in her hands. She had thought she understood Felix when really, she had not known the full extent of his desperation to win her back. She could believe he had made a bargain with her grandfather to advance his career, but to give so much of the spoils of his success to them, to her, smacked of pride, too. Felix must have been mad to agree to such terms. Or desperate to prove he was not the fortune hunter she had accused him of being all those years ago.

CHAPTER TWENTY-FIVE

FELIX REMAINED in a foul mood and made little attempt to keep it from his face or his tone as he started another wasted day sitting about at Newberry Park. Despite Gabriel's suggestion that he should try to recapture Sally and their lost love, he could not fathom why she would share what they did together with her future husband.

He had taken her at her word that no one would know about what they'd done together, and he was more disappointed by her behavior than words could say. It was one thing to be unfaithful but quite another to gossip about it. It cheapened her and him.

He had been so cross about it yesterday that he had gotten good and drunk with Jennings, which was unusual for him, in the hope of forgetting the entire affair. He had slept the indulgence off at the inn until the duke's staff—Morgan and Rodmell plus stable hands—had fetched him home again as the new day started.

The duke cleared his throat. "I understand you kept a woman on board during the summer of 1812."

A little gasp escaped Sally, and he was pleased. "What of it?"

The duke seemed taken aback by his tone. "You kept her

confined to your cabin for three weeks and would not let her even come up on deck for air."

He folded his arms across his chest. Everything the duke said was true, but none of that had been in his report. "Was that a question?"

The duke pursed his lips. "Young man, keeping prisoners, particularly females of reportedly lovely proportions, in cramped conditions is ungentlemanly conduct. Especially when she is the widow of your enemy."

"The conditions were not cramped for her. She was particularly small and found my quarters completely charming." Felix ground his teeth. Someone on board his ship had talked, and if he had to guess, he could only assume that Lieutenant Laurence Ford had been spying on him at the duke's request. But why? The duke had maintained his support for his career even after Sally had broken with him. What did his love life, or lack of, have to do with his command? "I treated her with the respect and privacy I had hope my own wife would receive if I had one to be taken aboard an enemy vessel."

The duke stamped his cane on the floor and bellowed, "Forcing her to be your mistress is hardly respectful."

He was not the least bit intimidated by the duke's bark since he was innocent of the charge. In fact, he was feeling decidedly reckless about his future. Keeping women on board went against the grain for many captains. However, in this case he had had good reasons for keeping the woman restricted. Reasons he did not wish to share while Sally was in the room. "She would feel that my discussing it with strangers to be a betrayal of the worst sort." He glanced at Sally. "I gave her my word that I would never speak of her."

"Was she your mistress, Captain?" the duke pressed. "And how many others have there been that the admiralty would equally disapprove of?"

The duke's tone was harder than it had ever been, and although Felix wished to ignore the question, his honor would not allow it. He had worked too hard to rebuild his reputation to let a lie unravel it all.

"I never touched her," he bit out. "We had been nine months at sea without shore leave, and she was exceptionally beautiful and sweet. She kept to my cabin—very happily I might add—to keep out of the path of my lusty crew until circumstances allowed her to disembark. I disapprove of keeping women on board as a rule."

The duke expelled a huge breath. "Why is that, Captain?"

"Women are a distraction, both to the captain and to the men under his command. A woman has so little to do, and it would be easy to misunderstand a harmless jest as a flirtation in close quarters when tempers often grow short, and the comfort of home and sweethearts are far away."

The duke raised one brow. "I happen to live in a society full of distracting women, so I can assure you their location hardly matters."

"That is indeed true." He glanced at Sally briefly. "However, there is also the danger of attack at sea that is another strike against having a woman on board. In battle, all hands must defend the ship and most women are unequal in strength to an enemy intent on harming them. They must find sanctuary within the ship, and if the ship were to fall and they alone were to survive, they would face an eager welcome from unscrupulous men."

"You mean they would be imposed upon," Sally said in a sickened voice.

He nodded. "Madame Velay was lucky that the *Selfridge* captured her husband's vessel. She was entirely safe from indignity on board my ship, as any woman could expect to be."

The duke peered at a letter before him. "She married your physician."

"Yes," he added, noting another detail that had not been part of his dispatches. Laurence was going to be peeling barnacles off the hull of the ship with his teeth when Felix got back on board. "I had noticed a few looks between them, and when she asked me if it would be all right to invite the physician to call on her, I allowed it. He was a bachelor and a gentleman."

"And your other women?"

"There have been no other women, Your Grace," he said in a tone that he hoped brooked no further discussion on the topic. There had never been anyone since Sally. "My personal life is not for further discussion and is hardly relevant to how I run the ship or protect my king and country."

"Yes, of course. But the way a man feels about women is especially telling of his character in general. If he chases after everything he sees, helpless women and even servants, then he does not place much value on the one he has rightfully married."

The duke's gaze landed on Sally and remained there a long moment.

Felix snorted. "I have had little time for socializing. The admiral prefers to keep the *Selfridge* at sea and away from England."

"Yes, I had noticed my son has kept your ship far from shore, despite discussing otherwise with him on several occasions, much more so than any other frigate of your line." A corner of the duke's mouth lifted in a half smile. "Sally, note that the captain's loyalty to king and country is unquestioned, as is his faithfulness."

Sally started but made hasty notations on the page. Felix kept silent. The duke was fishing for a flaw in his character. Examining his personal life in the hope of shaking out some deep, dark secret. He had none that the duke likely did not already know about, but that book and all it contained would be open for public scrutiny if the duke chose to share the details with others. Who knew what they were really writing about him?

An interruption took the duke from the room, leaving Sally alone with him. He thrust out his hand. "Show me what you have written."

Sally was slow to comply, but eventually she stood and passed the journal to him. He was surprised to find it an accurate account of the interview today, so he flicked back to the beginning. Brief and to the point, and remarkably close to what he remembered. He tossed it back in her general direction, reluctantly impressed that she caught the journal before it hit the floor. Felix could not even look at her and examined the high shine on his boots instead.

"What is wrong?" she whispered, sliding into the chair by his side.

"Nothing, my lady."

"You do not seem very happy today."

"I am not. I would much prefer your aunt to take notes, but I am in no position to argue with Rutherford. Don't you have a new betrothed somewhere to entertain?"

"He has gone shooting with Uncle George." She sat back a little. "Why would you not want me to know how good and kind a man you are to a woman in need?"

"So, you can laugh about my old-fashioned notions with Ellicott? I would rather a ball to the chest. Kill me now and be done with it, madam."

"I would never laugh at you. You are an honorable man."

"And what are you? A woman of similar character?" He checked behind them to ensure they were still alone. "You told him about Thursday night."

She blushed, her hand coming up to cup her own cheek. "I spent what remained of Thursday night, after I had left you, tossing on the chaise in my sister's room because of our argument. My sister and I talked for a while, but I could not get to sleep. I did not tell him of your illness. I have not told him anything about you at all still."

He shook his head. "Why would you lose sleep over what I said to you?"

"Because I do not understand why I am still drawn to you when I have agreed to marry Ellicott," she whispered and then dropped her gaze.

His ears buzzed as if a sudden gale had sprung up.

Sally stared at her hands, twisting an obscenely large ring on her finger. He had not seen the piece before, so he concluded the earl had given it to her recently to mark their marriage. "Are you having second thoughts about marrying him?"

She swallowed. "Did you enjoy your visit to Lofton Downs?"

"Why would you think I had gone there? Oh, for heaven's sake! Do you really believe I would take up with another woman just because we disagreed?" He scowled at her. "I went to the tavern to see how Captain Jennings was getting on. We drank the day and most of the night away. The duke's grooms fetched me back at some ungodly hour this morning. I have no intention of taking up with your friend."

"Oh, I thought..."

"Yes, I can see what you thought. Your friend was quite the flirt the other night, but you know me, or you should." Felix could not stop grinning as Sally's startled gaze lifted to his. At the same time, she slipped her ring on and off her finger. He leaned closer to whisper, "I am not interested in Lady Duckworth for more than friendship, and then only because she means so much to you."

Sally bit her lip. "I am terrible to have doubts, but I do not seem able to stop. I catch myself staring at you in case you are gone the next moment. When you were fevered, I was so frightened, then you left suddenly, and I did not know what to think. I cannot stop myself from imagining the worst."

"I am still the same man at heart that you knew six years ago." He leaned across the space between them and pressed his lips to her cheek briefly. "I am only capable of thinking of one woman, and that has always been you."

He sobered. Declaring himself would do him little good. Sally was still engaged to be married, still not free to be with him openly, but her confusion gave him hope. If she could be jealous of a little flirting aimed at him, then that meant she might still have stronger feelings for him she'd not yet revealed. He might yet have time to convince her to cry off.

But then what? Ask her to wait forever or marry her by special license against her family's wishes, only to abandon her to wait for a return that might never come if he were killed in the next battle? That was not the life for her. She belonged among her family where she would be loved and kept safe from harm.

Could he even marry Sally and return to war without breaking her heart again?

He rubbed a hand over his face, conflicted in a way he had never expected. Yes, he wanted Sally with a desperate ache that never went away. But he did not want to leave her behind, disappointed, lonely, and wondering if he lived. She could not come with him.

"Say something." Sally whispered.

"I think doubt is natural." He paused. "But you have a chance for a home and love with Ellicott. It was never my intention to make trouble for you."

"I know." She smiled. "But trouble seems to follow wherever you go."

He took in her expression. "Steady on, sweetheart. Trouble seems to follow you too."

She pressed her fingers to her temple. "I had hoped to have grown out of my impulsive nature by now. However, it seems I am doomed to make the same mistakes. Perhaps in another year I will have grown out of my rash temper."

"Do not." He smiled, losing the last of his anger. "It is one of your most endearing qualities. You are unexpected and bold and entirely too delicious not to kiss as often as can be managed."

She laughed at last and grasped his arm. Warmth flowed into him, and he leaned in to deliver a kiss. Unfortunately, the doors creaked open behind them at that moment, and he jerked back in his seat even as Sally bounced out of her chair to stand.

"Excellent," Rutherford exclaimed as he returned. "Now that problem is taken care of, where were we? Ah yes, I want to hear how you managed to lose your masthead and still win the day."

"I would like to know that too," Sally agreed, her eyes shining with unguarded interest. She took her seat and reopened the journal. "My brothers do not believe you did it without help."

The duke groaned loudly as he sat.

"Well, we did. My officers have christened it the Hastings Maneuver," Felix confessed, watching the duke lean heavily on his canes. "Might I fetch you a drink, Your Grace?"

"Yes, why not." The duke sat with an oath and wrung his hands together. "My old bones are aching like the very devil today. A shot or two of whiskey might help ease the pain. Take one for yourself as well. We have much yet to talk about."

He nodded, and glanced at Sally, wondering how long she might stay.

CHAPTER TWENTY-SIX

SALLY SANK into the empty space beside Felix in the drawing room later that day. "How are you enjoying your stay at Newberry Park, Captain?"

"Quite well indeed," he replied companionably. In a softer voice, he added, "I gather we are still pretending not to know each other as well as we do."

"I think that would be best for the present. I hope you do not mind." Sally glanced across the room to where her future mother-in-law sat and her intended stood. The two people she most wanted to avoid tonight were never far enough away. She had so much to say to Felix and could not help but feel time was running out. "My grandfather has asked me to present a proposal. He wishes to offer you a position at Newberry Park."

His brow rose. "I am already in the service of my country. What more could he want from me?"

Nerves beset her as she answered. "He wishes you to make your home at Newberry Park after the war."

Felix's eyes widened and he glanced around. Grandfather was noticeably absent from the family tonight. "Does he now? Hmm. I thought he was up to something but could not put my finger on his scheme at first."

"What do you mean?"

"It has become all too clear that your father did not summon me to Newberry Park. I am here only because the duke wishes to see me. At first, I thought he meant to punish me with news of your engagement, but that must not be it after all. That enquiry into my character is quite the charade though. What position does he mean to offer?"

"Estate manager. The position comes with living quarters, the estate manager's office for yourself—all within the great house—and a goodly sum of money and respect."

"I see." He sat back, crossing one leg over the other. He was informally dressed tonight in dark coat and trousers and quite handsome out of his naval uniform. "Managing the estate is your role, is it not?"

"It has been until now, but once I marry, I cannot be around enough to do any good. My grandfather has not advertised the vacancy and has told no one else of this offer as far as I know."

"Newberry would be the poorer for your absence. You have done so well. I know your mother is enormously proud of you, and of Louisa too." He glanced around. "But I do not truly need the income of the position. I am wealthy enough to live how I like. There is much that could be done at Newberry, particularly hiring more staff to ease the pressure on the old, and I could help with that I suppose. When Maitland returns, he will undoubtedly want to do things his way."

"You have considered what Newberry needs already?"

"Only in passing. I could not help but notice a great many things need to improve. For example, your sister and cousins should not be hauling baskets of fruit about. If there were more able-bodied gardeners in service, they would never have to."

Sally shifted uncomfortably.

"How do you think I should answer him? Should I take it or not?"

"I could not say." She swallowed. "Mother says you do not have a home."

"I do not yet. For the past few years, whenever I was able to come ashore, I have stayed at the Fladong's Hotel in London. It has been good enough for a bachelor."

"But one day you will want to have a family."

"I already wanted that," he said quietly, and her heart skipped a beat. "With you, in fact. But that does not seem likely anymore, does it?"

Her eyes stung. He had said he wanted her, but she had not realized just how deep his intentions ran. If she had not been engaged when Felix had first come to Newberry, would she have said yes to Ellicott straight away? Would Felix have offered for her hand again?

So far, they had managed to patch up their differences, but she was a long way from trusting her heart to him.

"I think you should consider it," Sally murmured. "You are liked by everyone here."

His hand twitched toward her. She stared as it came to rest on the cushion beside her, and the compulsion to take it overwhelmed her momentarily. Everything would have been so easy if she had married him. No family but a brother. No home of his own. She could have gone on as she was, managing the estate alongside Felix, visiting her sister in the middle of the night when she was troubled. Felix was an easy man by and large and had never been demanding of her time and attention. He understood her devotion to her family better than anyone.

She took a deep breath and glanced across the room. Ellicott was talking again, remarking on the features of the new home she would live in with him. A place she should yearn to see. But she could not imagine herself as his wife and living anywhere but here at Newberry with Felix.

Felix hissed suddenly and she glanced at him quickly. He lifted Horace from his legs, leaving tiny claw marks in the black fabric of his breeches. "Even your cats seem to like me. Perhaps a little too much."

Sally removed Horace from his grip and their hands brushed around the cat's middle before he pulled away. "It is good to know they like you. I have to leave them behind now."

"That seems unfair."

"Ellicott has dogs, so it will be safer for them. I could not bear to place them in harm's way." She hugged Horace a moment, then let him leap from her arms. "So how long do you think you might remain ashore this time?"

"I have still no idea, but I am not anxious to return to my ship. Not anymore." His gaze warmed, and a sensuous smile curved his lips, making her think of how warmly he regarded her when she'd been strewn across his bed.

When he flicked his tongue over his lips, she could not keep her eyes from him. "You are not wishing to go back?"

"What do you think?" he said in a deeper tone that struck her senses like the flick of his tongue against her most intimate places. "I would like nothing better than to get to know you all over again, sweetheart."

She blushed as she pressed her knees together, drowning in his heated stare. She was powerless to prevent the reaction, not when she wanted to rediscover everything about him too.

"Sally, come over here and tell this old fellow how lovely Shropshire is in the summer," Ellicott called out.

Sally closed her eyes to break Felix's hold on her, sucked in a sharp breath, and then let it out softly. "Please excuse me, but do give my grandfather's offer proper consideration. It would be good to have you here, and I would like to see you again."

"I will be waiting."

Sally stood and hurried to her betrothed before she made any promises. If she was going to reconsider marrying Ellicott for Felix, she had better decide and quickly. Breaking an engagement would be expensive and embarrassing for the family at this late stage.

She smiled at Ellicott. "I could not say, having only ever visited your home in the autumn."

"The autumn months are lovely too." Ellicott took a drink from a passing waiter and then tossed back the entire thing. Sally frowned at the empty glass. Was that his fifth drink this evening?

Uncle George moved away as Ellicott curled her arm about his and held her at his side. He led her to take a turn about the room. "What were you whispering to Captain Hastings about?"

"A message from Rutherford," she said, noticing Felix was watching them. "Nothing of importance."

"He is a dry fellow. Hardly ever see a drink in his hand for all he is meant to be a sailor."

He drank, of course, but she had never seen him indulge to excess. Not like Ellicott had done on numerous occasions in the past year. She had overlooked his lapses because she had wanted to marry him. Now, though, it was his least appealing attribute after his strong dislike of cats. "I would not know."

"It hardly signifies. I see your young and handsome neighbor, Lord Cameron, is back again. Does the earl have his own room too, or is it just sailors who are invited to rest their heads where they do not belong?"

Sally ignored the question about Lord Cameron as he did have a guest chamber here, having stayed so often in his youth. She was pleased to see Felix and Lord Cameron seemed to have hit it off immediately. If Felix became the estate manager after she married, they might have a great deal to do with each other in the future.

She switched the subject to family. "It is good to see my uncle so high-spirited tonight. Ever since William made landfall, he has not been himself. I swear, only my cousin's amateur theatricals and musicales made him laugh these past months. His foot has been aching terribly these past weeks too, but it is clear he is feeling better tonight."

"You mean the foot that is not attached to his leg anymore?" Ellicott laughed as they reached the most distant point in the room. "My dear, what an eccentric family you have to complain of something that is not there."

She bristled at the term eccentric and was thankful her family were so far away. "I love them all the more for their little quirks."

"More than just a little quirk in some. Your mother wails about your absent brother's day and night, your sister hardly comes out of her room without a book, your younger cousin squeaks whenever she sees me, and you and your aunt Penelope run the whole of the estate with hardly any help. I told Rutherford he simply had to hire a proper steward, but he claims he already has someone in mind. I think he just agreed with me so I would go away."

Probably. She coughed quickly. Her grandfather would not have liked to be told what to do by someone who was not part of the family yet, not to mention younger. "He does have someone in mind."

"Really?" Ellicott waved over a footman and obtained a fresh glass of port. "Who?"

Sally should not speak of the matter openly. Not until Felix had accepted the challenge of managing the estate for her family. "He has not told me the name, but I know he is serious about hiring someone."

Very serious if he thought a position of steward might tempt the captain to retire to the quiet of Newberry Park. He must have an enticement in mind that he had not told her about to sweeten the deal. What else could tempt Felix to stay?

Ellicott drew close, forcing her to look up. "Mother mentioned there was another captain staying in a guest room. The infamous Captain Jennings. My dear, your family really does consort with the most interesting characters."

"Captain Jennings is not a guest now. He visited my grandfather briefly, but then returned to his rented rooms at the village."

"The village inn, you say? How provincial." The sounds of keys being struck drifted in from the music room. "Ah, wonderful. Another musicale," Ellicott murmured. "Let us hope it is your sister and not your middle cousin. She is much too fond of the dramatic for my taste."

"Audrey chooses music to suit her mood rather than the popular choice of the crowd."

Ellicott scowled. "Then I swear she must have been in a black mood every single day I have been here. Shall we *join* the family amusements yet again?"

Sally rose, bristling at the sarcasm in his tone, and followed everyone else into the music room, stopping at the doorway when Ellicott did. It was foolish of her to have expected him to appreciate every member of her family. Audrey was so young and could be easily hurt by a cutting remark. She hoped her cousin never realized Ellicott disliked her choice of music so much.

Everyone else was seated and facing the pianoforte. There were three chairs remaining at the rear of the room, but she waited for Ellicott to lead her there.

Ellicott leaned close, drawing her against his body. His hand slipped lower to her hip and caressed her. "On second thought, let's slip away while we have a chance."

"My absence will be noticed."

Ellicott scowled. "I wonder if you will notice mine."

He strode off in another huff that was entirely her fault. She considered chasing after him, but what good would that do? She did not want to be alone with him. She was not even sure about the marriage.

"Are you going in?" Felix asked in a voice that carried into the music room.

Aunt Pen turned in their direction and gestured to the remaining chairs impatiently.

Sally nodded. "Yes, of course I am."

She led the way, aware of Felix at her back. She took the middle seat, and Felix took the end, leaving the isle row for Ellicott to claim if he ever came back.

She did not want to be rude, so she smiled at Felix. "Have you heard much music?"

"Some. Your brother is quite proficient on an upturned ale barrel." His eyes danced with mirth.

"He always did like banging things." She laughed at the memory of their childish theatricals in this very room. "After an hour of play, my ears used to ring."

"That still happens on board." He smiled broadly and then bent over. When he sat up, he had Arturo in his hand. "Not my boots, little beast."

He passed the squirming cat to Sally. "I think this is yours too."

"Yes. I am sorry."

"Don't be. It is in his nature to protect his own." He smiled softly. "Do you still play the harp?"

Sally settled the grumpy cat beside her feet and untangled a length of yarn she kept inside her glove for such moments. She dangled it beside her chair, and Arturo was distracted enough to leave the captain's glossy black boots alone and swat at the toy instead. "You can be easy. I have ceased torturing family and friends in recent years."

"I would not have called it torture exactly." He tugged on his ear lobe a few times. "It was more a long and drawn-out savaging of the eardrums."

Sally shrank into her chair. He had teased her many times in the past that her playing could be used to defeat the French. She frowned at the memory as her middle cousin caressed a few keys of the instrument. In truth, she had stopped playing because of his remarks. She had begun to doubt herself, and not just in music. "Everyone is safe now."

"I am only teasing you," he whispered.

"Of course, you are."

He fidgeted. "You are the only musician I could ever sit still for on the harp."

She faced him. "The truth is better, Felix. You hated my playing."

A few of the candles were extinguished to add atmosphere to the room, and then Felix leaned closer. "I adored teasing you, just as you tease poor Arturo there. That is not the same thing as disliking your playing, and you know it."

"I do not know anything." She shook her head and shifted her attention to the pianoforte. "We never really knew each other, did we?"

CHAPTER TWENTY-SEVEN

"YES, WE DID," Felix insisted. "And I will prove that I am exactly the man you said yes to once."

She met his gaze, yearning for what they'd had but afraid to commit herself. Things were different now. Sally had never been comfortable harboring doubts, but she had plenty. Did she love him or simply love what he made her feel? There was no easy answer, so she kept quiet and kept her feelings to herself.

They were silent as Audrey commenced to play. As Ellicott had predicted, the tune was mournful and full of dramatic melancholy that sent a chill sweeping through her body. Audrey really did use music to cast her emotions on those around her, whether they wanted to feel them or not.

Sally nibbled on her finger, seeing her cousin's state of mind with new clarity and concern. Audrey had always been an odd girl, too serious and yet timid despite her importance to everyone. How would she fare in London society in her first season? Would she be celebrated or ridiculed the way Ellicott had hinted she might?

As the piece ended, she glanced at Felix in fear of his reaction.

He stood immediately, a wide smile on his face, and clapped, leading everyone else to join in with him.

He grinned down at her, and for a moment she was overwhelmed by his excitement. "My word. William had mentioned she played well, but I had no idea she was so good. At last, a pianist with substance and not the usual fluff and air pieces so often played in London."

She stood slowly, aware that every inch of Felix was so near and yet so far away. "Truly?"

"Oh yes. She is simply wonderful," he said, grinning and his blue eyes alight with passionate conviction. He had looked at her that way once. On the day she had accepted his proposal. "Warn her chaperones they will need to beat Audrey's suitors back with a very heavy club when the girl makes her come-out."

His confidence in Audrey's prospects relieved her mind greatly, but it did not prevent her from being besieged by regret. He had claimed to love her once. Could he love her that way again? Could she ever forget and forgive?

Sally wanted, more than anything in her life, to find out what was real between them or just a memory. Around him she was herself, and he never made her feel that was wrong. They talked, they argued, they laughed together easily and made love as if it was the most natural thing to do. What would it feel like to join him in his room again? Was it love she felt from him or just attraction? He had threatened to have her if she sought him out, and she was so tempted. Very tempted, because the thought of him touching her intimately made her ache even in a crowded room.

He caught her staring and raised one brow. "Is the cat savaging your ankle?"

"No, I was just considering what you said today and..."

She had waited for Felix, and now that he was here, she was not sure she could bear to let him go. She knew what she needed to do.

She wanted everything Felix had promised her younger self they could be together.

He frowned, searching her face. "Sally?"

Now was not the time. "We should congratulate my cousin on her performance."

Felix let her lead the way, praised Audrey till she blushed, then began a lively conversation with Lord Cameron and Louisa. "Tomorrow at eight o'clock would suit," he said finally.

Sally turned, catching Louisa staring at Felix with wide eyes. "You cannot fight each other."

"Why not?" Lord Cameron asked. "A man can get rusty if he does not practice."

"I am not much in need of practice, so fair warning. I will test your limits." Felix sauntered off with a smug smile on his face.

Louisa grabbed her arm and shook her. "Sally, Hastings has just challenged Lord Cameron to fight him with swords. You must put a stop to it."

Sally understood why Louisa was worried, but she did not share her fear. Cameron was proficient enough with a sword not to be a danger to himself or Felix. The young man who had stayed with them after his father's tragic death and had cuddled on her lap as she read him stories as a child was more than capable of taking care of himself now. But it was natural to feel concern for him. "What is wrong with a little harmless practice between men? Our brothers always fought against each other and included us too. If they were here, they might do the same."

"But Cameron is no match for a seasoned captain."

Sally was looking forward to the match. She would make sure to return from the fields just to have the pleasure of watching Felix stripped down to battle against an opponent who was not trying to kill him. "Felix is hardly going to do more than draw a little of his blood. At the very worst."

Louisa moaned, clutching her head. "Grandfather will put a stop to this."

"Grandfather will likely watch too," she called out to her sister's retreating back. "Once you tell him about the match."

"Do you think he will," Lord Cameron asked, his tone excited for tomorrow. "Will the duke watch?"

"I do believe he might." She shared a grin with him. "You have grown so dashing that we love watching everything you do. Let's hope the captain spares your pretty face from ruin though."

The young earl blushed a deep shade of red. "I wish you would not say things like that to embarrass me."

"Why not? It is the honest truth, dearest Cameron. You should get used to adoration. Many ladies will agree with me when you meet them in London. I have heard a great many sighs from the local lasses too, even if you doubt me. Just ask anyone."

"I did." He pulled a face. "Your sister laughed as if the idea was ridiculous."

"Well, she is a few days older than you. A wise and elder influence," Sally said, rolling her eyes. "But she still thinks of you as a little brother."

"And will never let me forget it either." He glanced around. "I heard from Louisa that you will move away soon to marry Ellicott. Newberry Park will not be the same without you."

Sadness filled her at this first good-bye. She could not tell anyone she was having doubts until she had decided what to do about them. "Thank you, Cameron. I will miss you too, but we will see each other often in London, I am sure, especially during the season."

He pecked her cheek as if he really were a member of her family, a sweet, shy little brother, and stepped back quickly. "But where is your betrothed? I should congratulate him on winning one of the most beautiful women in the district."

"You are too kind." She glanced behind her to point him out.

Ellicott had not returned. "I do not know where he has gone unfortunately."

"Well, perhaps I will see him tomorrow morning." He grinned. "Good night, Sally. I will expect to see you tomorrow too and to hear you cheer me on."

He swung his arm in a mock sword strike and started saying his good-byes to the family before collecting his mother and hurrying out.

Around her, her family chatted and mingled with an ease she for once did not feel part of. Troubled by the feeling of displacement, she slipped from the room and approached the butler. "Do you know where Lord Ellicott went, Morgan?"

She should really talk to the man about her conflicted feelings. She was not being fair to him.

Morgan winced. "I could not say my lady, but he did ask for a carriage."

Ellicott had left the estate without telling her! And to do what at this hour?

"Thank you." Sally slowly ascended to the family wing, pondering how men kept running away from her. Felix, though, kept returning. She found herself at his door. Light flared beneath, proving he was still awake. Was he waiting, hoping she would come to him again? Hoping to start over with her?

She wavered a moment, then tapped once. Sally let herself inside, only to have Felix catch her up in his arms and sweep her off her feet. He kissed her, and thoughts of her engagement to Lord Ellicott fled.

CHAPTER TWENTY-EIGHT

FELIX PINNED Sally to the door and turned the key in the lock. "I thought you would never come."

He brought his mouth down on hers before she could respond and kissed her hard and long, the way he had been aching to do for days.

Sally wriggled and he gave her room. "I wanted to talk to Ellicott," she whispered.

"Ellicott?"

She nodded and moved away from him. "We never promised fidelity."

"You and Ellicott?" Anger built in him. "So, you said."

"How can I marry one man when I am attracted to another?"

"It is possible to be attracted to more than one person at a time," he suggested, still hoping she had not come to put an end to their affair.

"And if he discovers I am only attracted to one man particularly. How would that feel?"

"I do not understand."

She wrung her hands and moved away. "I have not been as bold with him as I was with you. As I am with you still."

Felix's legs wobbled. "You have not shared his bed?"

"No. But he wants me to."

A stupid smile swept over his face. He had the advantage if Sally kept coming back to him and turning aside her intended husband. "Is he pressuring you?"

"Not the way he might have done. I have managed to put him off. I told him I did not want to set a bad example for my sister, and he believed me."

Felix perched on the edge of the bed. "He thinks you are innocent?"

"He suspects I am not, but I have managed not to tell him the truth."

There was a wealth of pain underlying her word. Things that were *his* fault and could not be changed. "You should have told him about me."

"I *should* have told him, and I do not know how to do it now or if it is better not to if I am having second thoughts."

That was all he needed to hear. Felix tossed her over his shoulder and carried her to the bed like a barbarian. He was desperate to keep her in his life no matter what happened to his own prospects.

He deposited her gently on the mattress and threw himself down beside her. "I am glad. I cannot stand the fellow."

And he meant that. Watching her on Ellicott's arm had been painful. It was driving him mad the way he had spoken to her too.

She curled up on her side, facing him. "Well, I never imagined you could have reason to like him."

"He is not right for you," he told her, sliding his fingers along the edge of her face. "You are different around him."

"I know."

"Always be yourself with me." He leaned in to kiss her softly. "I love the woman you are deep inside, but I can accept you might not want that anymore."

She toyed with his shirt, rubbing the material between her fingers. "I do not know what I want anymore."

"That is enough for me."

"I missed you, Felix," she whispered. "Why did I never see you again?"

He pulled her close. "Wasn't that what you wanted?"

She nodded and looked away. "I drove you away."

They must never have told her the truth. As much as he hated to whine and complain, she deserved to know he had not been given much of a choice in leaving her. "No, Rothwell drove me away."

She looked up at him, confusion clear in her expression. "What does my cousin have to do with us?"

"Rothwell took pains to send me back to my ship that night in quite a state. I was warned to stay away from you, by him and others ever since. Since Rothwell used his fists to do the explaining the first time, I did not wait onshore long enough for your brothers to find me and deliver their own similar warnings."

"Oh God."

"Water under the bridge," he promised her, meaning every word. "We cannot remake the past, only our futures. Make love to me tonight?"

"I thought you would not ask my permission. That you would take me no matter what I said to oppose you if we were ever alone again."

"I was a fool to say that. I could never force you to do anything," he whispered, stroking the fine hair around her temple. Allowing his love for Sally to expand and thrive. "Not even to forgive me."

He wished she would, but for now having her in his arms, in his bed, was enough.

"Make me remember what we were like before, Felix."

He drew her more tightly into his arms and held her close. "Gladly."

She leaned her head against his chest and allowed him to loosen her gown. He eased it over her shoulder and kissed her skin. "I always loved this moment. Undressing you."

"I preferred the ones after our clothes were gone."

"I remember that very well." He smiled down upon her, loving her with every part of his soul. "I do not want you to be disappointed in me. Give me tonight, and we will see if reenactment matches our memories."

He slid his hand down her back, squeezed her bottom, and jerked her hips forward. He was already hard and aching. He had always been like that around her. He rotated his hips a little, grinding her sex against his erection.

"Yes," she whispered, fingers curling around his head.

Felix rushed to undress her fully, carefully laying aside her gown and underthings at the foot of the bed. When he turned back, she helped him to undress completely too, and they quietly lay down side by side again before they began to kiss.

The taste of her was the same as they moved into a rhythm of kissing and brushing against each other. They had done a lot in bed together in the past, arousing each other to the point of madness. Tonight was no different as he cupped her breasts and took one nipple into his mouth. He sucked and teased until she moaned, pulling him closer with one arm.

Her other fingers wrapped around his length and stroked him firmly, the way he had taught her to excite him years ago. She was, quite frighteningly, even better at arousing him than she had been before.

He switched breasts and lavished her with attention, doing his best to ignore the skill and enthusiasm of her hand.

He slowly moved his hand down, sliding over her curves until he reached her thighs. He brought one leg over his and then slowly teased his way between her legs. Sally sped the movement of her hand as he caressed the opening of her body. She was wet already, and his finger slid inside her easily. She arched her back and gasped as he teased her with one finger before adding another, then he added a little twist to every thrust, making his thumb brush over her clitoris.

They curled closer together as they pleasured each other with their hands, and the present was not exactly as passionate as their past. All-consuming bliss surrounded them. A cannon could probably be fired, and they would not miss a stroke.

Sally kissed him and did not stop until he was moments away from completion.

She clenched around his fingers, gasping his name as her body shuddered in the grip of her release.

Her grip eased a little, but all too soon she was rushing to bring him off. Sliding her hand up and down his length, brushing her thumb over the tip in a way that made him insane.

She cupped his balls.

Felix groped for the sheet beneath them, yanked it up just enough to cover the head, and spilled his seed into the cloth. He panted hard, lost in the wonder that was making love to Sally again.

God, he loved her. He had never stopped wishing for these stolen moments. Never stopped hoping that one day he would have a second chance to win her back.

After a moment, Sally snuggled into him. "Felix?"

"Yes, my dear?"

"That was actually better than I remember."

"For me too." He kissed her brow. "For me too."

He kissed her soundly and curled around her, determined never to let her go no matter what obstacle was placed in his path next. They had to figure this out somehow.

They had the rest of their lives ahead to love one another.

CHAPTER TWENTY-NINE

HE WOKE TO LOUD PURRING. Felix opened one eye carefully and stared up into the face of Sally's largest cat. "Hercules. What the devil?" He shoved the cat aside. "Who let you in?"

To his complaint the cat said nothing, and unafraid of his poor welcome, continued purring very loudly as he nosed about Felix's hands. He glanced at the door and found it ajar. "All right, I am up," he called.

He dragged himself to a sitting position and glanced around the empty room. The sun was beating at his windows, casting bright stripes across the floor where it peeked through the drapes. He felt good. Comfortable. "What time is it?"

"Long past rising," a hesitant female voice whispered through the crack of the door. "You'll be late for your practice against Lord Cameron if you do not move soon."

"Lord Cameron, of course. Thank you for reminding me." He thought a moment, trying to pinpoint the owner of the voice that he still could not see. "Louisa?"

"Do not hurt him." Whoever it was rushed away without revealing her identity. He could not blame her. He was naked under the sheet. He had spent the night making love to Sally, and he must have fallen asleep first. He had never heard her leave his bed, but he was glad she was gone. He wanted her, but he did not want her family to be disappointed in her behavior.

Behavior he happened to crave.

Felix threw himself from bed, jerked his trousers on, and then quickly closed the door properly so he did not shock anyone who happened to walk past. He threw water onto his face and then shaved before dressing in clothes he did not mind getting a little cut up. Not that he expected Lord Cameron to possess great skill with a blade. He was looking forward to an easy challenge and offering instruction rather than a battle of life or death.

As an afterthought, he tucked the cat under his arm, walked from the room, down the staircase, and took the cat outside with him to the terrace.

Sally was waiting, hand on her hip. "Where was he this time?"

"Waking me." He grinned as he dropped the cat onto the top of the stone wall she stood beside. This morning she seemed impossibly more beautiful and irresistible than ever. "Some adventurous soul let him inside my bedchamber to ensure I got up in time."

She lavished attention on the cat, then looked him over. "I thought all captains rose with the sunrise."

"Must be the country air and the energetic late nights," he said. His weariness was entirely due to having Sally waltz back into his bedchamber. Satisfying her hunger had been a wild ride. "Has Lord Cameron arrived?"

"He is speaking with the duke round the corner, through the study window."

Felix grinned. "As good a vantage point as any. We can practice on the lawn below the study."

"I think Cameron's nervous." She bit her lip, and Felix considered leaning in and kiss her good morning.

He resisted the temptation by sheer force of will. "There is nothing to be nervous about. I meant to ask you last night, what has become of Lord Ellicott?"

"He had business elsewhere."

"Business? Well, his absence last night was my gain." He stroked her cheek softly. "And I hope yours too."

"Yes. I think so. Felix, we need to talk."

"We do, but it will have to wait until I have tested your neighbor's skill with a blade." He strode off, shrugging out of his coat so he could face Lord Cameron with the fewest impediments to his movements. "Good morning," he called and then looked harder at his opponent. He laughed. "What are you wearing?"

"Protection," Louisa quipped with a smug smile. "He is not accustomed to fighting as navy men do."

"We are sparring, my lady. I am not obligated to slice him to ribbons at the first provocation." He pointed at Lord Cameron. "Take that lot off or yield now."

"I told you he would not like it," Lord Cameron complained to Louisa as he shrugged out of the specially padded waistcoat and arm guards and tossed them to a waiting servant.

Felix found his spot on the grass below the duke's study and waited for his rival. Louisa apparently had more than a few hushed words to say to the young earl, but whatever was said was endured, though with a mournful expression by Lord Cameron.

When they parted company, Louisa ran to her sister's side and the pair stood arm in arm. He saluted them and faced Lord Cameron.

The young earl appeared a little more nervous now than before.

"We start at half speed," Felix murmured and then explained how the morning practice would proceed.

"Very good, Captain." Lord Cameron flexed his arms when he finished and then prepared to fight.

"Let's begin." Felix had trained many young men within the confines of the ship's narrow layout. He had taught them how to avoid entrapment, how to use the ship's rigging and timbers as shields, and not traps to hamper their movements. Fighting in a pretty, open garden afforded no such impediments. A wild, uncontrolled swing could cut deeply.

The young man was much more skilled than he, and Louisa, had given the earl credit for. Very soon he urged Lord Cameron to fight faster, and they battled around the garden until a fine sweat beaded his temple. A crowd had gathered, servants and family were placing bets, and some were hanging from upper windows and calling to each other. Drawn by the sound of weapon strikes, they gossiped and gasped depending on who appeared to have the upper hand.

Lord Cameron caught his heel in a divot and fell backward over the short, clipped hedge that surrounded the garden. He went down hard and groaned as his head struck earth. Felix surged forward, believing the man had dealt his head a severe blow. As he leaned over him, Lord Cameron raised his sword arm and swung.

Sally screamed as the blade sliced his shirt.

"Victory," Lord Cameron crowed, pulling his arm back quickly so Felix was not impaled upon his blade, and tossed the weapon away.

Felix found his breath at last, then checked his sliced shirt and the skin beneath, knowing from experience an injury often did not feel bad until a moment or two has passed. The shirt was ruined, but nothing more perilous had occurred. "No harm done."

Lord Cameron rested his head on the gravel path and puffed. "Had to do something to best you," he complained. "Even if you were holding back, I could not have lasted any longer."

"Well played." He helped Lord Cameron stand and then shook his hand. "If I ever need practice, remind me not to come to see you anytime soon. You are deceptively modest about your skills, my lord."

Lord Cameron grinned, his pride full and obvious. "Thank you."

Morgan rushed over. "His Grace wishes to see you both in his study."

Felix sighed even though he was growing used to the duke's urgent summonses. If he agreed to work for the man, he would be answering them for all the days that remained of his life. "Tell him we will join him as soon as we are presentable and have our breath back."

"Very good, Captain. My lord."

They parted to redress.

As Felix was shrugging on his coat, he became aware that Sally stood nearby. Everyone was off congratulating Lord Cameron on his fine show of skill and cunning victory, but she crept closer, one hesitant step at a time. "Sally?"

"Did he hurt you?"

Felix glanced at his stomach. "The shirt will need a few stitches, but it is not dire."

"Leave it out and it will be repaired," she told him, her hands clenched at her waist. "He could have killed you."

"No. He might be proficient with a sword, but he is not a killer. He was always in control."

Sally chewed her lip. "I almost died when he swung."

Felix approached her, bringing his sword with him. Sally was pale, her eyes wide with lingering fear. "You should not worry for me. I know what I am doing."

"I don't. Not anymore."

Although he should take every care with her reputation, he touched her arm and squeezed. "Come to me again tonight, and I will remind you."

Felix knew what he was doing. He was winning Sally back—one indiscretion at a time.

Morgan returned, his expression apologetic. "Captain?"

"I have to go now unfortunately. The duke wants me."

The corner of her mouth lifted in a rueful smile. "I know the feeling."

"Hold that thought. I will be back as soon as I can." He grinned and then strode off, collecting Lord Cameron on his way to the duke's study. Whatever the duke wanted he could have, as long as they were both of the same mind where Sally was concerned.

He wanted her and would have her back.

There had to be a way.

CHAPTER THIRTY

FELIX TURNED his head to view the dark cat sitting beside him. "So, what did you do to warrant your summons?"

The cat commenced to groom himself, uncaring of his exalted location before the duke's desk. Cats were creatures indifferent to proper behavior. Lord Cameron had only stayed long enough to be congratulated and had been ushered on his way.

"Ah, Hastings, thank you for waiting."

Felix stood quickly at the unexpected voice, surprised to find Admiral Templeton had returned to Newberry. No one had warned Felix, and the admiral had been gone so long Felix had stopped asking when he might be coming back. He had also been too full of anxiety over Sally, keen to know she had returned to her bedchamber undetected after their tryst last night to properly notice who had witnessed the morning's sword practice. "My lord admiral. I had not heard you had come home."

Admiral Templeton crossed to the sideboard and poured himself a drink. "My schedule changed unexpectedly."

Felix fidgeted, relieved the man had not returned last night. He might have come to his bedchamber door and discovered his daughter in a state no father should find his child in.

Admiral Templeton downed his glass and poured another. "Damn good of you to cool your heels like this."

Since the duke had not given him a choice in the matter, he wisely kept his mouth shut. Sally had said nothing so far about calling off her engagement, so he could very well be left with the pain of leaving without her once more.

"Now, to the matter at hand." The admiral strode across the room to a large table and sifted through the maps. "What do you recall of this region of the sea?"

Felix took a moment to study the map and then nodded. He sketched out his last journey in that region with the tip of his finger. "Shoals here and here. Deep water. This island has freshwater at the southernmost point." He pointed to a gentle curve in the topography. "We dropped anchor during a storm and then next morning awoke to find ourselves in paradise."

The admiral grunted. "Was the island inhabited?"

"Not at the time of our visit." He pointed again. "I placed men at these vantage points, and we saw no sign of other ships, smoke, or signs of human life."

The admiral grimaced and sucked his teeth. "Fredrick's ship is overdue to return. He should have traversed the same route as you did, but there has been no sign of his vessel."

"Could he have been taken as a prize elsewhere, or do you fear he ran afoul of a reef?"

"The reef. He is too smart to engage a ship he was not a match for. Far too cautious." The admiral tapped the map again. "According to all other reports and sightings in the region, this island is the most likely one to support life."

"I believe so." Felix rubbed his jaw. "He knew about that place too."

The admiral's brows rose. "How's that?"

"I bumped into Fredrick a few years ago, and he mentioned my stroke of luck to find the place. He had dropped anchor there, a year before me. If he needed to find shelter, it is likely he would have made for the island if he could. What is to be done?"

"That is a particularly good question. The admiralty will not sanction a search, and there are few captains willing to risk their career on such flimsy hope." The admiral tossed the maps away and returned to the decanter of whiskey.

"The duke insists the war is at an end. If Fredrick made shore, he could be well situated for an extended stay until help comes."

The tap of canes across the room had Felix spinning around to bow. "Your Grace."

"Felix, what trouble is my son luring you into now?"

The admiral flushed a dark red and mumbled an expletive.

The duke paused by the maps. "A long voyage, it seems. I might have something to say about that."

"Freddie's missing," Admiral Templeton explained.

The duke thumped his canes. "No. I forbid it. I will not support your sending the boy off on a fool's errand. You were the one to send Freddie south. You will find someone else to dupe into cleaning up your mess."

"Perhaps I should withdraw," Felix said, easing back from the confrontation between father and son.

"No, no. You will stay right where you are," the duke almost shouted. "You have already paid a hefty price for his foolish ambitions. He will not be sending the *Selfridge* to rescue a grown man because of more foolishness, and that is final."

The duke's jaw set stubbornly. Felix was familiar enough with that expression to wisely keep his opinions to himself. He did step back another pace to increase the distance between himself and the feuding pair.

Admiral Templeton rubbed a hand over his head. "She will blame me for this."

"Maggie already blames you for a great many things," the duke exclaimed coldly. "And that scorn is something you utterly deserve for the way you have neglected and embarrassed your wife over the years."

The admiral nodded, but his expression was sour. He slammed his glass down and stormed off. As Felix watched him go, he felt a pang of regret. Had retrieving Fredrick been all his summons had been about?

"I could have helped in the search," he told the duke honestly. "I would not have minded going. Fredrick is a good man. A good captain."

"He will be. One day." The duke collapsed into his chair. "Sit down, boy. You make an old man feel small."

Felix lowered his six-foot frame into a chair as swiftly as he could. As he settled, Sally's cat made the leap across the gap and landed heavily on his lap.

"Devil take it," he grunted as claws dug into his thighs. "Must you maul me?"

"He attacks everyone he loves. 'Tis part of his charm," the duke murmured. "It is patently obvious who he cares for. These creatures of Sally's are rather obvious about it, unlike their owner."

Felix met the duke's unwavering gaze and felt himself exposed. "I am sure that is not true."

"You and the cat are similar creatures. Direct and honest."

A strange pride filled him at Rutherford's praise. "Thank you."

"Young man, I have never met someone who exemplifies all that is good in the service or one so humble. Your actions do you credit, and you have my undying gratitude for the aid you rendered a fellow captain, even when I warned you not to."

Felix lifted his chin. "He was someone Sally loved. I would do anything for her."

"I know. That is why I forbid you to search for Fredrick. Your eagerness to please will only risk further heartbreak for her." He stretched across the table and held out his hand. "Safe journey to London and smooth sailing."

"That's it?"

"What were you expecting? A trial at arms? After that performance today on the lawn, I doubt I would last a full breath. No indeed, Sally has enough facts now that she will make the right decision or not. She will not fall prey to fabrications of idle gossip or her father's agenda ever again."

Felix stilled. "You did not bring me here to question my command but to hold my character and behavior with women up for scrutiny. Why?"

"The young are often prone to overexcited nerves, especially when it comes to a man's behavior and affections. And when there might be another woman involved, the more said the better to clear up the misinformation filling her ears."

He stroked the cat's head. "This has nothing to do with my command and everything to do with Sally. That is why she was there to hear it all. Why have her offer me a position?"

"You would make an excellent addition to Newberry and the family."

He drew back in shock. "You do not want Sally to marry Ellicott."

"Obviously not. He is rash, impulsive, and—"

"She is not in love with him," Felix added.

"How could she be when she was already in love with you?" The duke scowled. "But what choice does she have but to settle? It is not as if she could hope a distinguished captain would give up his career, passing his ship off to another captain, on the off chance she would see reason before it is too late."

Felix licked his lips, considering this new development. "I have thought of it, but if she still marries Ellicott, I will have nothing."

"The offer of making your home here stands. I have done everything I can to save her from her own foolishness. I could use a good man to eat breakfast with now and then too." He smiled. "Now, do not let me keep you a moment longer. I am sure you have much to think about and much to do this evening before you leave for London at first light. And also, precious little time left ashore to find a solution to the problem of what to do with Gabriel Jennings. He requires a ship, and you could have a tough time convincing just anyone to step aside."

"Thank you." Felix smiled. "Thank you for allowing me this chance to win her back."

"Keep her this time." The duke rubbed his eyes. "That is enough for today, Captain. If you would be so good as to send Morgan to me, I would appreciate it. Take the cat out too."

Felix hooked the cat under his arm. "Of course."

"Wait, a word of advice from an old man. Only the very lucky get a second chance in love. Do you feel yourself lucky, Felix Hastings?"

"I believe so," he answered honestly.

"You should work on that as quick as you can." He waved Felix away and then held his hand to his brow.

The man looked bone tired, and Felix swiftly found Morgan and sent him to attend the duke. At the stairs he came face-to-face with Sally's betrothed—a man he actively tried to avoid.

Lord Ellicott raised his snooty nose in the air as he glanced at the cat in his arms. "Cannot abide cats," Ellicott pronounced as they passed each other.

Felix paused to watch him go as Hercules began to purr loudly. He scratched the beast under the chin. "Now that is one more thing in my favor. She has to love me all the more for appreciating you."

CHAPTER THIRTY-ONE

SALLY LET herself into Felix's dark bedchamber and shut the door, finding herself alone. He had not come up as yet, but she was too nervous to wait until the house had gone to bed entirely before seeking him out. Something had changed. She could feel it in the air, and although he had not said anything, she feared she knew what was coming.

He was leaving.

She prowled the room, stroking Felix's possessions, then took up his uniform to hold to her face.

"Do you still do that? Touch everything?" Felix asked as he joined her after closing the door quietly. Even in the dark his smile was dazzling, and deep in her heart she wished he would always look at her that way.

"Occasionally," she whispered.

"I have something to say to you, and I fear you will not be happy," Felix told her, frowning.

She took a breath. "You are leaving."

"Yes, tomorrow."

She had expected it, but the news made her sad anyway. "At dawn?"

"Yes. I have sent word to Jennings to expect me, and we will make our way back to London and to the admiralty together."

"Not running straight to your ship? I am impressed."

"I promised to help Jennings regain a command, and then I will go."

"Of course." Her eyes stung. "You are an excellent friend."

"Am I still a terrible man?"

She met his gaze, pained by his questions. Part of her still wanted to scream that his ship ranked first in his responsibilities, but the other reminded her she was still marrying another man. There were only a few days left to change her mind. "No," she whispered. "I do not think that anymore."

He kissed the top of her head and began to strip off his evening attire. "Your father finally talked to me today. Freddie's ship is missing. He should have returned months ago, and your father asked me to sail off to find him."

Sally enjoyed the view of Felix removing his clothes. There was comfort in being alone with him at a time like this. Contentment and familiarity. "Father has said nothing. I do not believe mother knows, or she would have mentioned it at dinner."

"Your father does not want to tell her, or does not know how to."

She was not surprised after all she had learned of her parents' marriage this week. "She will not take it well, but since the admiralty is keen to rescue Freddie, she will feel a little better."

"His request has nothing to do with the admiralty. It is your father who requests I abandon the fight against the French and search for Fredrick alone."

She swallowed. Her father had asked him to abandon his duty. It was shocking to her that he would. "And will you?"

"No. I serve our country, not your father's personal agenda. He has only a vague notion of where Freddie might have found port. For all I know, his ship was taken by the French, or simply blown quite a distance off course. I have faith that Freddie will find his own way back to English shores, and so does your grandfather."

She faced him. "What does my grandfather have to do with what you do?"

"Everything." He studied her in return, his expression set in determination.

She took a step toward him. "How did you keep your command six years ago when our engagement ended?"

"Rutherford cleared my way." He took a chair. "Sally, I have wanted to captain a ship since I was a lad, well before I joined the navy. I never hid my ambition from you. Asking you to marry me was not planned, it was not a scheme, but of course it did speed up my promotion. The admiral could not bear to have his eldest daughter married to a mere lieutenant no matter how much she professed to care for him at the time, so he took steps to arrange my advancement when a ship suddenly became available."

Sally had loved Felix. She had begged her father to approve the match, and he had been furious with her for breaking the engagement. "And what of your arrangement with my grandfather? My mother has a theory that my grandfather extorted a share of your prize bounty in return for keeping the promotion. Is she close to the mark?"

"Yes." He pulled her into his lap and held her. "We made an agreement that Rutherford would take half my portion after I became captain, and he will continue to do so as long as I remain captain of the *Selfridge*. Nothing your father schemes now can change that arrangement."

Her breath caught as Hastings nibbled her neck, and she could not hold on to her anger. "It all seems so reasonable now, but I felt betrayed."

"I desired you then, Sally," he whispered. "I desire you still. I am hopelessly, completely smitten. I am the same man."

She turned into his arms and kissed him fiercely to stop him sounding so sensible.

He held her close, tight against his body, and explored the contours of her back with his big hands. Sally shuddered as he gripped her bottom, and she threaded her fingers through his hair as they made love with their mouths and tongue.

When they drew back, he was smiling. "Dear God, I missed being able to do that." He lifted his attention to her hair and unwound the ribbon around it.

"Surely there were other women," she whispered.

He dropped the ribbon to the tabletop. "No one else. The first night I met you, you wore a coronet of stars in your hair. Since that day, I have only had to look up to feel you near me. To see the path ahead was not always easy, but I never forgot that the place I called home was you."

She could not believe it. "You waited."

"Of course, I waited. There never could be anyone else for me but you."

The last of the moorings gave way, and her hair tumbled down her back. "Now you are the way I remember you." He brushed his thumb over her bottom lip. "Red lips, slightly mussed hair."

She blushed, recalling what came after. Their fight and heartbreak was etched in her soul. "And then I asked you a question."

"That I answered honestly." He pushed her hair aside and popped the first button of her gown.

"And I ended our engagement."

"You ended our engagement." He kissed her shoulder, softly at first, and then peppered more toward the base of her ear. "My wonderful, darling Sally. Still salty, too."

She laughed and gave him a little shove. "You suggest I dared exert myself to run to your room tonight."

"Well, if you have not yet, then you certainly will exert yourself before the night is through." He grinned widely. "I plan to have you any way you will let me."

Her breath left her in a rush. "Felix!"

"I might have been faithful and chaste, Sally, but I never stopped conjuring up new ways to make you mine."

Sally touched his face. "I thought of you every day. I worried where you were. I dreamed of you in my bed. When you never came back, I found pleasure elsewhere."

His eyes widened.

"I was not faithful to you," she confessed.

He glanced away, his jaw clenching. "But you said you and Ellicott had not..."

"Another man." She shivered under the weight of his shocked expression. "I needed to feel again, but it was not right with him."

Felix kissed her temple without saying anything against her decisions. She was grateful because she regretted that one night of rash judgement enough as it was.

"I missed you, Felix," she whispered. "I missed you so badly."

He nodded and held her in his arms without saying anything further about what she had done.

Her relief in his acceptance was staggering. She leaned her head against his chest and allowed him to finish loosening her gown. She stood and stepped from it and then dragged him to his feet. She pushed his waistcoat aside, revealing the man of her dreams and nights to come. He was so broad in the chest that he overwhelmed her a little at times, though she hastened to unbutton his shirt so she might run her fingers over his skin. When she unbuttoned the fall of his trousers, he pulled his shirt over his head and threw it aside.

Sally ran her hands over his hard chest possessively, relearning his body. She pressed her face to his warmth and inhaled the scent of him. How long had she waited to be reminded that desire began with a first glance and grew until all she could do is feel?

All her life.

"You make a man weak at the knees, my love," he whispered as he caressed her breast.

"You are still standing."

"Not for long." He picked her up easily and carried her to his bed where he gently laid her down before he finished undressing himself. He climbed in beside her, naked, and cuddled her against his long body. He seemed in no hurry to strip off her remaining clothes.

Sally, however, was not so complacent. They only had tonight before he might be lost to her. She turned her back to him. "Unlace me."

"Gladly." He fiddled with the strings, and she sighed as the garment went sailing across the room to land with a thud against the windowsill. He eased her chemise from beneath her bottom and slowly crept it up to her waist, taking his time. "I always loved this moment."

"You told me. I could get used to it, too."

He laughed and threw the chemise away to join the corset by the window.

He cupped her breasts from behind, and she tossed her head back against his chest and moaned at the pleasure of his touch. He tugged her so she reclined fully against him, his hands shaping her breasts, his fingers teasing her nipples.

It was heaven in his arms. This was the only place she had truly belonged and wanted to stay.

But pressing against her back, hard and hot, was the part of him she had longed for most.

She turned in his arms and drew him down on top of her. She was impatient and needy, and Felix did not seem to mind that about her.

He parted her thighs and settled his hips between them. Sally tugged him up until the head of his erection rested against her sex. She met his gaze and tears filled her eyes at the emotions on his face. "Lover, come into me."

"As you command, sweetheart."

He eased into her body slowly, a little at a time, and when he was fully seated Sally was panting and climbing out of her skin. It felt right with him. It always had.

He eased one of her thighs over his and slid deeper. When he withdrew, she held her breath, counting the seconds until his next thrust. He built her arousal slowly, a touch at her breast, her hip, the brush of his thumb across her lower lip between kisses that drove her wild. Sally clutched him, spellbound by her feelings, captive of his careful loving.

When she came, sobbing as her body clenched around his erection, he held her so tight she knew she would never give him up no matter the obstacle. She quieted and eventually he drew back.

His eyes were soft and full of love. "I will always love you, Sally, even if you marry that fortune hunter of an earl. I just want you to be happy."

"I am happy now. Like this. With you."

"And if tonight is all we have left?"

She pressed her fingers to his lips. "It will be time well spent. I love you, Felix. You are the only man I could love."

He drove into her hard. "Say that again."

"I love you; I love you," she chanted to his every thrust. "Come home and marry me. Don't make me wait forever."

He groaned and spilled his seed inside her body. His arms tightened like a vise around her body as he held nothing back. "I will. I will be back. Never ever doubt it. You have my word. I will marry you and give you everything you could ever want."

All she needed though was his arms about her and his love.

CHAPTER THIRTY-TWO

SALLY BRACED herself and then swept into her grandfather's study. As usual, he was seated behind his large desk, but for a change he was gazing pensively out the window at the Newberry Park gardens. He seemed to be brooding, and that was not likely to make her request any easier to confess.

"Good afternoon, my dear," he murmured after casting a quick glance in her direction. "I thought today of all days you would be too busy for me."

"I would never be too busy for you. I was up early and made my rounds as usual."

"That seems to be going around lately. Even young Felix could not suppress his habit and rose early, called for his carriage, and left after a few pretty words and a promise to visit again." He heaved a sigh. "I like him. I will miss his presence at breakfast."

Sally fought to hide her smile. Without even trying to, Felix had won her rather particular grandfather over completely. That boded well for what she wanted to do and the reasons for her decision. "Grandfather, I need your help."

His eyes lit up with kindness. "In what, child? Another stitch on your wedding gown?"

"No." She clenched her fingers together tightly at her waist. "I would like to not marry Lord Ellicott next week."

His gaze narrowed. "Or on any other day, I suspect?"

Sally bowed her head, then quickly nodded. Sally had known, as soon as she had woken that morning, that marrying Ellicott was a decision she would regret her entire life. Marriage was forever. Love was forever, too. And she already loved Felix so much that the idea of never being with him again was breaking her heart. Marrying Ellicott would have declared that love meant nothing to her, when in truth it was everything that mattered. "I know this must be a shock to you."

"A broken engagement at this late a date will cause Ellicott, and the family, a great deal of embarrassment. We were lucky last time that the arrangement with the captain was a private affair and easily hushed up." His gaze pierced hers. "Give me a good reason."

"Well." She squirmed. "When it comes right down to it, I just do not like him enough to spend the rest of my life with him."

"You do not like him enough?" The duke stood with a groan. "My dear child, you were the one who accepted Ellicott's proposal. No one forced you to the match. You stood before your father and mother in this very room and assured them he was truly what you wanted."

"I know. I did feel I could marry him at the time. After all, not all marriages start with love," she protested.

Her grandfather ambled around his great desk, supported by his two canes. "Your mother will likely have palpitations at the scandal a broken engagement will cause. There will be no end of wailing on her part."

"Mama is always emotional, but I believe she will understand my reasons for changing my mind."

Her grandfather stopped at her side. "She will be pleased you are not going away, and frankly 'twill be a relief to all of us not to be robbed of your company."

"I will marry one day, Grandfather."

"Oh, so there is to be a gentleman in your future?" He clucked his tongue. "Another relief. You are much too spirited in nature to be a spinster all your life. He did not deserve you."

She darted a glance at her grandfather, rather shocked by his confession. "I beg your pardon."

"Ellicott is a splendid fellow on the surface—witty, powerful, an excellent horseman on the hunt. But..."

He left the rest unsaid for so long that she had to ask. "But?"

"He has not the faintest sense of family, of commitment. I have come to feel he will only make you miserable too." The duke gathered his canes in one hand and with the other reached out to cup her cheek. "He does not understand you at all."

"I am sorry I cannot love him." She bowed her head, unable to hold his gaze. "I have tried, but I do not feel enough for him."

The duke patted her cheek softly. "I loved your grandmother, and it took me a dozen years to win her hand. We were enemies as children, you know. I pulled her braid, and she threw lemons at my head. I hope you will not have to wait that long to enjoy a rousing good fight with the one you love."

"You were both so happy. I remember how your faces lit up on first seeing each other whenever you were apart. I cannot believe you had any reason to argue. There was always a glimmer in your eyes when you were near each other."

"Your grandmother was a rare woman. She had no relations of her own by the time we married, and it took some time for her to find her feet among the family. But she did, and your mother did too, now I think about it. We are a rather hard family en masse." He laughed suddenly. "I imagine the man you do eventually marry will need to understand that while your name will change to his, you will always be a Ford down to the bone. Family first."

"I hope so."

"Never admit fault," the duke said. "Your grandmother always appreciated that one. She said it covered any number of social blunders or disagreements within the household."

The duke held out his arm to embrace her, and she clung to him a moment, reassured that no matter what anyone else said, her grandfather accepted her decision.

He bussed her cheek. "I will see to it, my dear."

"Thank you."

He pushed her away suddenly. "Now, about this other fellow. Are we acquainted?"

"Yes."

His eyes warmed. "And do I like him?"

She nodded. "Very much."

"I thought I saw a glimmer when Felix showed up on our doorstep." He leaned close and touched his finger to his nose, smiling at her shock. How could he know about Felix when she had only just decided to wait for him yet again? "Not quite so old and unobservant as you think, eh?"

Sally gulped. "You knew how I felt about Felix all along."

"Not in the beginning, but for some time I have noticed your interest was just a little too fixed on one particular ship and your brother Laurence's letters. When the engagement ended, I made discreet enquiries and learned your father had advanced Felix to the *Selfridge* simply to spite Admiral Greer. Despite the promise of his zeal and skill at command, the *Selfridge* was under-manned and under-gunned. I stepped in to ensure lives and the chance for success were not lost. Your father pushed him as hard as he could just to best another admiral."

Sally closed her eyes. Poor Felix. Even if he had wanted to stay, he had not been given a chance to escape her father and family. He had always meant to leave, but he had not abandoned her willingly. It was no wonder he had been angry. He'd had good reason.

The duke smiled. "Captain Hastings proved himself in battle, child, won a fortune and distinction with the sole intent of impressing your family and you. He has lost years with you, but let us hope he does not get himself killed when he returns to face the French. He has promised to lease Torre Cottage from me upon his return, and you know how hard it is to find agreeable tenants."

"But you promised me the dower house to live in."

"I promised you could live in the dower house if you wed the best man in England." The duke shrugged. "When Felix returns to shore again, you have my blessing to move there with him after the wedding takes place of course."

Sally threw herself around her grandfather and squeezed him tight. "Thank you. Thank you. Thank you. Thank you."

"Well, do not get too excited about it now. Put on a sad, contrite face. We have a wedding to halt, and you cannot seem to be relieved about it yet." He held out his arm. "Help an old man to the white drawing room, and let us put this mistake behind us."

They made their way to the drawing room and found her betrothed and their mothers and Lord Ellicott were waiting. Her mother gave her an encouraging nod of approval, as if she knew what Sally was about to do.

"Lord Ellicott, might I have a word?"

He nodded, casting a questioning look toward her grandfather. "In private?"

"Outside on the terrace will do." She led the way, chose her spot, and then faced him. "I cannot marry you."

He tipped his head to the side, studying her without saying a word.

"Did you hear me?"

"I heard, but I am unsure I believe my own ears." He shook his head. "Are you telling me that after a year of flirtation that should only have led to matrimony, after all the arrangements have been made to accommodate your wishes, you have simply changed your mind?"

Very little had been done to accommodate her wishes. "I made a mistake."

"Like picking up the wrong gloves to wear to a ball?" He folded his arms across his chest. "Well, I do not accept that."

When she had broken with Felix, he had begged her to reconsider, promising that his love came from his heart and not because of any promotion. Proof that she was making the right decision came from Ellicott's lack of appeal to her heart. His jaw was clenched. His eyes narrowed, but distress at losing her was not one of the emotions he chose to reveal over her.

"I am sorry if this comes as a surprise to you, but you will see it is the right thing to do in the end."

"It's because of those bloody cats, isn't it?"

"Partly." She lifted her chin. "But mostly it is because we do not have any intention of loving each other. I deserve that, and so do you."

His mouth pursed as if he had eaten a lemon. "Love?"

"Yes, love. That feeling you have for another. When you cannot stand to be apart. That you will do anything at all to make them happy." She studied his blank expression, pitying him. "It's like that feeling you must have when your mother asks you to go out of your way to fetch her new dress from London. But magnified a thousand times for someone else."

His jaw clenched tightly again, and then he brushed past her to speak with the duke.

Sally let out a shaky breath, glad the first obstacle was over because there would be more difficulties to come. Gossip and mutual friends choosing sides. She would hold her head up because she was doing the right thing for both of them. She could only hope her decision would not affect the reception her cousins faced when they went to London for their season.

She turned around.

The Ellicotts were gone from the drawing room. Only her mother stood at the doorway. "Well, that went better than expected," Mama murmured. "The Ellicotts are leaving immediately. One can only hope the rest of the family can be as civilized and not make a fuss about the break."

"Doubtful," Sally said, realizing her mother was fighting a grin. "Everyone will have an opinion if they do not already."

An amused smile tugged her mother's lips. "In case there is any danger you might misunderstand; we prefer Felix to be your husband."

"Who is 'we'?"

"Oh, everyone," Mama waved her hand to encompass the estate. "Even the stable master spoke his piece against Ellicott."

Sally stamped a foot as strong emotions rose up and tears pricked the back of her eyes. "Did you all conspire to bring Felix back into my life?"

"Well, of course we did. Everyone but Penelope because you know how she detests scandal. We all agreed to help things along. Do you forgive us? We only want you to be happy. We all felt bad that we hadn't done enough to heal the breach before this, so your grandfather and I decided to step in before it was too late to save you from misery with Lord Ellicott, not to mention his mother's plans to spend your dowry on whatever nonsense she wanted."

She opened her arms wide and enfolded Sally in the second-best comfort in the world. "It almost was too late. She was to hang red curtains in my bedchamber."

"Oh darling, a fate worse than death itself," her mother said with a soft laugh, shaking her head in vexation. "A nice mother-in-law should have asked what color you would choose for your chamber."

Sally clung to her mother a long moment. "Thank you. Thank you for meddling."

"It was our pleasure." Her mother cupped her head, holding her tight. "I think you will both be incredibly happy together upon Felix's return. He loves you so much."

"I hope so." She sniffed, struggling with her feelings. "I love him too, but I do not know how I will bear another long wait."

Her mother drew back and passed over a handkerchief. "You will do what you always do. Keep busy, and who knows, perhaps the wait will be much shorter than you imagined."

"The war cannot last forever," Sally whispered hopefully as a figure inside the drawing room claimed her attention. Aunt Penelope had come, her face pale.

Sally hugged her mother and whispered. "Do we have smelling salts nearby?"

"Behind the elephant statue on the mantel. Why?"

"Aunt Pen must have heard the news. She looks as if she might faint from the scandal of my second failed wedding."

"We will catch her should she fall," her mother whispered. "It is what our family is best at."

"Indeed, it is." Sally smiled and then strode to her aunt to explain.

CHAPTER THIRTY-THREE

AFTER BEING MADE to cool his heels for five and forty minutes in the secretary's office, Felix was finally admitted to Admiral Greers office. He took a deep breath as he swept into Admiral Greer's office with the reluctant Jennings close on his heels. The dark-paneled chamber was cluttered with more maps and folders than Felix had ever expected. A short man sat behind a large desk, poring over even more papers. "Admiral, thank you for seeing me at such short notice."

The overweight Greer raised weary eyes. "Captain Hastings, what an unexpected honor." Greer cast a glance behind him. "You! What the devil are you doing here?"

"Admiral Greer." Jennings nodded, doing his best to appear contrite. Felix had warned Jennings that a certain amount of humility on his part would be needed today if they were to have any success.

"He is with me," Felix said.

Greer appeared very unhappy and shuffled some papers around. "Well then, take a seat. What can I do for you?"

"I have come to ask, to plead, for Gabriel's reinstatement as captain."

Felix gestured to Jennings to come closer and sit down.

Greer sucked his teeth. "Is that so? Did he convince you he had not meant to shame me?"

"Actually, I meant to shame myself," Jennings said in a faint voice.

Greer adjusted his bulk in his chair. "And you did a fine job of it I must say."

"And he is sorry for the trouble he caused," Felix added. "For everyone, but especially to you. It was not well done of him, but grief and drink robbed him of his dignity that day."

Jennings said nothing to correct him, and he was grateful not to be contradicted. It had to be said that Jennings had been a fool. It had to be easier if someone else said it for him.

Greer's gaze finally settled on Gabriel, his eyes hard and assessing. "You, sir, are lucky not to have faced me on the field of honor."

"I know," Jennings said quietly. "And yet I would not have deserved the expense of the shot, let alone the burial."

Actually, it was probably Greer who was lucky that Jennings was incapable of answering his door when the seconds had called that night. Jennings had been so under the weather that it was said he had oozed from his chair without any semblance of having bones within his limbs. And Jennings had stayed that way for fully eight months. Tubby Greer had not come out from behind his desk in years and likely would have been incapable of matching Jennings's former skill with a sword or pistol. Two lives had probably been saved thanks to his inebriation.

"I will vouch for him," Felix added. "He has changed."

"Why should I believe you?"

"It is not as if I can lose my late wife again," Jennings remarked.

"I have made my peace with her loss and vow never to let love affect me again."

Greer grunted and turned his attention to Felix. "He is reinstated at half pay."

"Half pay?" That was not enough, but it was a starting point for negotiations. Felix wanted Jennings to command a ship again. During the journey to London, he and Jennings had talked about his future if this meeting went badly. The only way for Jennings to prove himself again and put the past behind him was to find an active profession. He was best suited to command a frigate.

Greer took papers from a desk drawer, scrawled a signature, and handed them to Jennings. "Give these to my secretary on your way out."

The reinstatement had come so easily that perhaps Admiral Greer had always meant to reverse his decision if given the opportunity without the loss of honor. He nodded. Greer had at least some compassion in his soul. Felix sat forward. "What about a ship?"

"There are none"—Greer scowled—"so even if he was sober enough for sailing his way out of a mere hip bath, there is nothing more that could be done."

"There must be a ship somewhere," Felix protested.

Jennings grasped his arm. "Hastings, you have done enough for one day."

It was not enough. "What if a command were to become available today?"

Greer's eyes narrowed, and then he shook his head. "Planning to murder a fellow captain? That is one way to do it, I suppose, but terribly untidy."

The sarcasm was not amusing, but there was a way. Felix's solution was not simple and would cause strife within the admiralty, but he was the only captain who had means and motive to make the offer. He took a breath. "What if I step aside?"

"Hastings." Jennings gasped, almost leaping from his chair. "What the devil are you suggesting?"

Greer turned his full attention on Felix, eyes alight with amusement. "You would resign as captain of the *Selfridge* for the sake of a drunkard's soul?"

"For my own," he insisted. "But only if Captain Jennings assumes command."

A devious smile curled Admiral Greer's lips. "Well, well, well. Do I sense friction between you and your esteemed benefactor? What will the Duke of Rutherford say? He likes to throw his weight and money around the admiralty."

If Felix returned to marry Sally, there probably was not a lot he would say against his resignation. "There has always been friction, but in this I feel I have the Duke of Rutherford's complete support."

Jennings gulped. "What are you doing?"

"Taking that risk we talked about." He studied Jennings. "No doubt Rutherford will expect the same terms as he attached to my agreement."

"Half your prize and to stay away from the Ford ladies." Jennings considered that for quite some time before nodding. "I can live with his conditions. But are you sure?"

"Never more so." He turned to Greer and smiled. "Now, Admiral, tell me how much blunt it will take to get my friend aboard the *Selfridge* as soon as possible and underway as captain. I am willing to grease as many wheels as is necessary. What do you want?"

"Information." From another drawer, Greer fetched a fresh sheet of paper. His smile was utterly cunning. "Captains, please resume your seats so we can make this official."

EPILOGUE

One month later

NO MATTER HIS LOCATION, mornings were Felix's favorite time of the day. Newberry Park grounds and staff were stirring to life. Chimneys sent up tendrils of smoke from various parts of the distant great house. The Fords would be rising soon and going about the business of being a family.

But without Sally in their midst, the day by necessity was a little less bright. Her marriage would have come and gone, and she was miles away.

"Why, Captain Hastings, you look the very image of a country gentleman." The duke smiled as they met on the grounds of Torre Cottage. The old man seemed particularly spry today as he navigated the white crushed-shell paths that circled the cottage, twirling his canes as if he had no need of them.

Felix glanced up at the house. "And that is what I am, what I will be once the final paperwork is done. I resigned my commission and have come to take up residence."

"Indeed, you have." The duke chuckled. "I was the recipient of the most irritated message from my son a week after you left, so I had some idea to expect you. It seems you only left Newberry to tender your resignation, but you also solved the problem of what to do with Captain Jennings at the same time. Giving him your ship with my apparent blessing was a masterstroke. Very neat of you."

"Jennings needed an occupation, and he has traversed that trade lane more times than I have. He will be the best man to keep an eye out for Fredrick." Felix smiled and swung the gate open to his new abode. Thanks to listening to Sally's hopes and dreams for this place, he had a list of chores to carry out before the house was habitable and ready to accept visitors. Not that he expected many.

A small black face peeked at him from under the nearest shrub. He crouched down and held out his hand. "Is that you, Hercules?"

The beast crept out slowly, hissing, avoiding the duke and his swinging canes.

"Overgrown rats, every last one," the duke complained but he was smiling.

"They have a certain charm." Felix smiled as the creature came close enough to receive a scratch. He scampered away to the undergrowth of a large shrub as soon as he had had enough attention, and Felix stood again. "If nothing else, my living here will offer a haven for the cats since Sally could not take them with her."

"Would it surprise you to learn there was no marriage?" the duke asked.

Felix froze and then faced the duke. "She called it off?"

"Seems a wise choice on her part, considering she is in love with you." The duke pointed his cane at Felix's chest. "But I knew as soon as she saw you and you cleared the air that she might change her mind about marrying that fortune hunter. I expect news that I will bounce a great-grandchild on my knee before the year is out."

"Ah, Your Grace?" Felix frowned at the duke. The old man was far more devious than he had given him credit for. "How long had you been planning our reconciliation?"

"Ever since you sent the breach of promise back. I knew then you had not played my granddaughter false. And I know our Sally's nature. A woman in love has a certain look about her," the duke advised sagely. "I understand the impediments that made it seem like you walked away the first time. You were young and foolish, but do not think I will allow it a second time."

"I am not going anywhere. No matter how many times Rothwell or her brothers hit me for making yet another mess of her life." He glanced around him and smiled. "I am home to stay."

"Good. Come for breakfast tomorrow."

"I would like permission to call on Sally," he told the duke.

"You do not need my permission. I expect it of you. And I am also sure she will show herself soon enough." He turned back momentarily. "Oh, and I took the liberty of arranging this. Just a trifling convenience that will make your homecoming so much more enjoyable."

Although intrigued, Felix tucked the letter into his coat pocket while he waited for the duke to leave in his carriage. He would read it later. He picked up another of Sally's cats that had appeared at his feet. He scratched the white ball of fluff beneath the chin and looked up at what passed for a cottage in this part of the world, a place that would become his new home. It was, overall, a bit smaller than his ship, but his living quarters were bound to be a vast deal more comfortable.

He would have a proper large bed here, and hopefully Sally would be in it very soon.

As he stared at the six front windows and high-pitched roof, he discovered a fire was burning inside.

Puzzled, he advanced on the door. "Hello," he called out, expecting a servant to appear. "Is anyone at home?"

There was a rush of footsteps inside, then all was quiet.

He let himself in, allowing the cat to wander where he would. To the left was a quaint little sitting room, decorated in rich hues of blue with white piping on the cushions. To the right was a dining table, and to his surprise it was set for two.

He smiled. "Sally?"

She peeked around the doorframe, smiling broadly and with tears in her eyes. She was a vision in blue. His favorite color. She was so beautiful his heart skipped a beat.

"You came back to me," she murmured, a broad smile spreading over her face.

He hurried down the hall and embraced her. "For you. Only for you. I am home to stay if you will have me."

She shrieked and her arms tightened around him. "Yes, Felix. I will have you."

He spun her around and then set her on her feet. He touched her face, her lower lip, and then kissed her brow. "I thought you would not be here."

"I knew I could not marry Ellicott even before you left." She brushed the corner of her eye, wiping away a tear. "But I did not want to say anything and make you change your plans."

"I missed you."

"Felix, you were only gone a month."

"An eternity.

"I have been too busy to miss you," she confessed, wincing.

"Is that right?" He laughed and glanced around, approving of everything he saw, comforts that would make Torre Cottage their home when they wed. "I had thought this house had been left empty, but you have achieved so much."

"It took three weeks to refurnish the house to my satisfaction." Sally smiled as she glanced around proudly. "I have moved heaven and earth so you would have somewhere to lay your head on the night you came home."

"For us both to lay our heads." He took her hand in his. "Marry me, Sally. Marry me and this time do not leave me at the altar no matter what your father says."

"I could never be so foolish again." She leaned close. "I cannot live without you in my life."

They kissed, and it was everything he needed in life. She was the star upon which his world turned. He cupped her face. "Where are the bedrooms?"

Her eyes danced. "Upstairs and to the right."

"Want to show me where to find our bed?"

"Oh, Felix. That is all I want to do, but I might not let you out of my sight again."

He shook his head, and winced. "I promised to have breakfast with Rutherford in the morning, but since his last words to me had something to do with bouncing and great-grandchildren, he might forgive me if you were the reason who made me late."

Sally caught his hand and tugged him toward the stairs and the main bedchamber. "He might, but I would not count on it unless you plan to marry me tomorrow."

Felix thought a moment, then dug inside his coat, and extracted the paper Rutherford had handed him outside. He quickly flicked it open, laughed, and then showed Sally. "Well now. Is this not convenient? We appear to have a special license to marry, courtesy of your grandfather. He thinks of everything."

Sally pushed Felix toward the stairs. "He certainly tries, but I think we can handle the rest of our lives without family interference."

"I certainly plan to." He swept her up in his arms and hurried upstairs. "Let's go make some new memories, sweetheart, and then you and I have some work to do."

"We do indeed." Her smile was blinding. "Together."

The End

Seeking escape from a marriage minded miss, Captain William Ford makes a desperate bargain with the maid who helped save his life. He'll give her riches in return for acting the part of his lover—only to end up finding a lover who enjoys all the wickedness he craves.

London, 1814

Matilda Winslow blew a fallen lock of her hair from her eyes and then crawled under Captain Ford's bed to retrieve an item that had rattled to the floor while she'd been changing his sheets. She stretched to reach a strap that appeared to be wedged behind the headboard.

When tugging from beneath failed to free it, Matilda scrambled out again, frustrated. The captain was leaving very early the next day, returning to his ship and command, and she needed to finish this job. Mrs. Young insisted the bedding be changed before he returned to the house.

She wasn't supposed to be in his rooms at this hour. No one was.

The captain, when he was ashore, ran his home under a firm set of rules that no one dared cross.

Matilda considered her options. She couldn't leave it there in case it was important to the captain. The bed was too heavy for her to move on her own, and although she could call for help, she hated to do so. The other servants didn't like her very much, having decided from the beginning to make fun of her at every turn. Calling out to them was decidedly unappealing, so she had no choice but to climb onto the enormous bed, hoping she could reach the mysterious item without having to remake her morning's work entirely.

It was dark behind the headboard, and she thrust her hand into the narrow space.

She touched cold metal and jerked her hand back in surprise. Matilda peered into the gap and discovered the straps attached to a buckle. Puzzled by their presence, Matilda grabbed the item and tugged it into the light. It was not what she'd expected to find.

It was a horse's harness, but a strange design indeed if it was intended for a normal-sized horse. The straps were made of red silk, the buckles bright silver and definitely too delicate for any beast of burden. On further exploration, she retrieved a leather mask, not unlike a satin one she'd seen the captain wear to a masquerade ball recently. It was engraved with swirls and markings to define the eyes and was sized to fit the full way around the head, almost like a cap that laced at the back with more red silk ribbons.

Intrigued, she searched again and brought out a riding crop and cat-o'-nine-tails that appeared new. The latter gave her gooseflesh just to look at it, but the strands were so soft that she wasn't sure it could be used for punishment of any member of the captain's crew.

She sat back on her heels, flexing the crop between her hands, puzzled. Why would the captain keep such items hidden behind his bed? Surely, they belonged in his dressing closet with all his clothes, although some items deserved to be in the stables. She picked up the mask again and studied the item, running her fingertips over the smooth sections where his cheeks would rest. Beautifully made, and the leather was supple as if it was worn often.

Matilda scurried off the bed and moved to the mirror to find out, but when she saw her appearance, she nearly died of mortification. Her hair looked dreadful. She appeared a waif who had run backward through a briar patch.

Matilda quickly released her hair from the few pins she owned, smoothed the strands until they were tidy, and swept it up again into a neat and modest arrangement. Feeling better about herself at last, she lifted the captain's mask into place.

The leather was soft against her skin, and wearing it made it seem as if a stranger was in the room with her. It hid her identity so well she was curious to know more about the purpose. She'd never seen Captain Ford carrying it out the door on his way to a society entertainment. She probably should not pay so much attention to the handsome captain; as a servant, his comings and goings were none of her business. Nevertheless, she had long ago admitted the man was more than a little intriguing. He was quiet, he never yelled, but somehow his brief stays in the town house managed to terrify each and every servant so much that they fell over themselves trying to please him.

He was dangerous in a way Matilda could never quite pin down. He made her wonder if falling into her employer's arms might not be the scandal her upbringing told her it should be.

Through the eyes of the mask, she saw the door open behind her, and she gasped as she realized her employer had returned.

Matilda dropped the mask from her face and swept it behind her back, hoping to hide what she'd been doing from Captain William Ford.

His dark eyes bored into hers, flickered to the bed where her discoveries were still on display, and then back to her. His brow furrowed, which she'd learned was not a good sign. He was displeased, as he often was around her no matter how hard she tried to be unobtrusive. She couldn't have picked a worse day to linger in his room.

The click of the door lock was very loud in the room. "Miss Winslow," he said in his soft way, causing gooseflesh to rise all over her skin.

"Captain."

He came close. "What are you doing here at this hour?"

Matilda clenched the mask behind her back. "Making the bed," she explained weakly and then prayed he would not notice she'd failed to straighten the comforter from when she'd been standing on it.

"The bed is made, although somewhat imperfectly." He stopped a foot from her, and then his attention flickered to the mirror behind her back. His brow rose. "Show me what is behind your back."

"I. Oh. This mask?" She offered it to him, seeing no point of hiding it any longer. He must have seen she'd been holding his possession through the mirror's reflection, a major transgression for any servant. She'd been warned before not to touch his personal items. "It fell."

His expression grew cold. "And the other articles. Did they fall too?"

"No." She swallowed the lump in her throat when he would not take the mask from her shaking hand. "Only one item truly fell. I still have not retrieved it from behind the headboard. It is out of my reach, only I did not know you stored these other items there and recovered them by mistake. I promise to put everything back the way I found them."

His hot fingers wrapped around her wrist and held her in place. The mask dropped from her hand. "Too late for that."

His grip tightened, and her heart pounded. "Captain?"

One brow lifted. "Have I not issued clear instructions that I do not want servants lingering in my bedchamber?"

"Yes, captain." She shivered, too aware of his proximity and unyielding stance. "But I was ordered to change your sheets today."

"If that is true, then what were you doing standing before the looking glass?" His gaze narrowed. "Admiring yourself?"

Matilda licked her lips. Oh, she was in so much trouble. Mrs. Young would waste no time in turning her out for displeasing the captain on his last day ashore. She could not afford to lose this position. Surely, he had some compassion in him for a woman who'd only stolen a moment to neaten her appearance.

"I wanted to fix my hair," she admitted, glancing down in shame. "I was given no time to use in the mirrors in the servants' hall this morning and I did not know how frightful I looked until now. Mrs. Young believes servants have no business fussing with their appearance. I apologize."

"You always look beautiful, even when your ebony tresses are half falling down. Especially then." His lips pursed, and he released her. "Turn and look your fill in the mirror."

Startled by his suggestion, Matilda hesitated to obey. Staring at her reflection wasn't actually what she'd been doing. Her hair was tidy now, and she had just been curious about how she would look in a mask, having never attended a masquerade ball before.

She turned a little as Captain Ford placed a chair some feet before the mirror and sat facing her, hands on his thighs as if he was waiting for her compliance.

Waiting for her performance—as if she were a character in his very own private play.

He scowled. "The mirror, Miss Winslow. Look at yourself in it now."

To follow his orders meant she would have to stand directly in front of him. What harm could come of that since he insisted it was all right? She took a step, placed herself before the mirror, and stared at her reflection. She had always resented that her skin wasn't fair. She was too much like her mother in appearance, her father had often claimed with a hint of regret. Her saving grace was her eyes, her prettiest feature by far. She widened her attention to the rest of her appearance. A poor maid wearing a drab brown gown that did not flatter her complexion or figure stared back. She lowered her eyes, properly shamed before the captain. Overall, she was nothing special to look at. "You were making fun of me."

He frowned. "I'd never do that."

"Why not? Everyone else does." She complained and then bit her lip. Her employer wouldn't want to know about her problems, and especially not on his last day ashore.

"Everyone else is either a fool or jealous, Miss Winslow." He pulled a face. "You could wear sack cloth and still be the most remarkable and distracting woman in the room."

His words made her skin heat with a blush, but she smiled too. She liked the idea that he had noticed her, even if he was so far above her. But was unwise to think a captain in his majesty's navy could want to pay too much attention to a lowly maid when he was as handsome as William Ford. However, the way he scowled at her sometimes had made her feel so very insignificant. Did he not want to like her? He probably didn't. "Thank you."

"Now come here and sit on my knee," he said quietly.

She spun about. "Why?"

"Your punishment," he said calmly. "You cannot play with my possessions without consequences."

She blinked as he reached forward slowly to capture her wrist, his gaze fastened to her face until she blushed.

"I issue orders and expect to be obeyed in all things. Especially in the bedchamber." His brow rose. "Or do you imagine yourself above my rules? I do not like snoops, Miss Winslow."

"I'm sorry, Captain." He tugged, and Matilda stumbled forward. He eased her down on his knees. "It won't happen again," she promised as she clutched at his shoulders to steady herself.

Eye to eye, her pulse raced. He was so very handsome and sure of himself. The very thing Matilda never was around him. All of Matilda's senses seemed ready to fly apart just by being so close to him.

His gaze drifted to her lips. "Don't be sorry. But accept my punishment now and do as I ask in the future."

She nodded, breathless at the way he was regarding her mouth. "Yes, Captain."

His eyes widened and his tongue slipped out to wet his lips. "Yes, to what?"

Matilda wriggled on her scandalous perch; sure he would steal a kiss and more. "They say a maid who is foolish enough to fall into her employer's arms, deserves her ruin and the loss of her employment. I do need to be punished."

"Never consider that I could turn you out for any reason," he whispered, his breath hot against her throat. "What happens between us is strictly our business and will remain a secret. I will punish you, bring you pleasure, and that will be an end to the matter."

She squirmed even more as she considered what sort of punishment he might deliver that brought pleasure. She was not afraid of him. At the very least she might be expected to polish his bedchamber from one end to the other as punishment for her misadventure today, at the worst he might kiss her witless. Make love to her. Her sex throbbed with unexpected anticipation. "Very well. Punish me however you like."

No sooner were the words spoken than he flipped her over, so she dangled over his limbs. Matilda gasped in surprise as he held her there by placing one arm over and around her waist firmly.

His other hand connected with her backside the next moment, and she cried out, kicking at the shock of his idea of punishment. She expected ruin, not a spanking. "What are you doing, sir?"

"Captain," he reminded her. "You agreed to be punished in any way I deemed fit." He struck again, so hard that her eyes filled with tears and her face grew hot. "I do not want you touching that mask ever again. Never wear it. It is not for the likes of you."

"I won't wear it again."

He held his hand still on her bottom and kneaded her flesh through the gown. "Do you understand that a line was crossed today?"

"I understand," she whispered. "Captain."

"You continue to place yourself in my path, so there's nothing else to be done but continue as we are."

She frowned and clutched at his leg to steady herself. "I don't understand."

"You, and only you, have my permission to linger in my bedchamber for as long as you want. I'll make the arrangements before I go. You may touch any possession of mine except that mask and do your hair before the mirror. Mrs. Young is an old woman, threatened by your youth and beauty." His hand smoothed over her bottom, and she held her breath. "Look at yourself in the mirror now, Miss Winslow."

She turned her head as he pulled her skirts up and exposed the bottom he'd spanked. Matilda's heart began to hammer. A smile lingered on the captain's lips as he lightly touched her exposed skin with just the tips of his fingers. As the gentle caress continued, her face grew hotter and hotter.

"Look at me admiring you," he said as his fingers trailed along her thigh, sliding down over the gaping hole in the stocking tied below her knee. Matilda was transfixed by his gentle touch, by the devilish light in his eyes. He teased his fingers into her best stockings, widening the tear. "You must replace these after I'm gone."

His hand lifted slowly, and he brought it down sharply on bare bottom again and then continued.

Matilda gasped through it all, overcome by sensation, pain, and anticipation for the next strike. She clung to his leg, stunned, and fascinated by how his punishment affected her senses. An ache began between her legs, a sensation she'd never experienced before. She was breathless and restless. Captain Ford's face was a mask of severity now. He did not smile or look at her again. His attention was reserved for her rear and the red flush growing on her skin.

Suddenly he glanced up and met her gaze. His eyes were wild, dark, and focused solely on her. Matilda panted. He gripped her tingling bottom tightly, then turned his hand a fraction and used his fingers to part her thighs. His brow rose. "More?"

She nodded, but was unsure of what he'd do next. As his fingers dipped between, touching a place only Matilda had tentatively explored before in the privacy her narrow cot afforded, she closed her eyes. She was assailed by strange sensations that made her feel warm all over. As his gentle caress grew bolder, she could not help the need to push her body into his touch.

Purchase your copy to keep reading.

MORE REGENCY ROMANCE

Distinguished Rogues Series

Chills ~ Broken ~ Charity ~ An Accidental Affair

Keepsake ~ An Improper Proposal ~ Reason to Wed

The Trouble with Love ~ Married by Moonlight

Lord of Sin ~ The Duke's Heart ~ Romancing the Earl

One Enchanted Christmas ~ Desire by Design

His Perfect Bride ~ Pleasures of the Night ~ Silver Bells

Seduced in Secret ~ Yours Until Dawn

Wild Randalls Series

Engaging the Enemy ~ Forsaking the Prize

Guarding the Spoils ~ Hunting the Hero

Saints and Sinners Series

The Duke and I ~ A Gentleman's Vow

An Earl of Her Own ~ The Lady Tamed

Rebel Hearts Series

The Wedding Affair ~ An Affair of Honor

The Christmas Affair ~ An Affair so Right

...and many more

ABOUT HEATHER

USA Today Bestselling Author Heather Boyd believes every character she creates deserves their own happily-ever-after—no matter how much trouble she puts them through. With that goal in mind, she writes steamy romances that skirt the boundaries of propriety to keep readers enthralled until the wee hours of the morning. Heather has published over fifty regency romance novels and shorter works full of daring seductions and distinguished rogues. She lives north of Sydney, Australia, with her trio of rogues and pair of four-legged overlords.

Find out more about Heather at:
Heather-Boyd.com

facebook.com/HeatherBoydRomanceAuthor

instagram.com/heatherboydbooks

bookbub.com/authors/heather-boyd

goodreads.com/Heather_Boyd